THAT FIRST FRENCH SUMMER

THAT FIRST FRENCH SUMMER

Mandy Baggot

An Aria Book

This edition first published in the United Kingdom in 2020 by Aria,
an imprint of Head of Zeus Ltd

A CIP catalogue record for this book is available from the
British Library.

ISBN: 9781789546323

Typeset by Siliconchips Services Ltd UK

Cover design: Cherie Chapman

Aria
c/o Head of Zeus
First Floor East
5–8 Hardwick Street
London EC1R 4RG

www.ariafiction.com

Chapter One

August 2005

His skin was like perfectly browned toast, but with the smooth perfection of chocolate spread. It had been almost a week already and Emma still loved watching him. It was his athleticism and sheer passion for the game, even just in fun with the children, that she admired, gawped at and lusted after.

He was rangy, almost six feet tall, already with the muscular frame of a man. He couldn't be more than eighteen, could he? His hair was dark but flecked with gold from the French sun and his eyes were the colour of wet grass – cool and crisp, like giant green mirrors, looking into the soul of anyone that he met. Emma had said four words to him in six and a half days. *Bonjour* and *Oui, ca va*. Why hadn't she learned more French? Or why didn't she just talk to him in English? She knew he spoke it well, to the children he taught football skills to and to all the other girls who weren't too scared to approach him and demand his attention. They giggled and adjusted the straps on their tiny bikini tops, flicking their hair and gazing at him with adoration in their eyes. She didn't blame them. He was something of a god on their Riviera campsite. He deserved all their flirtation and amorous advances. She just wished she had the guts to join in.

'Brie baguette, Emma?' her father, Mike, called. He placed a plastic plate on the wobbly table in front of her and launched himself into the canvas seat opposite.

She didn't reply.

'Haven't you finished that book yet? You remember what Mr Devlin said. You must read the required text by the time we get back.' He bit down into the impossibly tough bread, made so by the blistering sun and the lack of refrigeration facilities in their four-man tent.

'I know, Dad. I'm getting there.' She slipped her copy of *Cosmopolitan* down from her lap and under the table as discreetly as she could.

Chaucer was one thing. But knowing how to put your eyeliner on properly when you were just feet away from the most gorgeous specimen you had ever encountered was far more important. Not that she had got close enough for Guy to have a chance of noticing her eyes, or the make-up outlining them. In fact, the closest they had got was at the clubhouse. Guy behind the bar, her behind her dad, waiting patiently for her Orangina. Her mousy hair un-styled and wet from the cold shower she'd just had.

She bit into the baguette. The fusion of bread and soft cheese warmed her all over and smothered her in gladness. She was so happy to be in France.

It was almost six months since her mother died and it was only on this holiday – her dad's attempt to get them out of the house and away from the memories of her mother's slow, painful demise – that she'd started to feel like the teenager she was. Living alongside cancer aged everyone. She could see it in her dad's face and feel it inside of herself. They were both changed forever. She was that little bit more grown-up and her dad… well, he was supposedly still grieving for his childhood sweetheart. Three weeks in France couldn't heal them completely, but perhaps it would plaster over the cuts and bruises, act like a liniment and give them the strength they both needed to go on.

Emma took a deep breath and raised her head towards the sunshine. France had so much going for it after all. They had the best food, the best weather and apparently the best-looking boys. They just didn't make them the same in England. Guy was bright and funny. He made everyone around him feel special just by being in his company. His voice was thick with a low, sultry accent and when he laughed it made her insides tighten. That had to be a good thing no matter how weird it felt.

She was contemplating actually taking a glance at Chaucer when there was a loud shout in French and suddenly she found herself with a football in her face, a baguette on her lap and her backside on the floor. The camping chair upended and lay next to her.

'You alright, love? Here, come on, let me give you a hand up,' Mike said, leaping from his seat and going to his daughter's aid.

He was beaten to it. As Emma slowly began to realise what had happened, an olive-skinned hand was taking a delicate hold of hers, as if handling the most fragile of objects.

'I'm so sorry… We play too hard… I should take more care,' he said, his hand resting in hers.

She couldn't speak. His beautiful face was only inches from hers, his blanket of chestnut-brown hair flopping forward over his cut-glass eyes. He could have been reciting Shakespeare and she wouldn't have heard it. She was struck dumb, mesmerised by his spell. All she could see were his deliciously full lips as he mouthed the word *care* and all she could feel was the slight pressure of that tanned hand in hers.

'You OK, love?' her dad said again looking at her bewildered expression with concern.

He probably thinks I've taken a blow to the head, Emma thought, realising her blue eyes were wide from staring at the French boy and her mouth was parted in a rather pathetic pop-star groupie kind of way.

She closed it and struggled to get to her feet. He helped her. He took her arm with one hand, righted the camping chair with the other and then, supporting her with both his hands, he lowered her into her seat. If she died now, gave in to the heart attack she was surely having, she wouldn't care. She'd be content to go just because he had touched her.

He picked her book up off the floor and ran his fingers over its cover, removing the dust.

'Chow-cer,' he said, looking at the illustration and trying to get the pronunciation right.

'Chor-cer. It's not my book of choice. I mean I have to read it, for school. It's for A levels, you know, exams,' she babbled. She knew her freckled cheeks were reddening. She knew it wasn't because the factor-thirty sun cream was wearing off. It was him. She was blushing. It was hormonal. Ally had told her all about it.

'I love to read. Not Chow-cer perhaps, I do not know. You think I would like this book?' he asked, flicking open the pages and observing the text.

The only thing Emma was observing was him. The way his fingers stroked each page, the way he was looking at the words. He looked at them as if they were important, as if they might move something in him.

'I'm not sure I like him, I mean his style of writing. It's all in really old English, like relic stuff. No one talks that way now. Well, apart from Mr Devlin who seems to revel in it. But he's like a character out of Dickens... on skis.' Emma added as Guy raised his head to study her.

He threw his head back and laughed, his green eyes alive, his hair drooping over onto his forehead.

'On skis? What is this on skis?'

'We just say it, in England. Well, me and my friends back home. It's just like saying someone is something and then a hundred per cent more,' Emma attempted to explain.

Why had she said that? Stupid Ally Thomas and her made-up phrases to try and sound cool. It didn't sound cool. Not when you were trying to explain it to a hot French boy you couldn't keep your eyes off.

'Like... how you say? The girl is beautiful – on skis,' Guy said, his eyes locking with hers.

'Yes, just like that,' Emma agreed, having to force the words up her throat.

'I'm Guy,' he said. He extended his bronzed hand towards her.

She knew this. Everyone knew who he was and what he was called. He was the pin-up of the campsite, the person everyone wanted to know and be known by. But she loved the way he pronounced it, to rhyme with 'key'. To her it was the best name in the world, oozing his laid-back coolness.

'I'm Emma,' she said. She took his hand and gave it a professional handshake she might have reserved for a careers advisor.

'I know,' he answered, smiling.

Chapter Two

Present Day

*M*arry *me.*
The words were bumping around in her head, stopping anything else from getting through. Sometimes when Emma replayed the phrase it filled her with excitement, joy and a thrill she hadn't felt for years. Then, when her mind repeated the question again it was spoken by a different voice. *Marry me.* It sounded wrong, almost like a jailor talking before the shackles were attached.

'Well? How does it look?' Ally Thomas barked.

'It looks like a gym.'

'Argh! Emma! A little more enthusiasm please! It is a state-of-the-art sports facility. A gym conjures up images of strongmen, puffing, panting and dumbbells. Here, at the Wellness Sports and Spa Fitness Centre we do not have stress and strain. We have motivational personal trainers. We have the latest in cardiovascular equipment and we have beauty treatments to rival a dip in the Icelandic mud baths,' Ally announced. She proudly puffed out her chest like an aroused pigeon.

The Wellness Sports and Spa Fitness Centre was brand new and being opened and launched that day. Emma was there because Ally was the manager. Ally knew nothing about sports and fitness, but she had a power suit and a loud voice and could organise the unorganisable. She wanted her best friend's opinion before the official opening in the afternoon. How things had changed in eight years.

Eight years ago, Ally had been all set to do a course in beauty at the college and Emma was destined for university. She *had* made it there, but at the time she'd had to prioritise.

Emma swallowed as she caught sight of their reflection in the wall-width mirror. Self-consciously, she scraped her blonde bobbed hair behind both ears. Compared to Ally she looked like Cinderella in the pre-ball rags period. Ally was dressed in designer wear, all coiffured and tweaked, not an eyelash out of place. Emma was wearing jeans she'd had for years and a much-loved, shapeless, cream, long-sleeved top. Money was tight and Dominic came first.

'So, are you staying for the ribbon-cutting?' Ally asked, checking her watch.

'No, I've got to pick Dominic up from swimming in...' She checked her watch. 'God, fifteen minutes. I'd better go.'

'No more rushing about for you in a few months. We'll be doing swimming lessons here, you know,' Ally proudly reminded her.

'I know, you've given me at least five leaflets about it. I've got to go,' Emma said, embracing her friend and trying not to crinkle her so obviously new suit.

'You and Chris are coming to the gala dinner tonight

though, aren't you? I've invited Councillor Martin. I know you're desperate to bend his ear about more funding for the school,' Ally said.

'Yes, we're coming. My dad's babysitting Dominic and we have a pass out until at least midnight. Later if I leave him chocolate Bourbons,' Emma said, grinning.

She'd been looking forward to the gala dinner since Ally told her about it. Usually the closest she got to dressing-up was when she decided her students at the school needed period costume to help them understand the era they were studying. With a young son and a boyfriend who worked unsociable hours as a taxi driver, nights on the razz were very few and far between. She only hoped tonight wouldn't be tainted by the question she still hadn't answered. He'd said the words, *marry me*, like he'd said them twice before. This time she had sighed heavily, patted his arm and taken a pile of towels up to the airing cupboard. She knew it wasn't what he'd hoped for and she wondered how long he would keep asking before he gave up on her.

'How's your dad's internet dating going?' Ally asked, opening the door and leading her friend back out to the balloon-adorned reception area.

'He's going on a second date with Velma the dog trainer next week,' she announced with a giggle.

'Blimey! I thought you said she brought one of her dogs along to the last date.'

'She did. Dad likes dogs,' Emma said.

'I'm saying nothing.'

'So, who's the celebrity you managed to con into opening this fitness and wellness spectacular for the prize of a money-off voucher for the butcher's?' Emma asked. She pushed open the main door and got her hair whipped up by the breeze.

'Ah well, I had got Jason Simpson. You know, England's number ten, scores loads of goals every week for Finnerham United. The kids absolutely love him, the women adore him, the men respect him, and I was clapping my hands together...' Ally began.

'He can't come, can he?'

'He's gone and done in one of those crucial ligaments or something and they're operating... today,' Ally informed her with a frustrated sigh.

'And?'

'And I'm left with some new guy they've just signed from France. Now what was his name? Guy. That's right, Guy Duval. He probably can't speak the lingo, no one will understand a word he says and, knowing my luck, he'll look like the back end of a bus,' Ally gabbled.

'Guy Duval,' Emma said. Her voice had dropped to a whisper.

Marry me. Marry me. Marry me. The images were already in her head: his dark hair, his emerald-coloured eyes, his bronzed hand reaching out to her...

'Emma, you're letting air in. It will play havoc with my climate control,' Ally said, taking the door from her friend's hand.

'I have to go,' she said, her voice almost failing her.

'I know, shoo! Go and get Dom and I'll see you later. I'll be the one with my hand up the French guy's arse being the ventriloquist if he can't speak a word of English,' Ally said, cackling out a laugh.

Emma managed a faint smile and hurried out of the

leisure centre. It couldn't be him! Duval in France was like Smith in England. There were hundreds of people in France called that, weren't there? And so he played football? So did lots of men. Lots of French men called Duval. No, it couldn't be him. It wouldn't be him.

Chapter Three

It was him. Google had a lot to answer for. Here he was, Guy Duval from the Riviera campsite, now looking at her out of her laptop screen. He was dressed in the bright blue of the French national football team, the gold cockerel motif looking resplendent on his chest. Everything about him was as she remembered it. She had never envied a cockerel before, but there it was, its feathers erect, a smug beak on it, festooned against that well-structured torso.

Why had she never Googled him before? She knew the answer to that. She had banned herself from thinking about him. When he broke her heart, she snapped. She'd left, she'd moved on and she had well and truly put him away in her past. It had to be that way. There were times when her thoughts had travelled back to those few weeks, usually when she had had too much to drink or after a bad day at school. The trouble was, she could still so easily recall how the French sunlight felt on her skin, how his hand had felt in hers. But along with the good memories were others she would rather forget. She'd been broken. He had broken her. You didn't Google people who took your heart and threw it away.

'Mum, can I have some more sauce?' Dominic called.

He was behind her at the table, hungrily devouring fish-fingers after his hour learning the intricacies of breaststroke at swimming lessons.

'Yes, of course, I'll get some.' She snapped down the lid of the computer before standing up.

'Will Chris be here soon? He's getting me some more cars today,' Dominic said. He raised his head and those eyes lit up.

Emma picked up the tomato ketchup and squeezed some onto her son's plate. He was growing up so fast. He was tall, with a dark brown mop of hair that constantly fell across his forehead. He had an infectious smile and those wide eyes.

It had been just her and her dad when Dominic came along, but they had managed. And Emma hoped they had made him feel every inch the special person he was. He might not have been planned for, but even the best plans usually have to be adapted. And, whatever the future held for her now, Dominic would always be at the centre of it.

'I don't know what time he's coming over. We're going out tonight though, remember? Grandad's coming to look after you.'

'Great! That means I can stay up late and play on the Wii with him!' Dominic said, peas falling from his lips.

'So that's what you get up to, is it?' She smiled.

'I always win. Grandad gets the buttons mixed up.'

'Why doesn't that surprise me?' Emma replied. She opened her laptop back up.

There were dozens of photos of Guy, all waiting to be clicked on. Most of them were football shots, him in action for different teams in France. But there was one picture that interested her in particular. In this shot he was wearing an expensive-looking suit and had his arm around the waist of a beautiful dark-haired woman. She had eyes the shape of almonds and a slender figure draped in a coral-coloured shift dress. *Madeleine Courtier* the caption stated. She was so pretty, so immaculately turned out. Ally would know the designer of the coral dress and who her hair was styled by. But it didn't need intimate knowledge of haute couture to see that this gorgeous woman was Guy's equal in looks and status. Footballers were like movie stars these days. He was a footballer and she, Madeleine Courtier, looked like a movie star.

As Emma looked at the photo, a burn manifested in the pit of her stomach, bubbling and boiling, reminding her of all the nights she'd spent reliving what had happened in France. There he was in a magazine, almost unaltered, his handsome face working the camera, the edge of his tanned hand just visible at the waist of this hopefully highly airbrushed female companion. He had made a fool of her.

She slammed her laptop shut. The noise made Dominic jump and his fork clattered onto the table.

'Mum!' he announced, his dark eyelashes blinking as he retrieved his cutlery.

'Sorry, Dom, sorry. I didn't mean to make you jump,' she apologised.

She ruffled her son's hair and then held his head close to her in an embrace.

'Is it Chaucer again?' Dominic questioned, turning his head to look up at her.

'What?' Emma asked, the name feeding a memory back into her head.

'Chaucer always makes you mad.'

'He'll make you mad too, when you're older,' she replied.

The doorbell rang and Dominic sprang from his seat like a greyhound out of a trap, racing to reach the door first.

'It's Chris! It's Chris! Hi Chris, have you got my cars?' Dominic bombarded as soon as Emma had opened the door.

'Dom! Let Chris come in, for goodness' sake. He's tired, he's been working and…' Emma started.

And there he was, her lovely boyfriend. Tall, slim, blond-haired and blue-eyed with laughter lines at the corners of his eyes. But she couldn't look him in the eye. They hadn't spoken since the *marry me* of that morning, and she didn't know if anything had changed.

'Hey, that's alright. You should know you can't keep a boy away from his cars… especially a yellow limited-edition Ferrari and a replica of Lewis Hamilton's winning racing car,' Chris announced, producing two boxed cars from behind his back.

'Wow! Mum! Have you seen these? Thanks, Chris they're awesome! Can I play with them now, Mum? I've had enough dinner,' Dominic said. He gave Emma the benefit of one of his heart-stopping beams.

'Peas or racing cars. I guess it isn't really a hard choice. Go on then,' she agreed.

Dominic raced off upstairs to his bedroom and within seconds the noise of cardboard being broken apart was the only sound to be heard.

'Would you like a cup of tea?' Emma offered.

'Tea? Emma, I've never drunk tea,' Chris said. A sigh escaped his lips.

'Sorry, I know. I just feel awkward about this morning and...' Emma's eyes dropped to her shoes.

'Well, don't. It was a spur of the moment thing. I hadn't asked in a couple of months, we were having a laugh with Dominic and everything and it just slipped out,' Chris said in a matter-of-fact tone.

'Slipped out,' Emma repeated, raising her head to look at him.

'Yeah, it wasn't especially important. It just sort of happened,' Chris continued.

'Right.'

'So, no need to feel awkward or anything. God, I could do with a beer. I brought some. Want one?' Chris offered, indicating the bag he was holding.

'Maybe in a bit,' Emma answered as he moved past her, heading for the kitchen.

She knew he was talking rubbish. Marriage proposals didn't slip out. They were well considered before they passed anyone's lips. Chris was trying to make her feel better and that was so typical of him. Whenever there was crisis or confrontation he smoothed over the cracks and pretended the problem had never even existed. You couldn't live like that forever, she thought. Eventually something or someone had to give. The question was, who would give first?

Chapter Four

This was his third attempt at doing up his tie. What was wrong with him? He let out a sigh and looked at his reflection in the mirror. Here he was, Guy Duval, international footballer, a world-renowned player just signed to a high-flying UK team set on winning the Premier League. He had the world at his feet – he had worked hard to get the world at his feet. So why wasn't he happy?

He attempted the tie again, trying to look in the mirror for guidance.

'Guy! The removers have cracked a bowl. The whole set is ruined! You must call them. We ask for compensation!' Madeleine's voice called from downstairs.

He dropped his hands down to his sides and sat on the edge of the bed. What was he doing? Where was he going? No matter where he was he was always at a loss. Nothing he did felt right. Eight years ago, he'd thought escaping was the answer. But what had escape brought him so far? He might be rich beyond his wildest dreams but when he looked in the mirror he still saw the face that disgusted him. He still held the memories that haunted him.

He felt the ache riding over him. The pain started like a flutter in his chest, crept its way upwards, taking a strangle hold on his neck, invading his shoulders, his back and then his head.

'Guy!' Madeleine called again.

'I will be there,' he finally responded.

'Grandad!' Dominic announced, jumping up at Mike as he entered the house.

'Hello, Dom. Hello, Chris. Don't you look smart?' Mike said, his eyes taking in the grey suit and retro paisley tie Chris was wearing.

'Do I? It's really itchy, this material. Friend of mine lent it to me. I don't have a suit. I mean, when does a taxi driver get to wear a suit?' Chris asked, adjusting his tie and looking uncomfortable.

'Chris and Mum are going to a ball,' Dominic announced. He rolled his eyes and yawned.

'It isn't a ball. It's a gala dinner,' Emma said, coming down the stairs.

'Wow! Look at you, love. You look smashing,' Mike said, taking in his daughter's appearance.

She only owned one smart dress and it had seen far better days. But a black dress circa 2007 wouldn't do if she wanted to tackle Councillor Martin about school funding. Ally had lent her the dress she was wearing now. It was a simple style, scalloped neckline, in at the waist and flaring out to the knee. The colour gave it the wow factor. It was canary-yellow and it brought out the deep chestnut-brown of Emma's eyes.

'*Smashing* makes me sound like some sort of successful clay sculpture,' Emma said, blushing as both men looked at her in appreciation.

'Your dad meant to say *gorgeous*, didn't you, Mike? But he's your dad, isn't he? *I* should be the one telling you how beautiful you look... and you do,' Chris said. His cheeks flushed.

'You can go out now,' Dominic instructed, taking hold of Mike's hand and dragging him towards the living room.

'Oh I see. You don't need us now Grandad's here,' Emma joked, smiling at her son.

'I thought you were going to go all mushy and kiss, that's all,' Dominic said, screwing up his face and poking out his tongue.

'No mate, we haven't had enough wine to do that,' Chris replied.

Emma swallowed and avoided reacting by gathering Dominic into a hug. Did he really mean that?

'Now listen, you be good for Grandad. Not up too late playing computer games and not too many Bourbons. And brush your teeth before bed,' Emma ordered.

'Have we got Bourbons? Fantastic,' Mike said, clapping his hands together.

'Bet I can eat more than you,' Dominic challenged.

'I've had years of practice,' Mike reminded.

'I think we should go. This sounds like hardcore biscuit-eating to me,' Chris said, opening the front door.

'We won't be back too late, Dad,' Emma said, touching him on the arm before she stepped out.

'That's OK, love. You enjoy yourself,' Mike told her, catching her hand and giving it a squeeze.

It was a balmy evening for mid-September. August had been one of the worst on record, spoiling the school break. Now the children were back in the classrooms, the temperature had risen and everyone was wishing they were still on holiday.

Emma could only imagine Ally's delight at a warm evening. It meant her friend could open the remote-controlled veranda doors leading from the function room out onto the deck. From there the guests would have a great view of the outdoor pool and waterpark-style lazy river.

'This suit is nylon, isn't it? I'm sweating buckets here. How long d'you think I'll have to keep the jacket on for?' Chris asked as they walked towards the entrance of the fitness centre.

'There's vicious climate control inside. You might be glad of it,' Emma answered.

There were paraffin torches leading the way. Two wine waiters stationed either side of the main door held trays of champagne.

'They will have beer, won't they? I mean freebies are freebies, but I've never been that keen on champagne,' Chris whispered as they approached the waiters.

'If I know anything about Ally it won't be the cava we're accustomed to,' Emma told him.

'Champagne, sir? Madam?' a waiter offered.

'Don't mind if I do,' Chris said, picking a glass up.

Emma helped herself to a glass and then stepped through the door into the foyer where people were mingling.

She noticed Ally at once. She was wearing a peacock-coloured dress with a feather fascinator in her hair. No one else could have got away with wearing something so elaborate, but she did and made it look stunning. Ally waved and headed over in Emma's direction.

'Ooo Em, you look fab! I said that dress would suit

you, didn't I? Hello, Chris, what are you doing with that champagne? You're not a champagne man now, are you? It's a free bar tonight. We have five different lagers, fill your boots,' Ally announced, holding her hand out to indicate the bar area.

'Good stuff, I'll get on over there then! Here, more for you, Em,' Chris said. He handed Emma his half-started glass of bubbly and hot-footed it over to the bar.

'Where on earth did he get that suit from?' Ally asked. They both looked as Chris itched around the waistband of his trousers while he waited for his pint.

'Oh don't! He's self-conscious about it enough as it is,' Emma answered with a giggle.

'Right, well, while he's busy getting lager and scratching, come and meet *the* hottest specimen of manhood I've seen since the chef on my last cruise,' Ally announced, taking Chris' glass from Emma and grabbing her by the arm.

'Oh, Ally I thought you were happy with Jonty,' Emma exclaimed as Ally led her along.

'He's never here! Him being a pilot is a pain in the rear! One day it's Germany, the next it's Fuerteventura… wherever that is. And I'm pretty sure he's spending intimate cabin time with Claudette the trolley dolly. He talks about her all the time… when he's with *me*! No, no future in that one. He couldn't even get me any air miles,' Ally said.

'Right, so who's the next victim?' Emma asked.

'Well, remember I told you about the footballer, the French one, the one I thought would look like Quasimodo…'

'Guy,' Emma said. The name almost caught in her throat.

'Emma, you have *got* to see him! He's divine! He looks like something that's been sculpted. Firm jaw, Roman nose, eyes the colour of a Grolsch bottle and a mane of hair any racehorse would be proud of,' Ally described, her voice full of excitement.

'But he isn't here, is he? I mean he cut the ribbon this afternoon, didn't he? He'll be halfway back to wherever footballers spend their nights, won't he?' Emma asked. As the words came out of her mouth, her eyes scanned the room like an assassin looking for its target.

'Of course he's here! He's here all weekend! No football, most of the players are away on international duty. Tomorrow he's spending all day teaching football to the local kids. Well, I can tell you I am going to be keeping a very close eye on his ball skills,' Ally said with a giggle.

'I should really go back to Chris. He doesn't really know anyone else here…' Emma began, holding back from Ally's determined walk across the function room.

'Don't be daft; he'll have a pint to talk to by now. Ah, here he is. Just look at that! Isn't he perfection?' Ally said. She sighed.

And there he was. Guy Duval. Her Guy. The Guy who stole her heart.

Dressed in a blue-black suit, his thick glossy hair sat just on his shoulders, he was engrossed in conversation with a wizened woman in a tangerine-coloured frock coat.

'Ooh God, he's been pounced on by Kathleen Dobbs! She's the chairwoman of the Fair Trader Association and hell, doesn't she talk! Are they talking French? Emma? Is that French they're speaking?' Ally hissed at her friend.

She couldn't be here in this moment. She couldn't let Ally try and introduce them. Suddenly she longed for the familiarity of Chris and his down-to-earth normality. While

Ally was busying herself scrutinising Kathleen Dobbs' wrinkled mouth, Emma fled back across the room, trying to avoid elbowing guests' glasses out of their hands.

She didn't stop until she found Chris. He was leaning on one of the pillars festooned with ribbons, one hand wrapped around his pint glass, the other at the collar of his shirt, scratching.

'There you are! Thought you'd deliberately deserted me in a room full of posh people for a second,' Chris said. He smiled at her.

'No, no, Ally just dragged me off to meet some woman from the Fair Trader Association. You know what she's like and this is her big night,' Emma said. She didn't dare to look anywhere except at Chris. The hairs on the back of her neck were standing up. It was like she could sense him.

'Well, she's heading this way with someone in tow,' Chris announced.

Emma buried her nose in her champagne glass and waited for the inevitable.

Chapter Five

'Emma, Chris, this is Kathleen Dobbs from the Fair Trader Association. Kathleen, this is Emma Barron and Chris... er... Chris...' Ally began.

'Chris Mason, lovely to meet you, Kathleen,' Chris said. He took hold of the frail lady's translucent hand and brought it to his lips.

'Oh I say, an old fashioned gentleman at last. These days most people want to kiss you on the cheek, or both if you're particularly unlucky,' Kathleen said, tittering with laughter.

Emma realised she wasn't breathing and almost sucked in the contents of her glass as she gasped in some much-needed oxygen. It wasn't Guy! Thank God!

'Although, I didn't mind the two kisses from the French gentleman over there. In fact, two wasn't quite enough,' Kathleen said. She let out a girlish giggle.

Emma coughed and hurriedly drank some fizz.

'He *is* rather lovely, isn't he? Speaks wonderful English,' Ally continued.

'And so handsome! When he told me he wasn't married I very nearly offered,' Kathleen said, a glint in her eye.

'I almost offered this afternoon when I saw him on the rowing machine,' Ally said. She let out a heavy sigh.

'So what time do we sit down to eat? I mean, Chris, you must be starving,' Emma interrupted.

She couldn't listen to any more of it. Ally and Kathleen Dobbs were talking about Guy as if he were some sort of rare species, a never-been-seen-before Adonis to be admired and adored. That wasn't the Guy she knew. He had made her give away her heart to him only for it to mean nothing. He was manipulative and detestable and she wanted to pretend she'd never met him.

'There will be a gong in approximately—' Ally checked her watch '—eleven minutes. I'd better mingle. Don't forget, free bar. Drink up and make the most of it.' She made off, surging back into the throngs of people.

'Eleven minutes! Right, well that gives me just enough time for a cigarillo. Bad habit I know, but when you've got to seventy-eight there's really nothing left to be good for,' Kathleen Dobbs said. She let out a cackle of naughtiness and shuffled off towards the exit.

'Good old gal,' Chris said, laughing as he put his glass to his mouth.

'I'm just going to the ladies',' Emma said. She needed to get some air.

'Are you alright, Em? If you're still thinking about this morning then...'

'No, it isn't. I'm not. I'm fine, honestly. I just need the loo. I won't be long,' Emma said. She smiled in what she hoped was a comforting way.

She needed a minute. She had to get out of the room, the same room that Guy was in, and think about this. He was in her orbit for the first time in years. It was the absolutely worst thing that could ever have happened.

Guy had done a double take when he saw her. It couldn't be. Emma Barron, the only woman he had truly loved, was here, at this moment, on this night. So many years had gone by, years in which he'd tried to turn his life around. Years of mourning something he would never get back. And here she was, looking not a day older than he remembered. Those eyes. Those chestnut-coloured eyes that had wept so many tears because of him and haunted his dreams since.

His heart was beating a rhythm he barely recognised. He wet his lips as he tried to gather his thoughts, still not believing that she was here

He had considered trying to find her many times but there was always something that stopped him. Pride was a factor. Then there was shame. What he'd done to her so soon after she'd lost her mother. What she *thought* he had done to her. Grief played a part too. He'd hidden away for almost six months after what had happened to Luc. And then, later, when the tears and heartache had subsided a little, he'd thrown himself into work. He'd trained hard and he had made himself into one of the most talented footballers in the world. But now it wasn't just about the game. He was in demand for so much more. There were modelling assignments and clothes endorsements, television interviews and promotional events. But he wanted it that way. Keeping busy stopped him from thinking.

He was afraid. Afraid to find her, to reawaken sleeping feelings and let himself be taken back to the time they had shared. He'd tried to put her to the back of his mind, knowing that if he'd found her, if she let him back into her life, he wouldn't want to ever leave it again.

And now here she was. *Merde!* He didn't know where she was in her life. He didn't know her situation. Perhaps she had moved on. Of course she had moved on. So had he... with Madeleine.

She was stood with a man tonight. A man who looked older than her. A man in a cheap suit. He did not want to believe she was involved with this man. Not when his own heart was telling him his moment had finally come.

Emma stepped out onto the decking and walked up to the wooden railings. There was the view of the lazy river Ally had told everyone about. The air was not the cooling balm that she had been hoping for. The warm humidity enveloped her.

Of all the people Ally could have got to open the fitness centre, why was it him? It was too weird to be a coincidence, wasn't it? But Ally didn't know. Ally didn't have a clue. Why would she? A guy called Guy that had never been mentioned after Emma returned from France. Even if she had accidentally mentioned him, Ally couldn't remember the names of her own boyfriends let alone any of Emma's.

'Emma?'

The sound of his voice sent a shockwave right through her. She couldn't respond or turn around. She was rooted to the spot, scared into a statue. She closed her eyes and held her breath. Perhaps if she were lucky she would melt with the heat, dissolve into a pool of yellowness right before his eyes like the witch in *The Wizard of Oz*.

'Emma? Is it you?' the voice said again.

She was biting her teeth together so hard her jaw was aching. She couldn't look into his face and see those eyes. She just couldn't. No, she would just stand still and look like she was nonchalantly gazing at the view.

A hand lightly touched her arm and then he was next to her, looking at her. Guy Duval, right in front of her. His dark hair framed his face. His green eyes gazed at her. His body was so close to hers.

'Emma,' he said, his voice barely more than a whisper. He leaned forward and kissed her first on one cheek and then the other before she had a chance to move.

'I... don't know you,' Emma said, her cheeks flaming.

Who was she trying to kid? This was ridiculous. Her heart was pumping like an engine and she felt sick. She couldn't pretend she didn't know who he was. Time had gone by but... you didn't erase people you'd been intimate with as easily as that. Especially someone you had planned a future with.

'It is me, Emma. Guy, Guy Duval. I know I look a little different? The clothes maybe?' Guy suggested, holding out one side of his beautifully tailored jacket.

She was trying to conjure up the contemptuous feelings she had for him all those years ago when he'd destroyed her. But all she could feel was excitement. She was thrilled that he was in front of her, looking more gorgeous than she had remembered. There was no more pretending to be done. He knew it was her. The game was up and it was time to deal with the reality of him being here.

'We fell in love,' Guy whispered.

As he said the words, every muscle in her being tightened. They were on a newly constructed deck, overlooking a fake river surrounded by local dignitaries quaffing Cristal, but she had been transported back to a French Riviera campsite and he was the eighteen-year-old heartthrob she'd stripped of his clothes. How could she pretend not to know him? Eight years wasn't a long time, and when you've bared your soul to someone, you never forget. You cling on to every memory you've ever made with them.

'Emma! Here you are! Ah, Guy, I see you've met my best friend, Emma,' Ally said, appearing at Emma's side and linking her arm through hers.

'Well...' Guy started, his eyes not leaving Emma's.

'Isn't he fabulous? He was so patient with the crowds today. There wasn't one person without a photo and an autograph,' Ally continued.

Emma nodded, gritting her teeth and trying to look anywhere but Guy's face. She could feel him looking at her. Those intense green eyes that reminded her of the deep, bottomless Mediterranean. The full lips so beautifully shaped as if they were just waiting to be kissed.

She fell off one of her shoes and grabbed Ally for support.

'Sorry! Not the champagne, the shoes. I don't wear high shoes very often,' she said quickly, trying to smooth over her embarrassment.

'Emma's a teacher. Always been a bookworm and now she has a whole class of students to listen to her prattle on about Shakespeare and—' Ally said.

'Chaucer,' Guy interrupted, his eyes locking with Emma's.

'Oh yes, I'd almost forgotten about him! What a total bore! In fact, his work was boredom… on skis,' Ally finished.

Emma swallowed and started to find her fingernails intensely interesting.

From inside the function room a gong was struck and people began to meander back towards the building.

'Right, I'd better get back in and help seat the less capable. You two are on table two,' Ally said.

'On the same table? Oh no, Chris and I are quite happy to sit somewhere at the back… not with the special guests,' Emma said in a strangulated voice. She grabbed hold of Ally's arm before she could leave.

'Emma! You get to look at *him* all evening. What's not to like?' Ally asked. She looked at Guy and gave him a coy little wave.

Emma's shoulders slumped as she watched Ally trot away to schmooze with local councillors and the MP.

'You teach? That is amazing. It is just what you wanted to do,' Guy said, sidling up by her.

'Yes, it was. You remember?' Emma asked, looking up at him.

'Of course. I remember everything.'

He took her hands in his and brought both of them to his mouth, touching his lips to her skin. As they made contact a spark crackled in the place his heart had vacated long ago.

Chapter Six

It was Yazz and the Plastic Population playing, one of her favourites. Circa 1988 but still cool. And what was an Eighties disco without Yazz? Sometimes she and Ally had put white swimming caps over their heads and with a hairbrush microphone, their jeans well below their belly buttons, they'd belted out 'The Only Way is Up' until Ally's mum banged on the ceiling with her Vileda super mop.

She was holding a copy of *The Canterbury Tales* in front of her face but she wasn't reading it. She was watching the primal mating dance going on on the dance floor.

Tasha and Melody were the A-list girls of La Baume. They wore tiny white skirts, baggy vests that fell off their shoulders exposing brightly coloured bras, and wedged heels. They were from London and that sounded the height of cool to the local boys. Wiltshire never really attracted the same amount of attention until you let it drop you lived within spitting distance of Stonehenge. Then she was on a par with Tasha, Melody and London. Or would be if she had wedged heels and a red bra.

They were gyrating now and pulling their elbows into their bodies every time Yazz crooned the word 'up'. And everyone was watching. The cute boy who hired out the clubs for crazy golf. The lifeguard with the tattoos who had winked at her again today. Several men over forty who should know better… and Guy. He seemed to be transfixed. His eyes were focused on the dance floor. His gaze on Tasha and her slim, tanned legs. On Melody and her ample bust.

'Why don't you go and dance, love? It's one of the songs you like, isn't it?' Mike asked, putting down his guidebook and turning to her.

'Not really. I mean it's alright, but…' Emma trailed off. There was no point explaining to her dad that dancing next to these two was akin to a Japanese kamikaze mission. She knew she'd be a laughing stock. When you were feeling fragile because your mother died, it didn't do to line yourself up for ridicule.

'I thought we'd go to Nice tomorrow. What do you think?' Mike asked. He took a sip of his pint.

'I thought you wanted to enter the darts competition?' Emma replied, putting her book on the table.

'Well, love, it's your holiday too. And I know how hard you've been working. You don't want to hang around the bar all day watching me lord it on the dartboard. I thought we could have a browse round the designer shops. We could have lunch there. In one of the posh places like you see on the telly,' Mike suggested.

Nice would be nice. She knew her dad was on a tight budget but they'd hardly left the campsite since they arrived.

It would be nice to explore a bit, discover parts of the real France, the scenery, the shops, the *saucisson*.

Emma nodded in enthusiasm and took a sip of Orangina as Yazz came to an end.

What was next on the playlist? Emma grabbed her book and put it up to her face as Roxette's 'It Must Have Been Love' began to filter out of the speakers.

Slow music would clear the dance floor. She knew the drill. Tasha and Melody and the other cool girls would slink to the edge of the room and lean seductively against the wall. They would chew the ends of their hair and look disinterested. Then very slowly, one by one, they would pair off with their male counterparts.

She smelt him before she saw him. That mix of sandalwood and perspiration, a trace of lemon and freshly baked baguettes. For a second she let her eyes flick over the top of the book and there he was, standing in front of her.

'Would you like to dance?'

He looked hopeful. He looked like he really wanted to dance, not like the desperate, can't-really-be-arsed-but-I-might-get-to-grope-you kind of look she was used to from the boys at home. His hands were coupled together and he was twisting his forefingers.

'No thank you. I mean… *non, merci*. I don't really dance,' Emma replied quickly.

'Yes you do! She loves dancing! Go on, love, don't you mind me. You go and dance,' Mike urged.

Guy was looking at her. She felt like Tasha and Melody and the whole room were looking at her. She had no choice. She just wished she didn't fancy him quite so much. She could tell what sort of guy he was, a love-them-and-leave-them type, and she didn't want that. She wanted to be special, not one in a line of summer romances.

He stretched out a tanned hand to her and her dad nudged her in the ribs and snatched *The Canterbury Tales* out of her hands.

She took Guy's hand and let him lead her to the dance floor. She almost heard Tasha's chin hit the floor.

She felt like Baby in *Dirty Dancing*. The square, educated girl, inexperienced in all things cool. And Guy was her Johnny Castle. The hippest boy at the campsite, the one person every girl wanted to lock lips with.

He put both of his arms around her waist and she followed his lead. He was hot and his skin was damp and dewy, but it was his eyes she couldn't stop looking at. They were mesmerising, hypnotic, soul-seeing.

There they were, dancing chest to chest in the middle of the floor, only three other couples on the peripheral. And Emma could see nothing, hear nothing, feel nothing but the heat from him. And there was *that* look in his eyes.

He took one of her hands from behind his back, placed it on his chest and covered it with his own. He lowered his face towards hers and Emma's breath caught in her throat.

'Will you teach me the Chaucer?' he whispered.

'I don't know, I...' Emma replied, trying to ignore how pleasurable his breath was in her ear.

'You say you are not sure you like him. I think you enjoy him and... I would like to know what it is you enjoy,' Guy continued.

'He talks funny,' Emma said.

'So do I,' Guy answered, looking at her.

She could feel his heart beating under the thin cotton

of his white short-sleeved shirt and she swallowed. She couldn't take her eyes from him. The line of stubble on his top lip and along his jaw. His long straight nose, slightly too large for his face. The dark hair falling over his eyes. She swallowed and nodded her head.

'You will teach me?' he asked, his expression animated.

'We can teach each other,' Emma responded, a tentative edge to her voice.

'You want to learn French?' Guy inquired.

'No,' Emma answered, her brown eyes challenging him for a response.

'It's *non*,' Guy whispered in reply.

Chapter Seven

Present Day

He was sat opposite her. He would get to look at her beauty for the entire meal. Now he had seen her again, he never wanted to take his eyes from hers. His hands were trembling, his whole body was aching. He felt how he used to feel when he thought that love and happy-ever-afters were possible. She knew a little about his past; she was the only woman who knew anything about that black time. She had been the light. She was the hope he'd clung on to until he'd had to leave it all behind. She had never given him a chance to explain. But then, he hadn't really deserved one. Would he have told her the truth if she had given him the opportunity? And there she was with another man. A man he already disliked, just because he was seated next to her.

He clenched the anger down and reached for the jug of water.

★

She was opposite him. Opposite was OK, opposite meant not next to. Their knees wouldn't accidentally brush and their elbows wouldn't connect when they ate. The only downside was that she had to look at him all night.

Chris was next to her and, after his two pints, was halfway down a bottle of red wine. But that was nothing compared to the whole bottle of white Councillor Martin had necked before the starter had come out. There was no way he was going to be remotely interested in discussing extra provision for the school when he seemed hell bent on sampling all that Pinot Grigio had to offer.

'So Guy, how are you finding things here in England? Bit different from La France, I bet! The weather for one. I mean today's been a scorcher but tomorrow it'll probably piss down,' Chris said, refilling his glass.

Emma cringed. Chris had no idea how to behave in different social situations. She used to be proud. Her boyfriend was who he was, no airs, no graces. He could be at an audience with the Queen and he'd probably ask her if she thought David Cameron was a fuckwit... and expect a reply. But now it wasn't endearing. Now it was embarrassing.

'I like the rain. It is fresh,' Guy said.

Fresh rain. Yes, that conjured up plenty of images. None of them clean. His eyes kept locking with hers like they were a compass, always swinging back to find north. It was giving her heartburn, or perhaps that was down to the prawn cocktail.

'I guess it's still the novelty factor for you. When you've had years of back-to-back sun, drizzles and downpours must certainly be different. You'll get sick of it though when it happens every bloody day,' Chris continued, slurping at his wine and prodding at a cucumber wedge on his plate.

'I like England. It has character,' Guy replied, putting a hand to his hair and pushing it back from his face.

' How long are you here for, Guy? Signed up to a long and lucrative contract, I hope!' Councillor Martin said. He wiped his sweaty brow with a napkin.

'Two years for the moment. We will see.'

Two years! Two years playing for a team only eighty or so miles up the road. It was too close for too long. France may only be a tunnel trip away but it was still another country, another lifetime.

'We should take Dominic to the football more, Em. He'd love it,' Chris remarked.

'Mmm,' Emma replied, poking some prawn cocktail into her mouth as quick as she could.

'Dominic?' Guy asked, looking up from his meal. His tone showed slightly too much interest.

'So, Councillor Martin,' Emma said quickly, changing the subject. 'Sorry, Geoffrey, you know what I'm going to ask, so let's get it out of the way. Is there any chance St Joseph's could get some more funding? The drama classes desperately need new books and costumes for performances. The parents have donated generously but there's only so much they can give and only so many times we can ask them without it getting embarrassing.'

'There are procedures to apply for extra funding I'm afraid. You have to apply, in writing. There's a form,' Geoffrey Martin said, sticking his finger in the remaining sauce on his plate and wiping it up.

'I know. I've applied. Actually I've applied twice this year already and no one responds to my phone calls,' Emma answered.

She was sick of being given the run-around by Geoffrey Martin's secretary. She didn't need an abacus to count how many messages she'd left for the councillor to call her.

'You tell him, Em,' Chris encouraged, refilling his wine glass.

'Well, I expect matters are in hand,' Geoffrey mumbled into his napkin.

'Maybe I could make a donation, to the school,' Guy spoke up.

'Oh no, Mr Duval, you don't need to do that. That wasn't what I was trying to do, I was just... well, the council should have provision,' Emma replied, her cheeks reddening.

'Not so hasty, Em! Who cares where the money comes from? You said you're in danger of having to perform *West Side Story* again this year! Believe me there's only so much "la, la, la, la America" I can take. Hummed it for over a week,' Chris informed.

'How much would be OK? Twenty-five thousand? Thirty?' Guy inquired.

He looked like he was going to reach for his wallet.

'Good God, son! They must be paying you a small fortune at that football club,' Geoffrey remarked. Others at the table sucked in their breath.

'No, really, you don't have to do that,' Emma said. Her heart was hammering against her rib cage.

'Maybe I want to,' Guy replied. He kept his eyes on hers.

'Christ, Em! Take the guy's money! If you don't take it for the school he'll just spend it on women and wine. Isn't that right, Guy?' Chris said. His fork clattered onto his plate.

'I would like to help. Perhaps we could talk, make arrangements,' Guy said, still only looking at her.

This was killing her. Just having him in the same room was killing her. She hated him. But why did she have to remind herself of that? He hurt her. But the sound of his voice and those green eyes were playing havoc with her insides. Her stomach was telling her she should vomit, while her heart was telling her if she didn't get a grip on herself it was going to bounce right out of her chest and land on Councillor Martin's plate.

'Isn't that wonderful news? No more *West Side Story*. Perhaps something lavish this year? I've always been fond of a bit of *Copacabana* myself,' Geoffrey said, wine spilling down his chin.

'Now you're talking! Feathers, fruit, skimpy sequined costumes for the ladies. I could invite some of the lads from the rank!' Chris said.

He sounded more enthusiastic now than when he'd got tickets for an AC/DC tribute band.

Emma wasn't listening to either of them. She was looking across the linen tablecloth at Guy and he was gazing back at her. She couldn't see the person who'd hurt her anymore. All she could see was the boy she'd fallen so in love with.

Her starter was whipped away barely touched and now in its place sat a large slice of beef wellington. She could hear Chris' lips smacking together as he devoured it like a bear feasting on a lone camper. To the other side of her, Geoffrey Martin was raucously blowing at his nose and then wiping the same napkin over his gravy-stained lips.

'Lovely grub, isn't it?' Chris said. He nudged Emma with his elbow.

'Yes, lovely,' she answered, turning the corners of her mouth up in an unauthentic smile.

'You two are married?' Guy questioned.

Emma stabbed at her main course, hit a pea and watched it roll off the plate onto Geoffrey's lap. He didn't notice. It seemed he was trying to attract the attention of a waiter because the wine had run out.

'Almost. Aren't we, Em?' Chris answered. As if to emphasis his point, he draped an arm around her shoulders and very nearly pulled her off the chair in his attempt at a boa-constrictor-style hug.

'Almost? You are... how you say... engaged?' Guy inquired further.

'No.'

'Yes.'

Emma looked at Chris and he looked back at her. She wanted the gong to sound to announce the end of this nightmare scenario. Chris laughed and squeezed her in even closer to him, her face right up against the damp polyester of the cheap material under his armpit.

'I'm working on it. I keep asking. Emma keeps not answering. I think she's worried my idea of a morning suit might be something Jack Sparrow might wear,' Chris said, still chuckling to himself.

'Jack Sparrow?' Guy asked, a puzzled look on his face.

'*Pirates of the Caribbean,* my lad,' Geoffrey filled in.

'Ah, Johnny Depp,' Guy answered, nodding.

Emma couldn't help but notice he had picked up the salt cellar and was squeezing it tight in his hand. She looked away again when his eyes connected with hers.

'I'm really impressed with the facilities here aren't you,

Geoffrey?' Emma interjected. She had to change the subject. She couldn't be doing this. She couldn't be talking with Chris about not being engaged. Not with Guy sat opposite her, nothing separating them but a pillar candle, three empty bottles of wine and some gerberas in a vase.

'Oh, top class, yes. Just what the area needs for our youngsters. The school will benefit I'm sure. I believe Ultra Leisure is contemplating free swimming lessons,' Geoffrey told the table.

'I am teaching the children tomorrow. Football skills all day,' Guy said. He took a sip of his wine.

'Really? How much is that?' Chris asked.

'Oh, it is free. It is a promotional event for the opening.'

'Christ, Em, get Dominic signed up. He would love it. Free skills from a pro. You can't beat that,' Chris said. He nudged her *again*.

If the elbowing continued all night she would end up with bruised ribs and a week wearing Deep Heat.

'We'll see,' she answered like Chris was one of her schoolchildren.

'*We'll see*?! It's a fantastic opportunity to learn from a real master. This guy plays for his country, Em, not to mention now playing for my favourite team, the Whites,' Chris continued.

'Dominic is your son?' Guy asked.

'Emma's son,' Chris replied with a grin. 'But I love the little fella to bits.'

'How old is Dominic?' Guy asked.

'He's—' Chris started.

'He's in Year Three,' Emma interrupted quickly.

'Loves football, doesn't he, Em?' Chris said, his right elbow connecting with her side again.

Emma raised her head and met Guy's gaze with a nod. She knew what he was thinking and now she felt sick.

He gritted his teeth together and put the napkin to his face to hide his mouth. Was her son seven or eight? He was finding it hard to breathe. Emma had had a baby, a son – was Dominic *his* son? Had she just told him he was a father without having to say a single word?

Chapter Eight

She'd excused herself as soon as there was opportunity. Every time he'd tried to get her to look at him she had either turned away from him or to that man, her boyfriend. He couldn't keep making polite conversation with him and the councillor. All that was running through his head was the thought he might have a child. He was ecstatic and furious at the same time. The one thing he was certain of was they had to talk.

'Mosquitoes,' Kathleen Dobbs announced, stubbing out her cigarillo into one of the ashtrays on the table.

'Sorry?' Emma answered, waving the smoke away from her face and clutching a little tighter to her wine glass.

'I've been far, far afield and despite what people say there's nothing as irritating as a British mosquito. They're silent, they're sneaky and they think nothing of sucking up your food before they attack,' she continued, her eyes weaving from side to side as if trying to single insects out.

'Have you been bitten? I think I have some antiseptic cream in my bag,' Emma said, unfastening the zip and rummaging.

'Oh no, dear, I have repellent. Just commenting on their

devious ways. The Mayor over there, he's been itching for a good five minutes,' Kathleen remarked.

'It's humid,' Emma said, peering over her shoulder and hoping not to see Guy.

She had left him and Chris at the table having an in-depth discussion about television replays for penalty decisions. She'd been glad to get out of the air-conditioned room because, muggy or not, the outside atmosphere was decidedly cooler.

'Are you alright, dear?' Kathleen asked her, scrutinising her instead of the flying insects.

'Me? Oh yes! Of course! It's been a lovely evening and the food was wonderful,' Emma began, tears pricking her eyes. The explosion of excitement she had attempted in her voice was far from convincing.

'I hear you're thinking of staging *Copacabana* at the school. Believe it or not, I was once a Lola,' Kathleen informed. Her eyes twinkled.

'Well, nothing's decided quite yet,' Emma began. She swallowed in a bid to stop the tears from escaping.

'If you need any help with costumes I would be only too happy to…' Kathleen began.

There he was! Guy. He was coming towards her from across the decking. He had a glass of red wine in each hand. Emma closed her eyes and clamped down on her tongue to try and prevent her taste buds recollecting Camembert and a soft Merlot.

'Those damn insects! I swear they're getting immune to DEET! I'm seeking cover. Don't stay out too long, dear, not if you value your skin,' Kathleen said, hurrying to the doors.

She felt like she was waiting for her turn at the gallows. He was steps away, moving towards her and there was nowhere to run. Her only escape route would involve a James Bond-esque vault from the railings into the lazy river. Even she knew that was ridiculous.

'I have some wine,' Guy said, holding a glass out to her.

'Is it Merlot?' she asked on autopilot.

It was like going back in time. She felt seventeen again.

'You remember,' Guy said. The smile that crossed his lips was one of almost relief.

'Of course I remember!' Emma shrieked 'You made me think I was special. Then you humiliated me!'

That voice wasn't hers. It was almost like a battle cry. A noise from deep within her, full of anger and despair.

Guy closed his eyes and very slowly shook his head.

'I remember every word you said to me. I remember every line you fed me and every touch and kiss that meant nothing to you. I remember it all! I wish Jason Simpson hadn't pulled whatever ligament he's pulled, then you wouldn't be here in his place!' Emma continued.

'You didn't let me explain,' Guy said.

His voice was soft and he gently took hold of her arm, guiding her away from the groups of people mingling.

'I don't care *now*! I'm older and wiser and I know how the world works. I was stupid and too young to know better. I don't want to remember what a fool I was. I don't want to remember the things I told you and the things we did together. I trusted you, I stupidly believed what you said, believed in us and you were... you were just playing games!' Emma carried on.

She drank the whole glass of red wine in one gulp and slammed it down on the wooden railings.

'I tried to find you' Guy began. 'I spoke to your father, I searched the entire campsite.'

'You had sex with that cow Tasha,' Emma hissed.

'It was not like that,' Guy replied.

'Didn't you hear me? I don't care anymore!'

'Then why do you shout?'

That was a good question. A very good question. She was seventeen then, she was twenty-five now. She was yelling at her first boyfriend who was also eight years older. She sounded unhinged. She sounded like she'd probably sounded back then. Immature.

'We should have dinner,' Guy suggested, taking a sip of his wine but still observing her intently.

'We've just had dinner!'

'I meant alone... to talk,' Guy replied.

'There's nothing to talk about! You're eight years too late!' Emma blasted. She couldn't control the anger. It was bubbling away in her gut, a mix of all her confused feeling now being expelled from her mouth.

'What about Dominic?' Guy stated, his eyes meeting hers.

'Ah! Here you are! Finally got served. They've got a bit of a rush on what with it being freebies. Ally's jumped behind the bar. It's all hands on deck,' Chris said, joining them. He sounded like a jovial Santa. It was completely inappropriate.

'We should go soon. We don't want to impose on Dad too much,' Emma said. Her cheeks were infused with colour and she tried to mask the bitterness in her voice.

'Christ, Em it's barely past ten! I'm sure he wasn't

expecting us back this early,' Chris said. He gave a snort of amusement.

'I'm not feeling very well,' Emma responded. She held her bag to her stomach and dropped her eyes to the floor.

'Shall I get you a glass of water? Is that red wine you've had? You know red wine doesn't agree with you,' Chris said. He shook his head and rolled his eyes.

'No, don't go. I'm fine, just the humidity I expect,' Emma replied, clutching at the sleeve of Chris' nylon jacket.

'I must go and speak with Jerome from Ultra Leisure. It was nice to meet you both, excuse me,' Guy said, backing away from them.

'Hang on, mate! Before you go... what time for the coaching session tomorrow? Dom is going to go nuts when we tell him,' Chris said.

'Nine-thirty. Registration and then we start with simple techniques and ball skills,' Guy replied. He looked to Emma.

'Brilliant! Cheers!' Chris said, waving his glass in the air in appreciation.

Emma watched Guy's every step. His expensive suit, the way he moved. She would know him anywhere, just from his gait. She had watched him so often back then, at first from a distance and then up close. It was if he was permanently etched on her brain. All those years dwelling on what he'd done had done nothing to destroy the feelings she had for him. She hated it.

'Dom's going to be made up about doing football skills with someone from Finnerham United, you know,' Chris said, swigging from his pint and spilling some on his tie.

'Can you take him tomorrow then? I thought you were working,' Emma remarked.

'I am, but you haven't got anything planned, have you? You'll only have to drop him off and pick him up. Guy isn't going to expect you to join in,' Chris said. He laughed.

She nodded and smiled feebly. Even a five-minute drop off was going to be five minutes too much.

He sat in his car, his fist in his mouth, his heart breaking. He needed to know if he had a son. Tomorrow he was going to see him. All those years apart with no contact, had Emma been raising his child? How could this have happened? Had he hurt her that much? She didn't even have the whole of the story. She only knew what she saw... what she thought she saw. If she'd really loved him she should have waited for an explanation. An explanation she should have known would have come. He had been in a dire situation. A dire, disgusting, situation he still had nightmares about. What had happened that day had cost him Emma.

He wiped at his eyes with his fingers and thought about Luc. If this was all true then Luc would have been an uncle.

Chapter Nine

August 2005

'Dad, would you mind if we didn't go to Nice today?' Emma asked.

It was almost ten. She had helped him cook blackened scrambled eggs on the camping stove and now she was watching him collect the plates and burned saucepan to take to the washing up area.

'Oh, love, I thought we had it all planned. You, me, yacht-gazing, boutique-shopping and baguette-munching,' Mike said. He looked over at her as he gathered up the utensils.

'I know but I want you to enter the darts competition. You missed the one last week and there isn't one the next. You should enter,' Emma told him.

She had been planning this speech since last night when Guy had kissed her.

After their smooch to Roxette, she had left the dance floor lightheaded, her heart fit to explode. She had sought refuge in the toilets to get her breath back. Guy, the campsite pin-up, the boy everyone wanted to get close to had danced with her. That was one in the eye for Tasha and Melody. They'd been green enough to rival the Incredible Hulk.

When she'd emerged, lip-glossed and breathing more stably, he'd been stood in the shadows, waiting for her.

'There'll be other darts competitions. There's the big one at the social club when we get home,' Mike told her.

She hadn't expected so much resistance. Her dad loved darts. It was the only hobby he'd kept up through her mum's illness. He'd escaped the awfulness of it by visiting the social club for a couple of hours on a Friday night while Emma sat with her mum. At least that was where he said he was.

'I want you to do it, Dad. For me… and for Mum,' Emma said.

'Your mum hated darts,' Mike reminded. The beginnings of a smile played on his lips.

'Yes, but she knew you loved it and she loved you. Anyway, I've got plans. I'm going to finish *The Canterbury Tales* and make a start on the notes before the Sumo competition this afternoon,' Emma informed.

'Sumo competition?'

'Daft people in fat suits. It sounds fun,' Emma said. She squinted her eyes as Mike moved and gone was her barrier from the sun.

'Are you sure, love? I know I said you should hit the books so you don't get behind but…' Mike started.

'I'm sure, Dad, honestly,' she insisted.

Guy was meeting her in less than an hour and she needed her dad gone before then. She was sick with excitement. It was a date, a proper date. And last night she had experienced a kiss like no other. Ally would be unimpressed, but for

Emma it was a milestone. The first boy she had *wanted* to kiss her, had kissed her.

He'd even been tentative about it. He'd held her hand first and stroked it with his long, tanned fingers. Then he'd entwined their hands and held them so firmly.

'Tell me you do not leave for a long time,' he'd whispered in her ear. 'Two and a half weeks,' she had replied.

And that's when it happened. He had looked at her, with those jade-coloured eyes and slowly, almost teasingly, lowered his dark head towards hers.

'Well, I'd better get on with this washing up then,' Mike said, picking up the tea-towel and washing-up liquid.

'Oh no, Dad, I'll do it. You should be practising. Limbering up for the games,' Emma told him. She stood up and grabbed the dishes from him.

'Are you sure you wouldn't rather go to Nice?' Mike checked, looking at his daughter with slight suspicion.

'Maybe we could go next week, plan it properly,' Emma suggested, clutching the plastic plates closer to her.

'OK, well, if you're sure. I'd better change my shirt and find those darts,' Mike said eagerly.

He'd finally left for the clubhouse forty-three minutes later and all Emma had managed to do before Guy arrived was run a brush through her hair, douse herself in body spray and put on her best sundress, yellow with tiny white daisies on it.

'*Bonjour*,' he greeted. The way he looked at her told her he appreciated what he saw.

'*Bonjour*,' Emma answered. She felt about ten years old.

'Thanne wolde I seye, goode lief, taak keep, How mekely

looketh Wilkyn oure sheep!' Guy spoke. His forced English accent was worse than Dick Van Dyke in *Mary Poppins*.

'God, you've been reading Chaucer!' Emma exclaimed

'You left it, in the bar. He speaks of how women feel, yes?' Guy asked, handing over her book.

'"The Wife of Bath's Tale" does. For me, that's the one that makes most sense. Well, as much as Chaucer can make sense,' Emma said. She blushed and inwardly cursed herself for over-analysing.

'Do you have allergic?' Guy asked.

'Allergic?'

'For food? Some people, they have allergic…' Guy began.

'Oh, you mean allergies. No, I don't have any allergies. I mean I don't like broad beans much but who does?' Emma said, smiling at him.

'I have *pique-nique* – is this how you say? Food – in a… *panier*,' Guy said, producing a wicker basket from behind his back.

It was so big Emma wondered how she hadn't noticed it before now. Except she hadn't been looking at anything but him and the tight, white T-shirt he was wearing, above a pair of jeans, cut off at the knees.

'Gosh,' Emma said, admiring his organisation.

'I thought we could sit by the river. We could fish if you like… I do not know… or read the Chaucer,' Guy suggested. His cheeks reddened.

'That sounds nice,' she said sucking in her stomach and trying to stand tall.

'To fish?'

'All of it.' She blushed.

★

'Why do fish eat bread? I mean it isn't what they normally eat, is it? They eat bits of yuck from the bottom of the riverbed, don't they?' Emma remarked watching Guy dangle a makeshift rod into the fast-flowing water.

'They think it is yuck. It looks like the yuck... on skis,' Guy told her. He looked up and smiled.

It was a beautiful spot. They had walked no more than ten minutes away from the site, off the track and onto grass near a river. It was hidden, from the track like an almost secret snake of silver, running through the land.

'Do you come here often?' Emma asked. She let out a laugh at her own comment.

'Why do you laugh?' he asked, carefully stepping back up onto the bank and sitting down next to her.

'Nothing, just a silly saying that's all. So, do you come here a lot?' Emma asked.

'*Oui*, when I have the time. I work every day at the campsite and at a hotel near here. Then I help my mother. She has a new baby and... how you say... *nous n'avant pas beaucoup d'argent*,' Guy told her.

'You don't have much money,' Emma translated.

'*Oui*.'

'Neither do we. That's why we're camping and not in one of the luxury lodges. My mother... she died a few weeks ago,' Emma admitted.

She'd tried to keep the pathetic, weak and sad tone out of her voice but had failed. The grief always took her by surprise.

'That is why you look so sad. Why you keep the beautiful

smile hidden away,' Guy said, reaching up and gently stroking her hair back behind her ear.

'I wish I was beautiful… like Tasha and Melody,' Emma mused. They had high-fashion outfits and accessories she could only dream about.

'The *prostituées* from the campsite? You do not be like them, they are *stupides*,' Guy told her.

There was real anger in his tone, an irate look in his eyes at the mention of their names. She wouldn't talk about them again. Not if it prompted a reaction like that.

'Well, I haven't really spoken to them or anything but they seem to—'

'They talk of nothing but boys and hair-changing and they spit their horrible chew gum on the Astroturf,' Guy told her.

'You're a very good footballer,' Emma said, changing the subject. She was secretly glad the other girls' multicoloured undergarments hadn't won any favour with him.

'I have trial next week, for OGC Nice. If I can get the time off work,' Guy informed. Pride coated the words and Emma felt her chest swell in admiration.

'Are they a big team? Sorry, I don't know much about football. Well, I know the basics but…' Emma started.

At this moment she wished she knew much more about it, like the offside rule for a start and how many players made a team.

'It is big team, yes. If they like me this could be a big, how you say… big *opportunité*,' he said, dipping the fishing rod back in the river.

'What does your father do?' Emma inquired.

'Tsk!' Guy spat, shaking his head.

The displeasure in his voice shocked her and she averted her eyes from him, worried she had spoiled the date. They hadn't opened the picnic basket yet and he hadn't tried to kiss her again.

'He is dead to me,' Guy responded. The way he said the words was brutal.

'He isn't around?' Emma asked.

'I do not know where he is. I do not want to know,' he replied, still shaking his head.

'But your brother? Your mother's baby?'

'His father is not around either,' Guy said, turning to look at her.

'I'm sorry,' Emma said, swallowing a ball of nerves and anticipation.

'*Non*, don't be sorry. I will look after him. I just need a chance, perhaps with OGC Nice,' Guy told her.

Emma smiled at him and he took hold of her hand and raised it to his mouth. He placed a delicate kiss on her skin and she let out a little gasp of delight and surprise.

'Are you… *faim*?' Guy asked, still holding her hand.

'Hungry? Oh yes! Dad made scrambled eggs this morning and they were really horrible… *très horribles*,' Emma said, using exaggerated hand gestures.

'*J'ai du fromage et du pain, des olives, des raisins locaux et une bouteille de Merlot*,' Guy said.

'Wine,' Emma said, a flush of adventure reddening her cheeks.

'You like red wine?' Guy asked, opening the basket.

'Oh yes, I do,' Emma said, smiling.

Chapter Ten

Present Day

'You have to leave again? This early?' Madeleine asked as Guy entered the kitchen of their four-bedroom house in Finnerham.

They had only moved in a few weeks ago but already, thanks to a team of movers the football club had provided, it was looking like a luxurious mansion inside and out. The lawns were mowed every second day and they had a fresh flower arrangement for every room brought on a Thursday.

'Yes, I teach the children today. Tonight I will be back for the football club party,' Guy said, picking an apple and an orange from the fruit bowl on the central island.

'You know I arrange for the couples clothing design today. This will be the second time I have to cancel,' Madeleine continued.

'I'm sorry. The football club ask me to fill in for Jason Simpson. I am new here. I am their face for promotion. I have to honour their commitments,' Guy responded.

'And what of my commitments? *Our* commitment, huh?' she huffed, one hand on the hip of her designer dress.

'I will make it up to you. Tonight, we will go to the party. Why not buy something new?' he suggested, kissing her cheek.

'New dress, new shoes, a bag *and* a coat,' Madeleine said, pushing out her bottom lip in an attempt to look affronted.

'Whatever you want,' Guy responded, picking up his kit bag.

Right now he would say anything to get out of the house. He had just over an hour to get to Finnerham and then he would be seeing his son for the first time.

'We need more goats' milk and we're almost down to the last guava. Could you call the personal shopper?' Madeleine called as Guy headed for the door.

Dominic yelled out in excitement when Chris told him about the football skills day, with apparently the world's greatest footballer, Guy Duval. Emma had never heard Chris this enthusiastic about football before. Now it was *the Whites* this and *Finnerham* that and by the time Emma had got Dominic in the car he was bouncing about with excited energy.

'This is so awesome, Mum! I can't wait to tell everyone at school,' Dominic said, kicking the back of Emma's seat with his indoor football boots.

'Well, some of your friends might be there. We're probably the only ones who found out about it yesterday,' Emma replied.

'Guy Duval's an awesome player. Did you know he

scored three goals for France against Austria in a friendly last month? I watched it on YouTube,' he continued.

'No, I didn't know that,' Emma responded.

She did know he had a birthmark at the top of his left thigh though. She didn't think YouTube would have a clip of that.

'He's played for OGC Nice, then Marseille, and Finnerham have just signed him for fifty million,' Dominic carried on.

'Fifty million? Pounds?! That's extortionate.'

'It's awesome,' Dominic replied, using the obvious watchword of the day.

When they reached the front doors of the Wellness Sports and Spa Fitness Centre they had to weave a path through the giggling mothers and sisters to get inside. As soon as Emma got Dominic through into the foyer she saw why. Guy was sat at a table with Ally, signing autographs and posing for pictures while her friend tried desperately to enrol the children on the day's course.

'Sorry, was that Adam Peters? Or Peter Adams? I can't hear myself think here. Shit, my pen's run out! New pen! I need a new pen! Milo! A new pen is needed!' Ally bawled in the direction of a shaven-haired youth loitering near the door to the office.

'Are you OK? Here, I have a pen,' Emma said, delving into her handbag and producing one.

She saw Guy look up, at the sound of her voice, from signing his name on the back of a leaflet about judo for an almost hysterical mother of a boy with a Mohican.

'Oh Em, we're inundated. Which is all good, don't get me wrong, but I've had two call in sick already. Milo hasn't even been inducted yet and as you can see it's chaos! I should be showing the children into the changing rooms but I'm stuck here enrolling,' Ally informed. Emma noticed a slick of perspiration on her top lip.

'Mum, you could help Aunty Ally, couldn't you? You do register and stuff at school. It would be easy for you,' Dominic piped up.

Bless him. He had good ideas beyond his years but she really wished he hadn't come up with one right now.

'I know, Dom. But it isn't quite the same,' Emma spoke quickly. She turned her body sideways to minimise her view of Guy.

'Oh, but it is! Here, you just write down the name and a contact telephone number for emergencies. Write the name on the sticker, stick it on the kid and send them to the changing area. Emma, please, I've got the hangover from hell after playing rummy with Kathleen Dobbs until the small hours. And if I hear another mother gush about Guy's *magnifique* physique I'm going to be sick,' Ally said.

'That's him, isn't it?' Dominic whispered. Emma looked to Dominic, not missing the awestruck expression on his face as he watched the football idol posing for photos at the other end of the table.

'Yes, that's him. If I didn't feel like death I would be sat on his lap. But right now I just feel like swilling out my mouth with antiseptic and then eating a bacon sandwich,' Ally said, fanning her face with her clipboard.

'Go on,' Emma said, putting her bag down on the floor.

'What?'

'Go on. Go! Go and do whatever you have to do. I'll book the kids in, stick the stickers on, whatever. Go before you make *me* feel sick,' Emma ordered, moving around to the other side of the table.

'You're a life saver, Em, really you are! Milo! Come hither!' Ally called, hurrying out of the crowds and beckoning her colleague.

His heart was in full palpitation mode. There he was. Dominic… he had to be his son. He was tall for his age, with hair the same colour as his own. It was brown, cut short at the back but longer on top. It flopped down over his forehead, just like his did. He could barely sign his name. He couldn't hear what the crowds were asking him. He was transfixed on this boy, *his* boy, just yards away from him.

'Could you sign my breast? It's a treat for my husband. He's a big Whites' fan,' a middle-aged woman asked him.

'Sure,' Guy answered. He wasn't looking as he moved his pen forward.

'Breast, love, not my flippin' navel,' the woman laughed, lifting Guy's hand higher.

There was a pillar in between them. A well-polished, chrome and mirrored pillar. If she leaned too far forward she could see dark hair falling forward over his face. If she leaned back she could see his football shirt tightening across the contours of his back. It was a no-win situation for her.

Suddenly, as she reached forward and stuck a label onto curly-haired Henry Palmer, she was aware of Guy getting up from his chair. A quick glance at her watch told her the session was due to begin at any moment.

Without really looking she could tell he was navigating the table, slipping his way through the bustle of chattering mums, grans and dragged-along partners towards her. Towards *her*!

'Emma.'

She knew he'd spoken but she couldn't raise her head. She also knew he was wearing shorts. She'd caught a fleeting glimpse of bronzed thigh when she'd dropped a sheet of name stickers on the floor. Seeing his face would be too much.

'And your name is Bradley, isn't it?'

'Brandon.'

'Sorry, Brandon,' Emma said.

She wrote the name in her best and slowest teacher's handwriting.

'Emma,' Guy attempted again.

'B-R-A... is it Brandon with an O-N or Branden with an E-N?' Emma queried, raising her head to look at the freckle-faced boy.

'O-N...I think,' he responded a look of puzzlement on his face.

Guy let out an exasperated snort of irritation and out of the corner of her eye she saw him head off towards the main gym hall.

'Shall I check with my mum? She's in the car park,' Brandon stated.

'Thanks for taking over with the signing-in. Here, cappuccino,' Ally said, sitting down next to Emma.

They were in the gallery café that overlooked the hall,

together with at least half of the excitable mothers from the signing-in process. They now had their noses pressed up against the glass pretending to be watching their children.

'I don't like cappuccino,' Emma reminded.

'Sshh, I know. Right now, the brand new, state-of-the-art coffee machine only wants to dispense cappuccino. I'll have to call the guy I guess,' Ally said, gulping her drink.

'What's the matter? Isn't he good-looking enough?'

'What?'

'Sorry.'

'What's the matter? You aren't hungover, are you? You didn't drink any red wine last night, did you?'

'What is it with everyone being so concerned about me drinking red wine?'

'Oh, would you look at him? I wish I was young enough and brave enough to put shorts on. I wouldn't mind brushing up on my ball skills,' Ally remarked, steaming up the glass with her breath as she moved her chair forward.

Emma looked too. There was Guy at the front of the hall, bouncing a football on his knee and talking to the children. His thick, dark hair was springing over his eyes with every movement. His chest was taut as he trapped the ball against it and deftly brought it down to his feet. She swallowed and turned her attention to Dominic.

He was looking at Guy like he was some sort of sporting god. His eyes were wide in concentration and he picked up a ball and tried to replicate the footballer's moves.

'So, did Chris enjoy the party?' Ally asked.

She could almost taste brie in her mouth. The scent of the memory engulfed her mind.

'Emma…'

'I never told you about the boy I met in France. You know, when I went there, after my mum died,' Emma stated, turning away from the view and facing her friend.

'That was years ago.'

'He was special.'

'He can't have been that special or you would have told me about him.'

'I wanted to tell you. I wanted you to make a voodoo doll of him.'

'I did make a lot of voodoo doll men, didn't I?'

'It was Guy,' Emma said.

'What was Guy?'

'The guy was Guy. Guy Duval,' Emma explained.

Ally was mid-swig and the hot coffee seemed to catch in her throat. She coughed.

'What are you telling me here? That you and that gorgeous Gallic hunk were once intimately acquainted?!'

'Yes... eight years ago,' Emma stated.

'Oh my good God! You and... *that*!' Ally exclaimed, taking another long look at Guy who was dividing the children into teams.

'He wants to talk and I don't want to talk and he keeps cornering me and I don't know what to say to him,' Emma admitted.

'Well, what does he want to talk about?'

'Dominic. And I'm terrified because he's in there with him now... and that's all Chris' fault,' Emma continued.

'God alive! Is he Dominic's father?!' Ally questioned.

'No! No, of course not.' Ally and her dad had been asking her for years who Dominic's father was. Emma knew Ally felt it was a breach of best friend commandments not to be in the know about it and Emma also knew her dad most definitely wanted a face and a name to blame for it. But opening up about it simply hadn't been an option. It still wasn't.

'Then what's the problem?'

'I think Guy *thinks* he's the father.'

'Then just set him straight.'

'I still have feelings for him,' Emma admitted. She hadn't thought about saying that. Her sensible side should have prevented her from saying that. But it was true. Without thinking too hard about it, just in the raw, most base sense, he made her feel how she'd felt when she was seventeen. It was like falling in love for the first time all over again.

'I think you'd better tell me everything…on skis.'

Chapter Eleven

August 2005

'We could swim... now we have caught fish,' Guy said. She was feeling lightheaded from the wine and full from the baguettes and cheese. She smiled, feeling content, warm and deeply satisfied for the first time in a long time. She lay back on the grass bank and stretched her arms behind her, flexing out her fingers, reaching out into the air. She almost felt free. Then suddenly her fingers recoiled as they made contact with something cold and wet.

She screamed and leapt up, wiping her hand on her dress. It was the fish Guy had caught and partially wrapped in the paper bag that had originally housed the bread.

He laughed at her, his green eyes alight with amusement. Then he began to peel off his T-shirt. The sight of his tight, brown body, the sun reflecting off the slight sheen made her insides unfurl.

'You swim?' Guy asked again.

'Do I swim? Or do I want to swim now?' Emma asked in soft tones.

'Swim now. Take off clothes,' Guy said, his fingers unfastening the button at the top of his cut-off jeans.

'Oh no, I don't think so,' Emma said.

'Why not?'

'I...'

Why not? Why couldn't she? No one was around, just her and him. She didn't have to be the person she was back at home. She could be anyone she wanted to be. This was her chance to escape her life for a moment. Here there was no house still tainted by death, no grief counsellors explaining all the stages she had to work through... and there was no Marilyn.

As the name came to mind she was struck by a feeling of rebellion. She stood up on her feet and hurriedly lifted her sundress. She knew he was watching and she liked it. She pulled the cotton fabric up and over her head leaving herself in a white underwire bra and high-legged cotton briefs.

He appraised her, from the ends of her toes to the top of her head, nothing escaping his gaze. And then he pulled down his shorts and threw them into the bank. They landed on top of Emma's dress.

She unfastened the back of her bra and let it fall down off her shoulders. She removed it from her arms, then stood before him, her breasts bare, her heart beating hard in her chest. She had never been semi-naked in front of a boy before and it was terrifying. She didn't know what to do. She didn't know what she wanted to do. It was frightening and exhilarating all at the same time.

'Come, we swim,' Guy said, holding his hand out for her.

Dressed in just her knickers, she took his hand and let him lead her into the water. Despite the heat of the day the water chilled her toes and she held her breath as he made her step forward, deeper, until she was past up to her knees and the water was on its way to being waist height.

'It's so cold! Gosh, it's cold!' Emma exclaimed, hopping from one leg to another and trying not to shiver.

'The cold is good. It is... how you say... *apisant*,' Guy said, still holding her hand.

'I don't know what that means,' Emma said.

'It makes you feel very good,' he responded, turning back towards her.

'Fish don't bite, do they?' Emma asked, trying to lighten the mood as he moved closer.

'*Non.*'

He stood opposite her, so close she could feel his breath on her face. It smelt of red wine, cheese and fresh bread. He put his hands on her shoulders and slowly, inch by inch, he moved them down her arms, his thumbs brushing past her breasts.

Her stomach fell down to her feet and she felt a bubbling sensation rising up inside her. She stepped forward and put her hand onto his chest. As she took a deep breath in, her fingers caressed the curve of every accentuated muscle in his lean torso.

He took her hand from his body and held it tight in his, stopping her exploration.

'Have... have I done something wrong?' she asked, her voice trembling with nervousness.

'*Non*,' he replied, shaking his head.

'Then...'

'We swim now,' he said, splashing her with water.

She let out a scream and hurried to splash him back as he raced away up the river.

'Hey! Wait! Slow down!' Emma called as she tried to run through the water. The muscles in her thighs tightened with every movement. She watched Guy dive into the water, completely disappear from view and then, yards ahead, bob up. She took a long breath, knowing she had to submerge herself and swim to be in with any chance of catching him. She braced herself for the cold and dived into the river.

Despite the warmth of the day the water was harsh and it felt like a thousand ice cubes had been thrown at her with force. She drew her arms back and forth in a front crawl, determined not to look silly. She was a reasonable swimmer and she wanted to prove herself his equal. She couldn't be worrying about the cold or the weed or the fact that fish might nibble her toes. This was her first date with a boy she really liked and she needed it to go well.

Then, all of a sudden, something was dragging her to the left. What was it? Guy? A river creature? Something else? Her arms were flailing, not aiding her movement at all and no matter how furiously she kicked with her legs she was being pulled left... and down. She panicked. She couldn't keep afloat. Her legs were being taken from under her, her whole body being dragged beneath the surface. She was fighting hard against the current but it was relentless. She was losing her strength. Her arms were like blocks of lead, her legs like useless strands of spaghetti, stringy and weak. The water seeped into her mouth as she struggled to take in air, trying to stay on top of the water but sinking and losing out to the force of nature.

Just as she thought she was going to lose her life in France, wearing nothing but a pair of cotton pants, she felt a pair of strong hands grip her abdomen. Her face was forced skywards and back up into the sunlight.

She gasped a mouthful of air and realised then how close she'd been to succumbing to the current. Her chest was heaving, trying to re-establish a comfortable breathing pattern. She dipped back down into the water and realised she wasn't quite safe yet. She kicked for the bank, summoning up every last ounce of energy she possessed.

Guy bobbed up from beneath her, gripping her again and pulling her to the riverside.

Finally, they reached the bank and were able to stand up in the water. Emma shivered as her skin pimpled with cold and the fright she'd just had. Without hesitation Guy pulled her into his embrace, wrapping his arms around her body, tightening his frame to hers to warm her.

'*Je suis désolé...* I am sorry. I did not ask that you swim well. The river... it is... how you say... *dangereux*,' Guy said, rubbing his hands up and down her back.

'I thought it was a very big fish... *un très gros poisson*,' Emma responded. Her chattering lips let out a small laugh. She'd been scared. Actually she'd been terrified, but it hadn't been his fault. And the sensation he was giving her now, his skin flush against hers, was more than worth a partial drowning.

He prised her away from him and she raised her head to meet his eyes.

'I do not want to hurt you, Emma,' he whispered.

'You won't,' she replied.

Chapter Twelve

Present Day

'So, let me get this straight. He *definitely* isn't Dominic's father.'

Ally had sat with her mouth hanging open since Emma started talking. It had started out being parted perhaps only an inch, then it had widened with every sentence until it was full-on agape.

'I said so, didn't I?' Emma snapped, taking a sip of her drink. It was cold.

'I know you said so, but you've just described this teenage boy, who's now all grown up and hotness personified, as the love of your life and yet I'm supposed to believe someone else is Dominic's father,' Ally exclaimed at great volume.

'Keep your voice down, Ally, please,' Emma begged. She looked toward the group of mothers nearest to them, worried they were listening.

'You know he's taken, don't you? A French supermodel no less,' Ally continued.

Yes, she knew. She'd seen the coral dress and the Botoxed face and Guy's arm around striking Madeleine Courtier.

'Yes, I know and I don't care. I'm not pursuing him. I'm with Chris,' she answered.

She couldn't have made the statement sound any more forced. It was like a recorded message.

'So what do you want? What's the real problem here because I'm not seeing it,' Ally remarked in a tone slightly below jackhammer.

Emma looked out over the sports hall as Guy began to demonstrate weaving the ball between cones. Her whole body contracted from looking at him, just like it had all those years ago. The feelings of resentment and fury were fast being diluted by the rush of passion that zipped through her every time she saw him.

'Who *is* Dominic's father? Are you actually going to tell me at all? Because it isn't like I've spent years asking, is it?' Ally said, snorting air.

Ah, there it was again – *that* same question. Having told Ally about Guy's existence in that first French summer now, she had to give her friend something. There was no way Ally would let it go until she had a little extra.

'The truth is, I have no idea,' Emma answered. She'd accompanied the statement with a shrug.

'What?'

'I don't know who his father is. You remember what I was like when my mum was ill. There were a few drunken nights at house parties weeks before she died I can't even remember. Then, after she died, Dad took me off to France to stop me drinking the contents of his wine collection.'

'What? No. No, you didn't.' Ally's mouth opened wider and her eyes narrowed with suspicion.

'That boy down there is proof that I did,' Emma said with a sigh. 'I was losing my mum. I was grieving before she left us. There were other parties, Ally. Parties you weren't at. Parties I definitely shouldn't have gone to.' She swallowed. 'Sorry.' She took another sip of her cold coffee.

'Em, tell me what's really going on here,' Ally begged. 'So you might not have felt you could tell me back then but, surely you can tell me anything now. Water's under the bridge, years of it. Let me in.'

Poor Ally looked wounded. She didn't want to lie, but Dominic came first. Just like he always had.

'It was a bad time, I did a lot of stupid things,' Emma replied.

The list of inappropriate things she'd done after her mother's death was vast, but she didn't consider all of them stupid. Some had even been well thought out. Not all had been successful and she had to live with those consequences.

'Em,' Elly whispered.

She shook her head. 'I can't.' She swallowed. 'And, truthfully, I don't know who Dominic's father is.'

Ally nodded, obviously not content but resigned to the fact she was getting nothing further. 'So, the problem here is, Guy's not the father but Guy thinks he was your first and you...'

'Had done it many times before we met,' Emma admitted with a nod.

'Well, you just need to shatter his illusions. Tell him he isn't the father and move on. Yes his pride might be dented, but we've all had our share of knocks.' Ally slurped up the last of her coffee. 'Has Chris proposed lately? Once a month now, isn't it?' She launched her empty cardboard cup into the bin.

'Yesterday,' Emma answered. She looked through the glass at Dominic. He was dribbling with speed and accuracy.

'No! What, after my free bar last night? God, did he end up on the shots?' Ally asked.

'It wasn't last night, it was earlier... in the morning... it doesn't matter,' Emma responded with a sigh.

Ally was listening but she wasn't hearing her. That was just the way she was. Ally was her best friend, her sounding board, the only person she had to talk to/at. But things were black and white in Ally's world. If you didn't like something you changed it. Ally didn't dwell on things. She made decisions and stuck to them. Emma thought too much. She'd always been guilty of thinking too much.

'So, what was he like? I mean, did he have the body on him he's got now?' Ally asked, a glint in her eye.

'Chris?'

'No, not Chris. Chris' body in that nylon suit is not something I want to have wet dreams about... no offence or anything.'

'Guy?'

'Yes, of course Guy.'

'What do you think?' Emma answered, a smile opening her mouth.

The boy had talent, already he could see that. It was so hard for him to concentrate on anyone else in the class when his son was stood in front of him. When he'd addressed the group, introduced himself and outlined what he was hoping to achieve in their session, the boy had looked up at him, his eyes wide with excitement and enthusiasm. He'd wanted to stop. He'd wanted to dismiss the other children and concentrate on his son. He had to be his boy. Watching him now, he still couldn't believe it. All these years, all the years of burying himself in the game, fighting his way to the top, being the best, staying the best, and, without his knowledge, he had someone to do it all for.

'Shall I turn again, Guy?' Dominic called.

Guy smiled at him and ruffled his mop of hair with his hand.

'*Oui*, go again,' he responded.

Chapter Thirteen

She heard the scream through the glass. She didn't need to look to know it was Dominic but she still did, hoping her ears were deceiving her. The visual only gave her confirmation. Without uttering a word to Ally, she leapt from her seat and fled the room.

Her heart was pulsating hard, throbbing a beat in her chest and her neck simultaneously. Her maternal instinct kicked in, concern for Dominic flooding every sense. By the time she reached the bottom of the stairs she was practically hyperventilating. She burst through the door to the hall, uncaring about anything other than getting to her child.

Guy was on his knees next to Dominic's prostrate form, holding the boy's leg with one hand and ruffling his hair with the other.

'What happened?'

The phrase came out of her mouth sharp and accusing.

'He is OK… just a twist,' Guy told her.

'And how could you possibly know that? Are you a doctor?' Emma yelled, taking hold of Dominic's hand.

'No, but…'

'Where does it hurt, Dom?'

'It's OK, Mum. It's not too bad now,' Dominic answered.

He gingerly bent his knee upwards. Emma caught the grimace and heard the creak.

'You're going to the hospital,' she said.

'I'm sure if I get some ice,' Guy began.

'Oh, you're sure, are you? Well, I think I'd quite like the opinion of a medical professional, not an amateur football coach,' Emma blasted.

'Mum! It wasn't Guy's fault. I just turned too quickly and—'

'Is everything alright? Come on, kiddies, it's rude to stare. Here, take some of the balls and kick and run or whatever,' Ally suggested, arriving in the room.

'We're going to the hospital,' Emma repeated, urging Dominic up from the floor.

'What's he done? Nothing broken is there? I could really do without a lawsuit in my first week,' Ally said, looking down at Dominic.

'Come on, Dom,' Emma urged, trying to help him up.

'Oww!' Dominic let out a screech of agony.

'Oh goodness. Shall I call an ambulance?' Ally reacted.

'No. Just leave him alone. Let me get him out of here and to a doctor,' Emma shrieked.

'Let me take him,' Guy said.

'No. I can do it,' Emma said. She tried to lift Dominic up but he was a dead weight and far too heavy for her.

'Emma, please. I can carry him to your car,' Guy told her.

'I don't need your help,' she insisted through gritted teeth. In an attempt to make a stand she lifted Dominic skyward, only to have him cry out in pain again. Some of the other children whimpered.

'I'm taking him to the car,' Guy stated firmly.

Worried for Dominic, Emma let Guy take over. With minimal effort he lifted the boy into his arms and headed out of the hall.

'Give me a ring, Em. Let me know he's OK,' Ally said, catching Emma's arm before she could depart.

She nodded. That was all she had the will for. She needed to be with Dominic, holding his hand and making everything better, just like she'd always done. She caught up to Guy.

'You'll be fine, Dom. Remember when Grandad tripped over the garden hose? He made all that fuss and it was just a sprain,' Emma said.

'It hurts a bit,' Dominic admitted, his eyes moistening.

'It's just the shock,' Emma said. She hoped that was all it was.

'Sometimes the body causes pain so it may repair,' Guy offered. He turned his back to the door, pushing it open with the force of his body. Emma tried to help by pulling one of the doors back but her effort wasn't needed.

'I shouldn't have turned so fast. I didn't listen to you,' Dominic moaned. He screwed up his eyes.

'It wasn't *your* fault,' Emma said. She caught Guy's eye and hoped she left him in no doubt just whose fault it was.

'Good footballers have to put up with the lows. We all have injuries,' Guy told him.

'It's the silver car... just there,' Emma indicated. She led the way.

'Have you had injuries?' Dominic asked him, raising his head.

'Of course. Just last week, before I move to England. I bruise my foot just by hitting the ball the wrong way,' Guy explained.

'And did you have to stop playing for a bit?'

'The physio say at least three days rest but…'

'You didn't, did you? You played.' Dominic's expression turned to one of boyish wonder.

'That's helpful, isn't it? He's injured and you're filling his head with suggestions about not resting,' Emma blasted.

'That was not what I meant…' Guy began.

'He's a child. They're easily influenced.'

She flung open the back door and started to push objects across the seat to make room for Dominic.

'He'll have to sit on his booster seat, but I'll move the seat right forward,' Emma told him.

Guy adjusted his stance, leaning in slowly to set Dominic down. The boy tensed his body as he met the seat. Guy removed his arms from underneath him and stepped back. Dominic looked pale but that wasn't so unusual when you'd had a shock. Guy reached forward, his fingers making contact with Dominic's dark hair.

'Thank you for your help,' Emma interrupted. 'We'd better go.'

Her words stung. He was being dismissed. She'd partially closed the door, stopping him from any further words or contact. This could not be. He would not let this be.

'We must talk,' he stated.

She shut Dominic's door, avoided eye contact. She had almost turned her head away completely.

'I have to get Dominic to the hospital.'

'Emma…please…tell me.' He reached out for her, his fingers gently grazing the skin of her forearm.

'I have nothing to say,' she stuttered.

'He is my son. Isn't he?' He couldn't help himself. He couldn't skirt around the issue anymore. He thought he knew but he needed to hear it from her lips. He wanted to hear her say the words, tell him what he longed to know.

'No, Guy. He's not.'

She saw him rock on his heels as the two-letter word hit him like a lethal dart. The light went out of his eyes, his shoulders fell and his hands sank to his sides. She swallowed. She shouldn't have been so blunt. She shouldn't have been deliberately cruel. *Had* she been deliberately cruel?

And then in a matter of seconds, his demeanour altered. He lifted his head, jutted out his chin and met her eyes with his. He took a long breath and she watched his chest swell.

'I do not believe you.'

The way he said the words burned her. He was angry. His teeth were pressed tightly together, that full mouth stretched into a furious, thin line of discontent. The dark eyelashes were hanging over his eyes, questioning and accusing.

His expression and the aura of resentment he was giving off was hurting her. She felt sick. She couldn't bear it.

'I need to go.'

She did need to go but whether it was for Dominic's benefit or her own was up for debate.

'We will talk, Emma. We need to talk,' he said.

She closed her ears to it, shut off her mind. She tried to concentrate on the matter at hand which was getting into the car and getting away. She couldn't go back there. She wouldn't let him remind her of that time.

She leapt into the driver's seat and closed the door on him. Her breathing came out in short, rapid pants. Her hands shook as she sought the ignition.

He placed his palm flat against the window. She jumped where she sat.

'Please, Emma,' he called from outside.

She turned her head, let herself connect to those pools of green, looking at her with such emotion. She couldn't look away. But she had to. With a trembling hand she started the engine. He withdrew his hand and she pulled the car away.

Chapter Fourteen

The rest of the morning blurred. He wasn't really present at the remainder of the training session. His mouth was working, giving out instructions and praise in equal measure. His body too was there, showing his pupils how to perform football skills. But his mind... Thoughts of Dominic moved around his head like a carriage on a Ferris wheel. Up and around, down, shaking and unstable.

He couldn't believe what Emma said. He *had* to be Dominic's father. He just had to be. If he wasn't, if she had been that close to someone else, it changed everything. It would tear up the precious memories. It would demolish all the feelings he clung to in his darkest moments. She'd whispered things to him; let him in on her innermost fears. Her grief, her jealousy, and all her insecurities. Or so he'd thought.

He sucked down some water as the parents began to arrive to collect their children. Ally had come in with the clipboard and was ensuring no one left without being marked off. He looked at his watch. He should head home. Tonight was an important function for Finnerham. There was a charity auction he was going to be paraded at. But he couldn't go without knowing about Dominic. Not only if he was better – but if he was a Duval.

'It's making it hot and the bandage smells.'

They were home. Two hours in accident and emergency was a record. Once, when Dominic was a baby, she'd been passed from nurse to nurse and spent almost five hours there. A wailing baby with a high temperature and not one person seemed to care. She'd been terrified. She was young and naïve; terrified that she had left it too long to get medical help for her son. Mike had driven them and then Marilyn had turned up. Perfumed, preened and wearing pearls. At one in the morning. The memory sent a shot of bile into her throat. She swallowed it down.

'Mum! How long does it have to stay on?' Dominic called.

She came back into the room.

'At least a week. You heard the doctor. And no football either.'

She put another cushion behind Dominic's back and lifted his injured leg onto the sofa. Just a bad sprain, nothing torn or broken they'd said.

'Are you hot?' She put the back of her hand on his forehead.

'My ankle is and the bandage is made out of that stinky stuff. It's like the one Grandad had on his arm when he hurt it at badminton.'

'I'll get you a drink. Hot chocolate?' Emma offered.

'Coke?'

'Dom...'

'Please.'

'Oh, go on then,' she gave in.

She flicked on the television and handed Dominic the remote control.

She was exhausted. After a late night and a morning of emotional turmoil she was done in. She switched the kettle on and opened the fridge. She took out the Coke and poured some into a glass.

Her mobile phone vibrated with a text message. She looked at the sender. Chris.

Did Dom enjoy the training?

She let out a sigh. She couldn't reply. She should call him. She should let him know about Dominic's ankle but she couldn't do it now. He would ask a load of questions and she'd feel uneasy. She still felt uneasy about what happened with Guy. He'd looked so determined, then so wounded and finally, furious. When he'd planted his hand on the window, a moment from the past had flashed before her. She had ached to say the right things. Not the truth, but the words to stop him asking. She'd never expected him to be here. He wasn't supposed to ever be in her life again. What she'd left in France was supposed to have stayed there and what she'd taken away wasn't meant to be shared.

A knock on the front door made her jump.

He should have been travelling back to Finnerham but instead he'd waited for Ally to leave the fitness centre. He was convinced a good friend would need to check up in person, make sure the boy was OK. She'd driven to a leafy suburb and parked outside a terraced home with Venetian blinds at the windows and a dark green front door. He parked across the street, not directly opposite, but close enough to see. He slunk down low in the seat, knowing his Range Rover probably stuck out like a sore thumb. He felt like a voyeur. Watching, he saw Ally knock on the door. His heart picked up pace as he waited. Perhaps this wasn't where they lived. Maybe this was another friend of Ally's or a man, a boyfriend.

The door opened a crack and he saw her. A look of relief seemed to cross her face when she greeted Ally, as if she was expecting another caller. Had she expected him? If she had, that told him everything he needed to know.

'God, you look bloody awful... on skis. It's broken, isn't it? It's broken and you're going to sue Ultra Leisure,' Ally spluttered when Emma opened the door.

'Oh it's you!' Emma exclaimed. Relief wrapped around her words.

'Is it in a cast? Please don't sue the leisure centre, Em. I'm really enjoying the job and it's great money...'

'Come in,' Emma said, opening the door wider.

'What can I do? There must be something I can do. How about free membership... for life,' Ally said. She wrung her hands together.

'It's not broken. It's just a bad sprain. He's fine,' Emma told her.

'Oh thank God! I was totally panicking. For a minute

I thought I was going to get fired and have to hang on to Jonty for a bit longer until I found another job!'

'And you're also relieved Dominic isn't going to be on crutches for weeks.'

'Oh, Em, of course. I mean that goes without saying,' Ally said quickly.

Emma let out a breath and put her hand to her forehead, pinching her eyebrows. She could feel the beginnings of a headache.

'Are you alright? You look a bit pale.'

'Yeah,' she replied. She didn't know what else to say. She couldn't think straight.

'I've brought Dom some chocolate. All that the vending machine could offer apart from sports drinks; I thought he might have had enough sport for one day. I could murder a coffee,' Ally stated.

Emma nodded.

'I'll go and give it to him. Then you can tell me all about it,' Ally said. She reached for Emma's hand and gave it a squeeze.

Emma was sure Ally thought she was a moron. What was it about her and this man? She was a strong, independent woman. A teacher and a pillar of the community. She marked GCSE homework, she taught Shakespeare and last term she'd even headed up an abseiling experience. She was not someone who should fall apart over a man... a boy from her past.

'Let me get this straight then. You told him, that he wasn't Dom's father and he didn't believe you,' Ally recapped.

'Sshh, Ally I don't want Dom to hear any of this. It was bad enough earlier. I shut the car door and luckily his leg was hurting him so he didn't ask any awkward questions but…' She picked up her cup of coffee and cradled it to her chest.

'He isn't Dom's father. You're really sure?'

'Haven't we been through this?'

'And you'd tell me the truth about this, wouldn't you?'

Emma lifted her chin, looked her friend directly in the eye.

'That was a really stupid thing to say. I'm sorry,' Ally backtracked. 'That was a bit of me circa back then.'

'I just really don't need this happening. I've got pressure at school, I've got Chris proposing every month, I've got Dad's internet dating to worry about and—'

'Why are you worried about Mike's internet dating? He's a grown man. It's about time he had a bit of fun, isn't it? What was the name of that girlfriend he had years ago? The one that looked like she'd stepped off the pages of *Woman's Weekly*? All light perm and acrylic jewellery,' Ally commented.

'Marilyn.' The word scorched her mouth.

'That was it. He hasn't had anyone serious since then, has he?'

'*She* wasn't serious. She was an interfering, busybody who took advantage of a grieving widower,' Emma spat.

'Right. Best left in the past then. Like you and the Gallic hunk?'

'There was a question mark.'

'What?'

'You put a question mark at the end of your sentence.'

'Yes Ms Grammar, I did. Is there one?'

'I don't want him here. My life is different now. He hurt me and I'd forgotten him.' *Liar.*

'But?'

As Emma put her coffee cup back on the table the letterbox rattled. The sound made her release her grip too soon. The cup circled on its axis, then tipped, spilling the remainder of its contents.

'Whoa! You need to relax. It's the letterbox. Probably the useless freebie paper with the coupons for Dominos that make their extortionate pizzas almost worth buying,' Ally suggested.

Emma got to her feet, ignored the fallen cup and walked from the kitchen. What had landed on the doormat wasn't the freebie paper. It was the page of a notepad.

Instinctively she knew who it was from. She bent down to pick it up. The paper was folded in two, her name written on it, a line underneath. She opened it up, reading the words.

Tomorrow night. 7.30 p.m. Café Rouge. Guy

Chapter Fifteen

August 2005

'I have to go,' Guy whispered. 'I have work.'

Emma opened her eyes. The warm sun on her face, the rays seeping into her skin always made her drowsy. Lying next to him, usually wearing her most flimsy outfits, was heaven. She felt so safe, so content, so happy.

This was their third date. After she'd almost drowned in the river they'd spent a second date together on the beach. She'd told her dad she'd met a new girlfriend called Sally. Sally came from Brighton (it sounded cool and was far enough away from Wiltshire not to continue the relationship when she got home) and she was studying for her A levels too. Mike seemed happy enough with the lie and had yet to ask to meet the girl. If he did ask she would think of something. She could probably find a willing teenage holidaymaker to pay.

Now, on date number three, they were lying in a honey-coloured field of corn having spent the afternoon walking through the French countryside, stopping to play ball now and then and chasing butterflies.

'What time is it?' she asked, reaching for his hand and the watch on his wrist. She hadn't noticed the watch before. It looked expensive.

'It is *cinq heure*,' he informed her. He took his arm away.

'Five. Where do you have to be at five? There's a game show tonight in the clubhouse but that's not until eight,' she said.

'I know. I have to work before, at the hotel and *ma mere*... she needs my help,' Guy told her.

'With your brother?'

'Yes. I have to work for him now,' Guy said. His beautiful eyes dimmed, his lips downturned and Emma reached up to take his face with one hand.

'You're a good big brother,' she stated. She softly brushed his forehead with her fingers, savouring the way his skin felt to touch.

'I want to be,' he replied, moving his lips to kiss the tips of her fingers as they travelled to his cheek.

'I want to stay here forever,' Emma stated.

As soon as the words left her lips she inwardly cursed herself. Why had she said that? *Stupid idiot!* This was their third date. He was gorgeous and she was lucky he was spending time with her! She'd gone and blown it! Everyone knew boys didn't like stupid girls who thought three dates meant always!

'There is a... how you say... *un monde entier*,' he responded.

'What does that mean?'

'The... land... the place...'

'The world?'

'Yes, *oui*, the world is big place. I want to see more than here,' Guy told her.

'I know what you mean. Until I came here I hadn't seen much more than the inside of our house for months. We thought my mum would want to go places, live her last days doing things she'd always planned to do. In the end she was just too sick to do anything but lie there and wait to die,' Emma explained.

She felt the pain in her gut, rising up into her throat, bringing the emotions with it. She was so fed up of crying. And boys on third dates were not interested in emotion. Well, actually, Ally had convinced her that all boys were interested in at all was getting into your underwear. And once they'd accomplished that, the relationship was pretty much doomed. Unless you wanted to give him a blow job. That was going to guarantee you at least six months together if you did it right.

'I am sorry for your mother,' he said. He brushed his hand through her hair and brought his lips down onto her cheeks in turn. It felt nice. It felt reassuring. Perhaps there might be a fourth date after all.

'We should read the Chaucer. If you want to be teacher you should work hard,' Guy said. He picked up her copy of *The Canterbury Tales* and opened it up where the page was marked.

'I hold a mouses wit not worth a leke, That hath but on hole for to sterten to,' Guy read.

Emma giggled. The text sounded terrible in class with Mr Devlin reading it. It sounded even more ridiculous read by a Frenchman.

'What does this mean? He talks of mouse… *souris*?'

'I know,' Emma said, unable to suppress her laughter.

'What does it mean?' Guy asked again.

'Basically it means don't put all your eggs in one basket. A mouse's heart is not worth anything if it has but one hole to run to and if that one fails then all is over. Something like that,' Emma explained.

'I do not know.'

'Everyone should have a contingency plan. In life things don't always work out how you want them to,' she said.

She sat up, brushed some imaginary dust from her dress and snatched the book from him. It was a shame Chaucer hadn't written about what to do if your mum died and your dad was seeing another woman.

'You are mad,' Guy remarked, watching her.

'I don't want to go home to how things are,' she let out. There were the words again, falling from her lips without any thought.

'You are still sad for your mother.'

'No. It isn't that,' she snapped.

'Emma… you must tell me,' he said.

Her breathing was erratic now. She was thinking about Marilyn and her heart was pumping the blood around her body so much faster than it should. That woman had been waiting. She had been waiting for her mother to die. Now she was sending messages to her dad. Texts ending in kisses just weeks after the funeral. What sort of person did that?

'Emma…'

'My mother was dying and my dad was seeing someone else. Some bitch called Marilyn,' she blurted out.

She felt the tears coming. She willed herself not to let

the emotion go. Things were going well. He liked her. She shouldn't be this wreck of a person. Why couldn't she just be normal? If she was normal, not a sobbing idiot, if she got a push-up bra and court shoes, she might be able to keep in touch with him when she got home. If she carried on the way she was he would move on to Tasha or Melody before the week was up.

She looked for something to wipe her eyes. Corn didn't look like it would make a good tissue. Before she could think anymore, the air flooded out of her lungs as he wrapped his arms around her. He held her so tight against his body and rocked her like a child.

Could she let it out? Could she let him see how fragile she really was? Back in the house, just her and her dad and the threat of Marilyn hanging over her, she had longed for her mother. She spent more and more time alone contemplating how her life was going to be from now on. What she wanted. What she didn't want. How much she hated what had happened to her. She was angry. She was mad at the world. She didn't know what to do. Who was Emma Barron now? Who would she become?

'I don't want to be the girl everyone pities. The girl who likes books too much. The girl who lost her mum,' she sobbed into his chest.

'What do you want?' he asked her, cradling her head with his hands.

'I want an aim. I want something for me. Something to call my own. I'm doing these exams but I don't know if that's what I really want. I don't know what I really want but it isn't a house shrouded in death and a father already looking for a replacement wife,' she bawled.

'We will find a way,' Guy said. His voice was soft, husky and warm in her ear. The words caressed her, filled her up with hope. This was a holiday romance. There was no future in it. But what he was saying soothed her. It made her feel better, gave her the consolation she needed, wrapped up her soul.

'We will make things better... *ensemble*... together,' Guy said. He interlocked their hands and her heart swelled. 'When I am with you... everything is better,' he told her. She felt his body contract with a shiver and he held on tight.

Chapter Sixteen

Present Day

His head was pounding and he deserved every second of the pain. He'd got back to Finnerham late. Madeleine had scolded him. Then, to placate her, he'd let her show him the products of her shopping spree at his expense. By that time he was desperate to throw himself into something… anything. The function was a blessing. He'd posed for photos next to the charity auction billboards outside the hotel ballroom. He'd done at least half a dozen interviews for television, newspapers and magazines. Then he'd hit the bar. Egged on by some of his new teammates and wanting to make a good impression he'd accepted every drink he'd been offered and bought plenty in return. Madeleine had seemed happy with the other wives and girlfriends clucking over their designer outfits and handbags. He'd wanted to blot everything out for a few hours but he should have known it was impossible. Emma and Dominic never left his thoughts.

He reached for a glass of water on the nightstand and

with a shaking hand he took a sip. It wet his tongue for a millisecond and then made him feel worse.

'Guy,' Madeleine called from the other side of the king-sized bed.

She knew he was awake now he'd moved. He took another mouthful of water and replaced the glass.

'Good morning,' he forced from his lips.

'You have too much to drink last night. There will be pictures on Facebook,' Madeleine scolded.

'We raise a lot of money for the charity,' he replied, putting his head back on the pillow and hoping it would silence her.

'I have to help you to the taxi,' she continued.

He sighed and closed his eyes. He couldn't remember a thing after the auction. He didn't really care what had happened.

'Gabriella wants me to talk about a lingerie collection,' Madeleine continued.

He didn't like her friend Gabriella. She was dating his new teammate, Daniel. Daniel was just about bearable on the field, but he didn't much care for the idea of socialising with him. He tried to think of something supportive to say but couldn't. Not that it mattered. Whatever he said would be wrong.

'This could be good for me. Her father is involved with a new film production company,' Madeleine carried on.

Again, he had no idea how to respond. He coughed.

'I do not know what is wrong. You want to move to England but since we arrive nothing is right,' she remarked.

Now he felt guilty. How he was behaving wasn't Madeleine's fault. Even after a year she barely knew him.

That was his fault. Their relationship was built on his success as a footballer and her desire to be in the spotlight. If his success should diminish he knew she wouldn't stick around. The worst thing was, that thought didn't bother him. They were seen together, they attended all the important parties together and they slept together. That was the sum total of their relationship. Making love with Madeleine was like taking part in an advanced yoga class followed by a spin session. It was all positions and deep breathing followed by sweating, shouting and shuddering. It was all about the physical. Emotions never came into it. Maybe that was his fault too.

'I am sorry,' he offered.

'I don't want you to say you're sorry, Guy. I want you to show me,' she stated.

A slender hand reached out for him, tracing its way down his back, stopping at the very bottom and teasing down his underwear.

He closed his eyes tight and bit his lip.

Chris let out a noise any warthog would be proud of. A flailing arm crossed over to Emma's side of the bed and hit her in the cheek. She resisted the urge to shout. Instead she placed his arm back down on the sheet and slipped out of the bed.

She'd called him last night and practically begged him to come over. She'd made a meat and potato pie, got in a case of lager and some wine and spent the evening looking attentive when he talked about his day. She even managed a laugh when he told at least half a dozen jokes she'd heard before.

She needed routine. She needed to be reminded of the life she had. The normal, everyday life she'd been living for the last eight years. This was where she belonged. This was the life she'd chosen. She'd chosen Dominic and her home and later she'd realised that teaching really was what she wanted to do. She was good at it. She would learn and grow through teaching. She would pass on her passion for literature to children; give them something to lose themselves in if life got too hard.

She made her way downstairs and headed for the kitchen. It was almost seven. Dominic would usually be awake. She could only assume the painkillers had made him drowsy. The dishes from the night before greeted her. There were also eight cans of lager and three wine bottles, all empty. No wonder she had a headache.

She turned the kettle on and opened the cupboard to get the tea bags out. That's when the note fluttered down and landed on the worktop.

There it was. The invitation. A one-line note she had to make a decision about. She smoothed her finger over the black, handwritten words, his name. Did she owe him anything? Definitely. Did he know she owed him anything? No. He'd betrayed their trust. He'd promised her everything and he'd let her down. They'd had a few weeks together but she'd believed him when he said he was going to be her world. He'd sworn he would. She had to make him believe he wasn't Dominic's father. But what happened then? Once he believed that would he leave them alone? And did she want him to?

She closed her eyes and breathed in. A moment of stillness and she was transported back to La Baume. The fine hairs on her arms all stood up to attention, almost feeling the heat of the French sun. For a short time she had been so very happy. She'd been released from all the pressures in her life. There had been too many pressures for a seventeen-year-old girl. Guy had relieved her of that worry. She had believed in him and his dreams. All he'd wanted to do was better himself and she'd had no doubt that he could. He wanted to learn everything. He saw the world as a globe of adventure. He wanted to travel, work hard, learn, see everything. His enthusiasm had been infectious and she'd got caught up in the fantasy. That's what he'd been. A delicious, teenage fantasy.

She heard Dominic coming down the stairs, moving a lot faster than someone with a bad foot should move. She pocketed the note into her dressing gown.

'Hey, Mum,' he greeted with a smile.

'Morning. How's your ankle?' Emma asked, standing up and giving him a hug.

'It's alright. Can I take the bandage off? And can I have a fried egg for breakfast?'

Chapter Seventeen

'I'm going to meet him.' She'd whispered the words so quietly even *she* hadn't heard them.

'Emma? Is that you? You'll have to speak up. I've got the coffee machine guy here sorting out the cappuccino issue. He's pumping and grinding with lots of long metal instruments, but he is hot! Think Kevin Bacon when he was younger,' Ally responded.

Emma shook her head. She'd debated about telling Ally and now she wished she hadn't made the call. She wasn't in the mood for her friend's exaggerated humour.

'I'll leave you to him.'

'No! Tell me what's going on. How's Dom?'

'He's tentatively playing bowling on the Wii with Chris. I've banned him from real sport for a while.'

'Good idea. Despite running a wellness centre, there are days when I can see that exercise definitely isn't for some people. There's a chap signed up for Boxercise I'm going to have the oxygen on standby for,' Ally continued.

Emma didn't respond. She'd made the decision to meet with Guy but it wasn't sitting well. In fact, every time she thought about it she felt sick.

'Did you say you're going to meet him?' Ally asked, suddenly translating the words she claimed not to have heard.

'Yes… at least I think so.'

'Well, I think it's a good plan. If you want a ring on your finger and a nice white dress to waltz down the aisle in then you need to give the ex the heave-ho and get him gone. Not that he isn't hot, because God he *is* hot but—'

'What makes you think I want to get married?' Emma interrupted.

'I know you keep turning Chris down, but that's because you're waiting for the grand gesture. The grand gesture you deserve. Knowing him, he's probably been saying the words over a pan of spaghetti hoops or in the ad break for Formula One.'

'Is that what you think?' She tried to steady her voice but she couldn't keep the wobble out of it.

'I think if Chris gets all dressed up, not in that terrible suit he had on the other night, and if he takes you out somewhere swish, gets the right flowers – you know, not ones from the garage – and gets down on one knee, you should snap him up. He's honest, he's hard-working and he loves Dominic. It takes a special person to take on someone else's child,' Ally finished.

Fury bubbled up inside her. Suddenly she was absolutely rage-ridden. She couldn't speak. Her head was throbbing. She wanted to slam the phone down.

'Emma?'

'You think… you think… Chris *will do*,' Emma stammered over the words.

'I like Chris.'

'You like him so much you couldn't remember his last name on Friday night.'

'Emma, I—'

'You think because I have a high mortgage, an average-paid job and an illegitimate son I should get Chris down the aisle because that's what I deserve. A kind, hard-working man who's putting up with my kid.'

'I didn't say that! Emma…'

'Well you're wrong, Ally. I say no to marrying Chris because he deserves someone so much better than me!'

With that statement made Emma replaced the phone and put her hands to her mouth, aching all over. Tears were slipping from her eyes already. When the kitchen door opened she hurriedly turned away and grabbed for the kitchen roll.

'Emma?' Chris said, looking at her.

The sleeves of his rugby shirt were rolled up to his elbows, he had a sheen of perspiration on his forehead and the Wii remote still in his hand.

'I'm fine. I'm fine. Just Ally and her latest boyfriend. The pilot. She thinks he's getting more than duty free from one of the air stewardesses.' She wiped her eyes and put on a smile.

'And it's upset you that much?' Chris asked. He didn't sound convinced.

'Well, she's a good friend and I don't like to see her messed about. She deserves someone nice, someone who'll look after her,' Emma added.

'She's lucky to have you worrying about her.' He put his arm around her and drew her into a hug. She let herself be warmed by his affection, closed her eyes and remembered.

'Dom's whipping me at bowling. You going to come and play?' Chris asked, letting her go.

'Yeah, in a second. Just got to iron his uniform for tomorrow,' she answered.

'Alright. But don't leave it too long because he's getting better with every turn,' Chris told her, grinning.

She smiled as he left the room again. Then she let the expression drop as she whipped up the phone.

'Hi, Dad. No, Dom's fine. His ankle's much better today. Listen, I know it's really short notice but would you be able to babysit tonight?'

'The reason we come here is because the management know just how to treat people like us.'

'No paparazzi,' Madeleine remarked, nodding.

'No paparazzi and no one without a significant profile. Last week an actress from *Hollyoaks* was asked to leave. Word is she had less than five thousand followers on Twitter.'

'The shame!'

Guy wanted to smash his head against the table and see what the management would do about that. He had endured four courses of food already at the over-priced quay restaurant and almost two hours of inane conversation about dress designers and California hotspots Gabriella and Daniel were going to visit on their summer holiday.

Daniel had consumed a bottle of red wine on his own and now Guy suspected the reason he kept disappearing to the toilets was for more than urination.

Guy hated drugs. Despised what they did to people. Those who thought they took them just for recreation were fooling themselves. They didn't just wreck your physicality, they poisoned your mind.

Daniel returned to his seat and beckoned the waiter to bring more wine.

'How about a Merlot, Guy?' Daniel suggested.

'*Non*, no, not for me. I will stick with water.'

'Guy had far too much to drink last night,' Madeleine told the couple.

'Didn't we all? Cracking night, wasn't it?' Daniel remarked.

'The food was a little overcooked,' Gabriella said, sipping at her glass of champagne.

'But we did raise a great deal of money for charity,' Guy added.

'Charity begins at home in my opinion. A lot of these so-called charities are just for people with no get up and go. You work hard, you make your own luck and the money rolls in. That's what we do, don't we, babe?' Daniel said snaking an arm around his girlfriend's shoulders.

Guy picked up his dessert fork and rolled it around his fingers. If he thought the management would turn a blind eye he would stab it right through Daniel's cocaine-speckled hand.

'So, what's on the cards for tonight? Casino?' Daniel suggested.

'That sounds fun. It is so long since we did that,' Madeleine said, turning to Guy.

'I cannot tonight,' he responded.

'Why not?' Madeleine's voice was sharp.

'I have to speak at the fitness centre. There is a... an exhibition this evening, all different sports. Some of us are talking about what sport means to us,' Guy said. He held onto his water glass and tried to look convincing.

'God that sounds dull! Rather you than me, mate. Oh well, another time. Shall we order dessert? What was that one with the truffles?' Daniel asked his wife.

'I can't remember what it was called but I do remember it was the most expensive dish on the menu,' Gabriella said with a laugh.

Guy forced a smile. *Idiots*. Was this what his life was to be from now on?

Chapter Eighteen

August 2005

'And now, the moment you have all been waiting for... Marco the Magician. Applause!'

The game show had been the lamest thing Emma had ever seen. Six red boxes and free raffle tickets for the audience. People with tickets corresponding to the numbers called were then invited on stage to choose a box. In some boxes were acceptable prizes, if you thought vouchers for the restaurant or a return visit to the holiday park were worth winning, and in the last box was a live snake that had almost escaped the grip of the host. Young children screamed and fled their seated positions on the floor in front of the stage and the game had been wound up pretty quickly after that.

Her dad had missed the whole event. His mobile phone had rung when the large woman staying three caravans along from them had been beckoned to the stage. He'd gone out to the lobby. Emma knew it was Marilyn. Who else would be calling him when he was on holiday? How could he think it was OK to be involved with another woman now? How involved with her had he been when her mother was still alive? She took a sip of her Orangina and picked up her book. It was *Dracula* by Bram Stoker. Another cheery read. At least this book wasn't written in old English.

'Vampires?'

Emma looked up and smiled, seeing Guy stood at her table. He was dressed up. He wore black trousers and a pale pink shirt that highlighted the darkness of his hair.

'Is that the same word in French? Vampire?'

'*Oui*,' he replied, sitting down.

'You can't stay here. My dad's here. He's gone to make a phone call and…' Emma started. She didn't want her dad seeing Guy. Although Mike had seen them dancing together the night they first kissed, she didn't want him to know she was involved with a boy. He would make a stupid comment about it. He would probably think, if she had a boyfriend, that it was OK for him to be moving on. It wasn't OK. And Guy was hers. She didn't want to share the knowledge of him with anyone.

'Will you have dinner with me?' he asked her, leaning forward across the table.

'Dinner? Tomorrow? Like another picnic?' Emma asked.

'*Non*. Tonight. Dinner. I know a place,' he whispered.

Her heart soared. A proper dinner. At a restaurant. Not barbequed sausages, lukewarm beans and a bread roll like her dad had been serving up all week. Her lips were moistening just thinking about it.

'You can come?' Guy asked her.

'I… I don't know. I want to, but…' She looked out into the lobby and watched Mike on the phone. He was smiling.

A wide grin crossed his mouth and then he let out a laugh that creased his entire face. He looked nothing short of joyful. It was wrong.

'At nine? Meet me at the back *entrée*,' Guy told her.

She looked up at him. His hair fell over his eyes and he smiled.

'I'll be there,' she answered.

Looking to check no one could see, he moved his hand across the table and touched her fingers with his. A spark of electricity left her stunned and sent a current running through her. It reached places that she hadn't known she could feel, inactive until now.

'*À bientôt.*' He left, made his way across the dance floor to the bar area.

A warm glow was filling her up, rising through her body as she watched him. And then it froze. She saw Tasha and Melody approach him. Tasha touched his arm. Her long, false-looking nails – painted red – were lying on his skin.

Emma swallowed, tried to get rid of the angry feeling that had invaded. It was spoiling the glow, putting out the fire. Tasha laughed. She threw her head back so her wavy blonde hair bounced about and took a step closer to Guy.

Emma dug her fingers into the tabletop. She hated those girls. They were so confident and uncaring and Tasha was touching her boyfriend. Well, they had had three dates, that made it official in her world. What else could she call him if not a boyfriend?

'Alright, love? Oh what's this? A magician? Smashing,' Mike said, settling back down in his seat.

She didn't reply. She was too busy watching Tasha's every move. She was still holding Guy and now her fingers were moving up and down his arm as they spoke. What were they saying? He'd told her he hated the girls. He thought they were superficial and pathetic. So why was he talking to them?

'Do you want another drink?' Mike asked.

Why was he letting Tasha hold his arm? Why wasn't he brushing her off? She wished she could stop looking but she was transfixed. Like someone watching a horror movie. She didn't want to see what was going on but she had to.

'You alright, love?'

Mike had leaned across her line of vision. She moved in her seat to watch Guy remove Tasha's arm and wave his hand in goodbye.

'Emma?' Mike tried again.

'Sorry, Dad. What did you say?' She held onto her glass and tried to will the heat from her cheeks.

'Is everything OK?' Mike asked.

'Yes. Just trying to get a better view, that's all,' she lied, turning her attention to the stage.

'Another drink?' Mike offered again.

'Oh no thanks, Dad. Actually, Sally's asked me to go to her caravan. She's got a load of snacks and some board games we're going to play,' Emma told him.

'Is she not here for the show?'

'No, she's having a late dinner with her parents. She said I could go round about nine… if it was alright with you.'

'What's the number of her caravan?'

'Er… I'm not sure… but it's the one right opposite the bicycle hire. I know how to get there,' Emma insisted.

'Don't you want to see the rest of the show?'

'Nothing could top the snake on the loose.'

'There was a snake?!'

'You missed it.'

She nearly said *you missed it because you were talking to your new girlfriend* but decided that wasn't the way to get him to agree to let her go and see her imaginary friend.

'Alright then, love but no later than eleven,' Mike agreed.

A thrill rode over her. Then she noticed Tasha and Melody were looking her way. They were doing that thing some of the bitches at her school did. Looking over, whispering to each other and then laughing hysterically.

'Could I have some money?' Emma asked her dad.

'Well... what for, love?'

'I just want to get some snacks too. I can't expect to eat everything Sally's bought and not bring anything. I thought I might take some fizzy orange too. The shop's still open,' Emma stated, checking her watch.

'Alright... here's five Euros. Will that be enough? Just trying to be a bit careful with the funds,' Mike said, handing the note to her.

'That's fine, Dad. I'd better go now if I want to catch the shop. I'll see you later.' She picked her book up from the table and stood up.

'No later than eleven,' he reaffirmed.

She smiled and made her way out of the clubhouse. What sort of wine could she get with five Euros?

Chapter Nineteen

Present Day

She'd lied to Chris. Not a white lie, like pretending that she liked a new shirt that he'd bought when really it was hideous, but a big, fat, blatant lie. She'd told him she needed to spend the evening marking homework. She knew Dominic would probably tell him she'd gone out when they saw each other next, but she had a plan for that. Ally would have a relationship crisis and need a shoulder to cry on. That would make two lies. Once she had started there was no stopping. When you'd spent most of your life hiding the truth it was second nature to lie, whether you wanted it to be or not.

'Thanks for coming over, Dad.'

She caught sight of her reflection in the mirror above the fireplace and shuddered. She'd made too much effort. She was wearing foundation, eye-shadow, eye-liner, blusher and lipstick. She hadn't made that much effort for the fitness centre opening. She was wearing an apricot sleeveless blouse she hadn't worn in years and a black layered skirt she last wore to the school prizegiving.

'You look nice, love. Where did you say you were going?' Mike asked, looking up from the TV magazine.

She hadn't said. She would have to tell another lie.

'To see Ally. She's on the verge of a break-up from her latest boyfriend. He's a pilot, works long hours and...' Same lie. Did that count as a third?

'He's spending too long with one of the air hostesses,' Dominic added.

'Dom!' Emma exclaimed.

'You said!'

'I know but you weren't supposed to be listening.'

'How's the internet dating going, Grandad?' Dominic piped up.

'Dominic Barron!'

'It's going alright, Dom. Not too bad at all. I've got another date with Velma next week and a dinner with a new lady I've been instant messaging with,' Mike replied.

'What's her name?' Dominic inquired.

'Rosemary.'

'Bleurgh!'

'Dom, you're being very rude. I'm glad you don't want Bourbons before bed,' Emma scolded.

'Oh, Mum!'

'She sounds very nice in her messages and we both like the Rolling Stones,' Mike informed them.

'She sounds lovely, Dad,' Emma said.

She was looking in the mirror and tweaking her hair. What was she doing tweaking her hair? What was she doing going to this restaurant to meet Guy. She'd said all she needed to say to him. Why was she torturing herself? It wasn't going to help. It could possibly make things worse.

'I bumped into Marilyn the other day,' Mike stated.

'Marilyn. Who's that?' Dominic chipped in.

Emma felt her hackles rise at the mention of her name. It brought back so many memories. She'd hated Marilyn. She'd been jealous and grief-stricken when they got together. She'd needed her dad's undivided attention and she'd made sure she'd got it. She'd driven the two of them apart.

'She's an old friend,' Mike elaborated for Dominic's benefit.

'An old *girlfriend*?' Dominic asked, giggling.

'I should go,' Emma said, looking at her watch. She didn't want Mike to say any more. It was enough that he'd seen her again. She didn't want to hear whatever came next.

'She asked after you, love. Asked all about Dominic too. I told her you were practically running the school,' Mike said, smiling.

The light was there again. His eyes were practically dancing. She knew he'd cared about Marilyn but back then it was too soon. She'd wanted him to mourn. He should have wanted to mourn.

'Someone told the Head about *Copacabana*. I think I'm going to have my work cut out with the costumes,' Emma said, picking up her handbag.

'Well, Marilyn is a dressmaker. You remember the little suit she made Dominic?'

Shit. She'd forgotten that. She needed to go before she

said anything else that would stir up memories. Seeing any more animation on her dad's face would open the floodgates to the guilt.

'What suit?' Dominic asked.

'It was white bloomers, a little shirt and a matching jacket. You wore it to your christening,' Mike told him.

'Urgh! Gross!'

She had a final look in the mirror and gave the front of her hair another flick.

'I'd better go then. Bye, Dom,' she planted a kiss on the top of the boy's head. 'I'll see you a bit later. Be good.' She opened the door to the hallway.

'Were you saying that to Dom or me?' Mike said, grinning.

She smiled at them both and then closed her eyes, shutting the door.

The worst thing was he didn't even know if she was coming. He'd arrived early and asked the manager for their most private table. Here in the UK the press were crazy, even more so than in France. At the moment attention was focused on Jason Simpson and his injury. It helped that he had yet to play his first game for Finnerham. Once that happened he would be back in the media spotlight.

He'd been given the menu and without looking at the wine list he'd ordered a bottle of French Merlot. The first glass had slipped down without him even realising it. He checked his watch again. It was just after half past seven. She was late. Or not coming.

He picked up the fork and twirled it around his fingers.

His hands were shaking. He didn't know what he was going to say to her, if she came. He needed to find out the truth about Dominic. Here, together, away from the noise, he would be able to tell if what she was saying was true. He took a sip from his glass of water and topped up his wine. No matter what she told him, he could handle it better than if she didn't turn up at all.

He beckoned the waiter and picked up the small vase on the table.

'Excuse me. Do you have any yellow flowers?'

She'd splashed out on a taxi. She'd splashed out on a taxi and hidden the fact from her dad and Dominic by driving her car down the street and calling one from the end of the road. She couldn't drive to the restaurant. Her hands were trembling and she wouldn't have been able to concentrate. Now, having paid the cab driver she was stood opposite Café Rouge wondering if she really wanted to go in. A drop of water on her bare arm told her it was starting to rain. Judging by the black clouds converging in the darkening sky above her, a thunderstorm was imminent. They needed rain. It had been too warm for too long and the ground was parched. As if sensing the drought she swallowed, urging moisture into her mouth. What was she doing? Why was she here? Whatever she said to him was only going to make things worse one way or another. There was no chance that this meeting was going to improve anything. She was going to tell him lies. He was going to try and wriggle out of how things were left between them eight years ago. She knew what she had seen. She still felt the betrayal. Yes, she'd been seventeen; young, inexperienced in love but... she'd believed in him. She'd believed in them. *Fool*.

The sporadic drops of rain started to become persistent and she needed to make a decision. Despite who she knew was waiting for her, Café Rouge did look inviting with its red and gold signage and cream drapes in the window. The interior promised sanctuary from the storm, a warm glow permeating through the glass doors.

She was starting to get wet from the rain. A couple ran past her, covering their heads with a handbag and a newspaper. She couldn't stand here forever. She stepped off the kerb and looked both ways.

Chapter Twenty

August 2005

She was a bit early. She'd thought the shop on the campsite would question her age when she tried to buy the wine but the cashier hadn't even blinked. Now she was sat on the low wall at the back exit of the complex waiting for Guy.

She could hear the host and applause coming from the clubhouse but it sounded far away. Here, almost out of the holiday park, it felt like a different France. Guy had shown her the forest, the river, the beach, the fields, all so idyllic, so peaceful. She didn't know how she would cope with going home. Wiltshire had its beauty, it was green and rural, but it wasn't France. Being here was healing her. She could feel it. He was healing her. He listened. He paid attention to her. He made her feel special.

'Psst!'

The noise startled her and she looked around to see where it was coming from. He emerged then, from behind a palm, smiling.

'You scared me,' Emma said, laughing as she stood up.

'Sorry.' He met her in the middle of the path, taking hold of her hands. Before she knew what was happening his mouth was on hers. His lips tasted of citrus and sun cream. She cupped his head with her hands, pulling him in closer, opening her mouth wider. She wanted to get as close as she could. She pressed her chest against his, felt the rise in rhythm of his heart. He broke away, out of breath, eyes wide, exploring hers.

'I... want to do that... *de tous les jours*,' he told her.

'Every day,' she answered.

'Every day,' he repeated.

'Where are we going?' she asked.

He was holding her hand and leading her through the woods. It was getting dark now, the brown bag with the wine in was getting heavier and she could barely see where her feet were going. Had she known he had a moonlit ramble on the itinerary she might have worn trainers. No, she wouldn't. Ally said trainers were for PE only... or shopping. The strappy sandals made her feet look slimmer and they were picking up a tan. Having slim, brown feet to show off was worth a few bramble scratches on her calves.

'We are here,' he announced. He drew back a large piece of foliage and Emma gasped.

In front of her was the most spectacular table setting she had ever seen. Not even something from a romantic movie could have compared to what was in front of her.

Just a few metres ahead was a table laid with a pale linen cloth, set for dinner for two. There was a lone candle in a glass holder in the middle of the table and a small vase of yellow flowers perfected it. In the trees above were white fairy lights, creating an almost magical glow. She put her palms to her cheeks and took a breath.

'Guy…' she started.

'Do you like it?' he asked, watching her expression.

'I… I… it's beautiful. *C'est beau*,' she said, turning to him.

'*Tu es belle.*'

He toyed with her fingers as he held her hand, smoothing the skin on each one and bonding them together.

'I don't know what to say,' she whispered. There were tears brimming up in her eyes but she didn't want to let them fall. This was by far the most wonderful thing anyone had ever done for her. And it was for her. *All* for her. Because he cared.

'Say you will eat with me. I have pâté, then… how you say… *poulet.*'

'Chicken.'

'*Oui* and *salade*. Then we have *mousse au chocolat*,' Guy finished.

'I can't believe you went to all this trouble for me.'

She was overwhelmed. This boy she had thought to be nothing more than a holiday romance was spending his time with her. Spending his money on her. Money he'd already told her he didn't have much of.

'Trouble?'

'Um, trouble… *difficulté*. No, not that. Um… *dérangement*. I think that's right.'

'*Pas de problème*. Please, we eat?' Guy asked, leading the way.

Her stomach contracted at just the thought of anything other than camp stove cooked fare. On the table for the first course was delicious looking bread and an individual terrine of the most fragrant pâté. Guy pulled out a wicker chair for her and she sat down.

'Thank you. Here, I got some wine,' she said, passing him the bag.

'Merlot,' he said, looking at the label.

'I don't know much about wine and Dad only gave me five Euros,' Emma said.

'It will be… *bien.*'

'Open it. Let's have some with dinner,' she urged. 'I got a screw top just in case.'

He smiled. He opened the bottle and poured wine into both their glasses. Then he whipped the cloth off another bottle stood on the side of the table. It was exactly the same wine Emma had bought. She let out a laugh.

'Great minds think alike,' she said, sipping some of her wine.

'What?'

'It's a quote. No one knows who first said it.'

'Is it the Chaucer?' Guy inquired.

'Oh no. It's far too straightforward for him,' she said.

'You like pâté?' Guy asked.

'Oh yes. Did you make all this?'

She took some bread and covered it with a thick spread of pâté. She sunk her teeth into it and savoured every sense as it travelled over her tongue.

'*Non.* I have a… friend?' he tested.

Emma nodded her head.

'He is chef at the restaurant,' Guy explained.

'This is gorgeous.' She swallowed her mouthful and had a large swig of wine.

'*Demain*… I have to… *essai de football*,' he started.

'Your trial. With the football team in Nice,' Emma guessed.

'*Oui*.' He drank some wine and looked across the table at her.

'Are you nervous?' Emma guessed.

He nodded and reached for her hand.

'But you're brilliant. I don't know much about football but you play so well and they'll see that,' she said, squeezing his hand.

'There are many people. Many people are good,' he told her.

'But you really want to play for them. You're passionate about the game. The children here love it when you teach them,' she continued.

'I have to be good. I have to get place in the… *équipe*.'

'You will. I know you will,' Emma said with confidence. She could see from his expression that this trial was a big deal to him. He was hanging all his hopes on it.

'But if you don't…' she started.

'I have to, Emma. I need to… for Luc,' he said. He withdrew his hand to take hold of his wine glass.

'I know you want to look after your brother but your mother… it's her responsibility and—'

'She cannot. She does not…' He shook his head hard and distracted himself by buttering some bread. He was upset. She didn't want him to be upset. Not when he had arranged this perfect meal in such a beautiful setting for her. She cleared her throat and held her wine glass up.

'I believe in you. And if this football team can't see the best player in the world standing in front of them tomorrow then they're idiots... on skis,' Emma stated.

He raised his head to look at her. His eyes brightened.

'To Guy Duval,' Emma toasted. '*Bonne chance pour demain.*'

He raised his glass, leaning forward to touch hers.

'*Salut!*'

'To us,' Emma translated.

As their glasses met she felt her whole body fill up with a warm, tingling sensation. It struck her like a thunderbolt. She'd never been this happy. He really understood her despite the language barrier. She'd told him all about her life, her mother, her books and he got it all.

She looked up. She watched him eat his bread, wiping his long fingers on the napkin. He was perfect. But could it last?

Chapter Twenty-One

Present Day

He'd been watching the door and every time it opened he'd held his breath. When she finally walked in it felt as if his heart had stopped beating. She was here. He was stunned. Had he really thought she wouldn't come? He'd wanted to believe but… his heart kicked back in. The thudding, drumming, slightly-out-of-sync beating moved from his chest up into his throat as he watched Emma shake her arms, ridding her skin of the rain.

She lifted her head, scanning the restaurant as the manager approached her. She looked unbelievable. So beautiful. She was still every inch the girl he fell in love with in La Baume. He stood up.

'*Bonsoir, madame*. Do you have a reservation?' the restaurant manager asked her.

'Yes… well, no… I'm meeting someone. Duval. He will have booked under the name "Duval",' Emma said. She shook the bottom of her blouse and droplets of water fell onto the tiled floor.

She lifted her head and it was then she saw him. He was standing at the very rear of the restaurant, gazing over the other tables and diners, directly at her.

'This way, madam,' the manager said, holding his hand out in direction.

She wasn't ready. She was here, *he* was here but she wasn't ready for this. Her stomach rotated and she sucked in a breath. Her feet wouldn't move. The manager was looking at her. She needed to do something. She tightened her grip on her bag and mentally gave herself a talking to. *You are not seventeen. You are a mother, a teacher, and a grown-up. He means nothing to you. He hurt you. You will not be taken in again no matter how good he looks.*

'Madam?' the manager asked for the second time.

'Yes. Sorry,' Emma said. She fixed a smile on her face and finally shifted her feet.

She followed the manager. Mimicking his step, she ducked her head slightly to avoid Guy's eyes. This was like a form of torture. She knew she was going to be sitting opposite him but she wanted to leave actually looking at him until the last possible moment.

Within seconds he was a few feet away. He was smiling at her, his napkin gripped in his hands. He was wearing a crisp white shirt and black trousers. As she looked at him a section of his hair fell across his forehead. He pushed it back behind his ear.

'Madam,' the manager said. He pulled the chair out for her.

'Thank you.' She sat down, moving her eyes to look at her plate.

'The menu for you, madam. I will give you a few moments,' the manager said. He handed the menu to Emma, smiled at Guy and then backed away leaving them alone.

She had to lift her head. Looking at the crockery wasn't going to achieve anything. But she knew what she would see. She wouldn't see the boy who had broken her. She would see the man she was still attracted to. She could already feel pinpricks creeping up her bare arms and it wasn't due to the rain she'd experienced.

'I have Merlot. Would you like—'

'Yes... please,' she interrupted. To get through this conversation she needed alcohol.

He poured some wine into her glass and put the bottle back on the table. It was then, as the bottle went down, she noticed the yellow flowers. Guy was watching her. Meeting his gaze, it was if he knew what she was thinking.

'I was going to have the Camembert to start,' Guy said. He cleared his throat and took another mouthful of wine.

'Right. The menu,' Emma said, realising she was still holding it in her hand.

'Emma...' Guy began.

'Not yet... please.' Her voice was faltering and there were tears on the verge already.

'I was just going to say... can we start again? Can we have dinner like old friends catching up, maybe?'

'Old friends.'

'I don't want to upset you. I think I upset you yesterday and I am sorry. I should not have spoken that way, with Dominic near. His ankle is OK?' he asked.

She nodded her head, reached for her wineglass.

'I have missed you.' His words were said in little more than a whisper. They waved over the table so soft and smooth but they hit her with full force. How could she respond to that?

'I'll have… the *moules marinières*.' She barely got the words out of her mouth. It seemed as if there was a rock between her lips, pent up emotion forming a real physical barrier. She cleared her throat.

'Emma…' he began again.

'What do you want me to say?' She swallowed down the threatening tears and replaced it with anger.

'I do not want to fight. I want to find out what has happened with you. It has been so long and—'

'It's been eight years.'

'I know.'

'We've changed.'

'Circumstances have changed maybe but—'

'*I've* changed.'

'Not to me.'

It was a dart to her heart. She couldn't avoid looking at him. This time she didn't want to avoid looking at him. Despite what he'd done to her, the depth of feeling she had for him engulfed everything she'd felt for anyone before or since. Sat just across the table was the love of her life. What could she do? What should she do?

'Are you ready to order?'

A waiter was at their table, intruding on the conversation, waiting for a response to his question.

'*Oui*. Camembert to start and the chicken tagine. *Moules marinières* and…' Guy started.

'The lemon sole,' Emma filled in.

Chapter Twenty-Two

He desperately wanted to make her feel at ease. Every time she reached for her glass her fingers were shaking. This was all his fault. What had he done all those years ago? The answer was simple. Not enough. He should have stood up for what he wanted. He should have dealt with the consequences of his actions and then pursued his dream. The dream he'd had since he met her. He wasn't supposed to be living his life with Madeleine. He had envisaged everything happening with Emma. His reality had got skewed and he'd stood by and let it happen. Was it too late to put things right? Was putting things right the proper thing to do? He pushed away his starter plate.

'I want to know about your teaching,' he said, pouring her another glass of wine.

She'd barely eaten. She'd watched him. They'd said very little. He'd commented on the weather and she'd asked ridiculous questions about football. She still didn't know anything about it and she didn't really want to. They were both circling around each other, avoiding the important questions.

'I've been at the school for four years now. I teach English,' she answered.

'Chaucer?' he queried. A smile flickered over his mouth and heady memories were forced into her mind.

'Sometimes. Not this year. This year we have *Othello* and Jane Austen… with a rousing rendition of *Copacabana* if Councillor Martin gets his way.'

'I meant what I said about the money. I would like to give something to the school,' Guy told her.

'Why?'

'Why not?'

'Because you know nothing about the school,' she challenged.

'I know you work there. I know how passionate you were about reading and literature. I would like to help. Is it wrong to want to give something?'

'I…'

He threw his napkin on the table and put a hand through his hair. He looked frustrated. She chewed her lip. She knew that she was making him like this because she was scared to say anything that mattered. She could have been having this conversation with her hairdresser.

'You say I am not Dominic's father. OK. If that is what you say then that is what I believe,' he stated.

Did he believe it? Did he believe it really? His tone sounded honest but his chest rose with hampered breaths that told another story.

'Where is he? The father.'

'Not around,' Emma answered.

She watched him take a long breath in. He held it there for what felt like a long time and then let it go through his nostrils.

'You and he were…' he began.

'It's a long story, Guy. You know my mother died. It happened then, before I met you.'

'But when we were together. You were…'

'I don't really want to talk about it.'

'So the things you say to me back then…'

'I was only seventeen. I needed someone… I said I didn't want to talk about it.'

She wanted to leave. She wanted to get in a taxi and go back to her dad, Dominic and a cup of coffee. That was her life. That was where she belonged. Not here with this guy from her past.

'I would have understood,' he said.

She could feel his eyes on her. So intense, so full of feeling. Just being near him stirred all those sentiments up again. It was dangerous to be here. She was flirting with disaster just by seeing him again, for so many reasons.

'Tell me about your career. Dominic tells me you're quite the international celebrity.'

She'd had to change the subject. His scrutiny was giving her goose bumps where she didn't even know you could get goose bumps. She needed to be mature. She had to be the adult here. Everything from their time together had been banished to the back of her memory and locked up for very good reasons.

'Celebrity. Yes, so it seems.' He took a swig of his wine and sat back a little in his chair.

'Finnerham have paid an awful lot of money for you to play for them. It must be very flattering,' Emma continued. She had to stride on with the questions or the spotlight would be back on her.

'Flattering? *Non*. Embarrassing, perhaps. I do not know if I am capable of being the player they deserve. The way we play football in France is very different to how the game is played here. I have taken the opportunity and I will be trying to learn as much as I can,' he explained.

'But you've played for your country and OGC Nice.'

'I had to make it there. I had to get there for Luc,' he stated.

She saw his fingers tighten around the wineglass and his gaze travel out to the mid-distance. Emma wiped at her mouth with her napkin and waited for him to continue.

'Luc died, Emma,' he stated.

'I'm so sorry,' she said, putting down her napkin.

There were tears in his eyes now. He was swallowing, trying to keep himself in check but she could see what was trying to break out from under the surface. Sorrow. Deep sadness over the loss of his brother.

He shook his head and took another drink. He paused before he spoke again.

'For a long time after you left I didn't know what to do. After Luc, my mother was drinking more and more. Then there were other... circumstances I felt I could not control. I had to try and pick myself up. I had to realise what was important and how to go forward.'

Emma managed a nod. His words were making her ache to reach out for him but she held back. It wasn't right to comfort him.

'I went to the local semi-professional team and I earned a place in the team. It was starting from the bottom but I needed to do that. Wherever it took me, if it took me anywhere at all, I had to make it because I'd worked hard and honestly.

Money can sometimes fall into your lap but money earned the right way is the only type worth having,' he told her.

'And you have a girlfriend.' She didn't know why that particular sentence had fallen out of her mouth.

'I suppose,' he responded with a shrug.

'What does that mean?'

'Madeleine and I... we don't have the right sort of relationship. It isn't the type of relationship I want. Do you remember?'

Did she remember? Of course she did. She could deny it all she liked but she remembered every detail of every moment they'd spent together.

'Then why be together?'

'Why are you with that man?'

'That man? His name's Chris. I'm with Chris because...' She had to stop. The truth was, she couldn't give him an answer. This was ridiculous. Why was she with Chris? Were they good together? Not especially. They were very different but they managed to pull off the family unit when they went out with Dominic. But that shouldn't be the answer. She should be saying something much more appropriate. Like he was her soul mate.

'He's kind. He's hard-working and he loves Dominic. Anyway, I don't need to justify how I'm living my life to you,' she snapped.

'You ask me about Madeleine and I told you the truth. I would believe it if you tell me you love this man, but you do not say that and I do not see it in your eyes,' Guy told her.

'It's none of your business what I feel for him.' She looked at the tablecloth and started to pick at one of the stitches on the hem.

'I want to see you,' Guy continued.

'What are you talking about? I came here tonight to…' She paused, facing him.

'To what?'

The air was so charged she couldn't breathe. All she could see were his green eyes, looking at her, beckoning her back to a time when she didn't know better. A time when she felt free, young, wrapped up in a dream of love and happy-ever-afters. She opened her mouth to speak but shut it again. She didn't know what to say.

'I know things are complicated, Emma. But the moment I saw you again… My feelings are the same. I know what you think I did to you… to us… but I'm asking for another chance.'

This couldn't be happening. All those years alone with Dominic. Struggling to get by. Begging the university to defer her place. Getting the teaching job she'd always wanted. Learning to give her heart again. And here he was, the man that broke her in so many ways, asking for a second chance. He was too late… wasn't he?

'Remember the story you read to me? Those two people who loved each other so much. She married someone else and he married someone else and…'

'Don't romanticise it. We're not Cathy and Heathcliff.'

'OK, maybe that was a stupid thing to say. I am trying to say how I feel but—'

'The lemon sole, madam and the chicken tagine, sir,' the waiter interrupted.

'Thank you. Could I please have a glass of water?' Emma asked. Her throat being dry was the least of her worries. Her heart was on fire.

Chapter Twenty-Three

August 2005

'No more food! I'm so full.' She moved her chair back from the table a little and held her hands over her bloated stomach.

'*Chocolat*,' Guy stated. He held up a large, round box filled with chocolates.

'Goodness, are they truffles? They must have cost a bit,' she said.

'Sometimes, I get… *cadeaux*… for doing good job.' He stood up. He shook out a blanket and laid it on the ground between two trees.

'Chocolate on the ground?'

'*Pardon*?'

'Nothing. It's nice.' She stood up, moved to where the blanket was positioned, throwing herself down. She stretched her arms out behind her feeling like a satisfied cat, warm and content. He sat down beside her.

'*Chocolat*?' Guy offered, showing her the box.

'Yes please,' she accepted, her eyes closing.

Guy took a chocolate from the box and placed it in Emma's mouth. She wasn't ready for it and she opened her eyes wide in surprise as it hit her tongue. Guy laughed and watched her, lying down and leaning up on his elbow.

She closed her eyes again and let the delicious, thick, creamy solid, melt with the heat of her tongue. It was so smooth. She let the fondant fold across her mouth. It was a sugar high. Then she felt something else. Guy's lips touched hers, so gently, feather-light kisses laid on the edge of her mouth, almost seeking permission to be there.

She reached up to place her hands in his hair. It was so soft between her fingers and she adored how it felt. She drew his face closer, opened her mouth to encourage him to deepen the kiss.

She felt him open his mouth wider, his tongue rolling over hers, colliding with the chocolate, creating an exquisite fusion of sweetness and sensuality. At that moment she knew what she wanted. This was her moment. This was the perfect moment she'd read about in Ally's *Cosmopolitan* magazine. She gently moved Guy back, reaching for the buttons on his shirt. She unfastened two and then her hands started to shake as he smoothed his thumbs across her cheeks and kissed her again.

'Guy,' she begged.

'*Qu'est-ce que c'est?*' he whispered. He brushed her hair back from her face.

'I want to…'

'Want to?'

'Take your clothes off. Um… *déshabiller?*' she offered. Her breathing was unsteady and despite the warmth of the night she was quaking. She drew back from him, afraid she had been too forward or said something out of place. What if he didn't want to?

He slipped off his shirt and reached for her, gently tugging her dress up and over her head. Straightaway a chill shot through her as she remembered not bothering with a bra. The straps had shown through her dress and it wasn't a pretty bra, it was a comfortable one her mother had picked out for her, all structure and no lace. It didn't have a place here.

Just from his gaze her nipples peaked. She'd never experienced a sensation like it and he hadn't even touched her. His eyes were travelling over every inch of her, taking in every curve, every part as if he were admiring a piece of art.

'Guy.' The voice that came from her sounded needy and desperate. That was how she felt. If he didn't touch her. If she didn't feel his mouth on her breasts she would die.

'*Tu es très belle.*' He reached out, ran his finger along her breastbone and watched her as she quivered under his fingers. She closed her eyes as his hand moved to her breast, smoothing the skin with his thumb and creating slow circles towards the centre. Finally he reached her nipple. It was already so hard and swollen, aching for him that when he touched it she let out a cry.

'Emma,' he said, letting her go.

'No. No, don't stop, please,' she begged, taking his hand.

He lowered her down onto the blanket and brought his head down to her chest, taking her nipple into his mouth. She closed her eyes and felt the heat rippling through her. She reached for his trousers. She wanted to get everything off. She'd never wanted to be naked with a boy before but now she needed it. She was ready.

She pulled at the fastening, undid the zipper and urged him to remove them. He swayed his hips, pushing the trousers down his body and finally kicking them off. He looked at her, his eyes wide, uncertain. She reached for his underwear, all the nerves she thought she'd feel about this situation taking second place to lust and the need to find out. She pulled at the elastic, inched the material away from his body until all of him was right there in front of her.

She saw him swallow as she looked at him. She didn't really know what to do but she longed to touch him. She brought her hand to his penis, touching it with her fingertips before holding it in her hand and caressing it with her palm.

Guy pushed her back down onto the blanket and met her lips with his. A hot, crashing, sensation as their near-naked bodies met. He peeled her underwear away from her and she shook as he touched her.

'I want you to...' She still couldn't bring herself to say the words. What were the right words for what they were doing? Sex? Making love? Doing it? Surely he would understand.

'*Je suis en train tombre amoureux de toi,*' he said.

His thumb was at the entrance of her vagina, gently probing, searching for something.

'What?' What did he mean? *Amour* was love. Was he saying he loved her? This was a holiday romance. That was all.

'Emma... *tu veux m'arrête?*' he breathed.

'Stop? Do I want you to stop? No. *Non.*'

His thumb pressed harder and she felt something in her shift. As he rhythmically circled the golden spot she could feel all this power welling up inside her. Like a blooming flower being warmed by the sun, about to burst open to display its petals.

She couldn't wait. She took hold of him and urged him forward, positioning her hips, letting him know, without any doubt, what she wanted to do. She shut her eyes and felt him push inside her. A second of pain and then what followed removed her breath. A surging, overwhelming rush boiled up as he began to buck against her. This wasn't what she'd expected, this was something much more. She felt terrified and excited in equal measure. He moved further inside her with every motion and she only wanted more. The buzz was building; it had taken over her stomach and chest. She couldn't breathe. She opened her eyes and looked up into his face, his beautiful, handsome face.

'Emma… Emma… I cannot…'

He was holding her hand as he moved, rocking her towards something she had no knowledge of. And then she was flying. Riding the river rapids, then shooting up to the stars as her whole body was washed with electric pulses that ignited every centimetre of flesh.

She couldn't speak as Guy cried out, squeezing her hand so tight. His body sagged. He leaned into her, burying his face in her shoulder. She ran her hand down his back, felt him trembling, a sheen of perspiration on his skin.

'*Je t'aime*,' he whispered.

She moved her hand through his hair, holding his body tight to her.

'I love you too.'

Chapter Twenty-Four

Present Day

He didn't really know what had come over him. He hadn't planned to say that. He hadn't planned anything, perhaps that was half the problem. But seeing her, having her with him again, it had stirred up so many feelings. Feelings that had never left him. He wanted to be that way again. How he'd been when he was with her was how he wanted his life to be now. Back then, when things had been so hard, so horrible, she was his salvation. He was a better man with her. He was the man he longed to be. An ordinary man. A good man.

She couldn't finish the fish. It was beautifully cooked and was drizzled with the most amazing sauce, but what Guy had said, coupled with being here with him, had her stomach tied up in knots. Giving it food was making the tension worse. In contrast, the red wine seemed to be helping. She drained her third glass then closed her knife and fork together on the plate.

'It was lovely,' she said, nodding.

'You have not finished,' Guy commented.

'No… I… the starter was very filling.'

He nodded and wiped his mouth with the napkin.

'So, how are you finding England? It's warm at the moment but you wait until the winter. We had snow last year.' She sounded jaunty. It was highly inappropriate.

'I have not seen so much of it. We arrive. We move in to the house. I come to the fitness centre. We have a charity party and…'

'What charity?'

'The football club is raising money to set up a youth organisation to run alongside their academy. They have had some funding from the English lottery, I think. Now they have to raise the balance to complete the project and pay for skilled staff to run it. It's so every child can have time to *be* a child. Play, learn something fun, keep off the streets,' he explained.

'We need something like that here. After-school clubs haven't really moved with the times. Mrs Morgan still runs origami,' Emma said. She smiled as she thought about it.

'Origami?'

'Making paper shapes… animals and, decorative things,' she explained.

'The youth club won't just be about football. There *will be* football sessions and the most gifted will have a chance to join the Finnerham youth team, but there will be all sorts of sports. It will not matter if you are good at sport. There will even be dressing up in Sumo suits. Everyone can do that,' Guy said, smiling.

'Like at La Baume,' Emma said, her voice soft.

'Yes,' he responded.

Simultaneously they both reached for the bottle of wine. Clashing fingers Emma withdrew her hand.

'It is empty. I will order another,' Guy said. He raised his hand to beckon the waiter.

'No. I don't think we should,' Emma said. She already knew she'd drunk too much. Her head was starting to cloud and she had that tingling sensation in the back of her head she always got with red wine.

'Why not?' he asked as the waiter came over. 'Another Merlot please.'

Why not? She didn't have an answer for that. Not a politically correct one anyway. The truth was if she had more wine she wouldn't be in control. She would feel a little too relaxed, off guard and vulnerable. She didn't want to feel vulnerable with Guy. Before three glasses of wine he had melted her reserve, after three glasses and more she didn't trust herself to say or do the right things.

'Have you been back to La Baume since…?' He left the question open-ended.

'No.' She shook her head with determination.

'I have a house there. I rebuilt my mother's house after she died,' Guy informed.

Emma drew in a breath. The shock of what he'd said hit her hard. She held the table with her fingers until her knuckles whitened.

'You remember how she drank?' He paused. 'Well, after Luc, it got worse. She did not see that as a chance to change or make something else of her life. She gave up,' he explained.

'Guy… I am so sorry.' She couldn't stop the tears now. Like raindrops they fell from her eyes and traced a path down her face. There had been so much pain.

'Oh, Emma, do not cry. Not for her, please.'

He reached across the table and took hold of her hand. With a tender touch he caressed her fingers with his, trying to soothe her.

She wasn't crying for his mother. She was crying for herself. But she had to say the right thing.

'No matter what she did. She was your mother,' Emma stated. Guilt was stabbing at her. This was her fault.

'But she does not deserve *your* tears. And she is gone. Maybe to a better place, maybe not,' he said with a shrug.

'I'm so sorry,' Emma repeated.

'*Non.* No, do not be sorry. So much of what has happened is my mother's fault. She is the one who should be sorry. And I do not think she ever was,' he said.

He was rubbing her fingers now, touching the skin with rhythmic strokes that could only be aimed to test her. She couldn't get lost in their reverie. She had to remain strong. She had to remember how he had betrayed her. But his hands felt so familiar on hers, so natural, like they were meant to be. And her heart was skipping. It skipped in a way it hadn't done since they were last together.

He took his hand away as the waiter returned with the wine. He waited for him to pour before he spoke again.

'Your father? Is he well?'

'Oh yes. He's fine. Perfectly fine,' Emma said. She dabbed at her eyes with the napkin, trying not to smudge her make-up.

'Is he with… the lady you did not like,' Guy began.

'Marilyn. No. No, he's not with Marilyn. He's actually looking for love on the internet.'

'Wow. That is… different,' Guy responded. He let out a laugh. Emma smiled.

'Does he meet the ladies or do they just Facebook?' Guy inquired.

'Oh no, he meets them. There's been a dog trainer and now someone called Rosemary.'

'You are OK with this?' Guy asked. He looked at her as if searching for her true feelings in her expression.

'My mother's been dead a long time now. He's not sixty yet. I suppose he needs something else.'

'You sound as if…'

'As if what?'

'Nothing.'

'I want him to be happy but…'

'You still miss your mother,' Guy said, nodding.

'It isn't that,' she snapped. Why had she overreacted like that? She *did* miss her mother. But by now, in her opinion, she should have healed completely… and she hadn't.

'It is not wrong to miss someone. No matter how long they have been gone,' he continued.

His comment couldn't have been more loaded, whether that was his intention or not.

'I know,' she whispered, meeting his gaze.

'Feelings are sometimes difficult to interpret. What feels like the right thing to one person might seem wrong to another,' Guy said. He pushed her full wineglass towards her.

'Your English is so good. How did you… did you take lessons?'

'I studied a little… after you left.'

'You were always very good but now you're… *magnifique*,' Emma said, smiling.

'And your French? Did you learn more?' he inquired.

'No. Well… with Dominic here I didn't have much time,' Emma admitted.

'I understand.'

'Do you?'

'Of course. To be a mother so young, it must have been hard,' he said.

How did she handle this? She'd had far too much alcohol to deal with this how she wanted to. If he made her dwell on how hard it had been she would probably cry again.

'I admire how you have raised him. He is a wonderful boy,' Guy told her.

'Could we have some coffee?' she asked, clearing her throat.

He wanted to take her in his arms and hold her close. She looked so fragile sat opposite him, her slender fingers toying with the tablecloth. What had really happened to her since they'd been apart? He'd thought about her often, but in most of those daydreams she'd been happy and content. Like she'd been in France. She didn't look that way now. She seemed troubled, concerned, like the weight of the world was on her shoulders. Was that his doing? Had he made her life complicated by turning up in it? Or was it something else? Something that was nothing to do with him. He wanted to know. He *needed* to know. Because he wanted to be back in her life. Right now he wanted that more than anything.

Chapter Twenty-Five

August 2005

She watched him as he pulled his clothes back on. They'd lain together for over an hour until time ticked closer to her curfew. She didn't want to go but she also didn't want her dad coming to look for her. How embarrassing would that be? And it would spoil it. This had been such a special night. She didn't want it ending like that, being dragged back to her too-small tent by her dad.

'Guy,' she said. He fastened his trousers and turned to look at her.

'I have to go,' she said. She'd pulled on her dress and was hugging her knees to her chest.

As the dark fell the temperature dropped.

He slipped his shirt over his arms and began to fasten the buttons as he came back to her. He sat down on the blanket and when the buttons were all done up he took her hand and brought it to his lips. His soft kiss shot a shiver through her.

'I do not… *Je ne veux pas que tu partis.*'

She traced a line down his face, stopping at his chin and

drawing him towards her. This gorgeous boy was hers. Even if it was just for the summer, he was hers. He wasn't a counsellor or a teacher. He didn't bang on about the grieving process. Here, with him, that part of her life didn't exist anymore.

'Guy... have you... have you been with many girls?'

She didn't know why she'd asked that. Was it because this night had been too perfect? Had he done all this before for someone else? Why would that matter? Everyone Ally had been with already had a history.

'*Quoi?*'

'Have you... I don't know the words... *amour* with other girls... like this?' She indicated the blanket.

For a moment, when he didn't immediately respond, she thought she'd ruined everything. She didn't really know what she wanted him to say. She was more or less certain it hadn't been his first time. He seemed to know what to do. He hadn't appeared nervous at all. And what he'd done had been more than *agréable*.

'I do not know... the words,' he began. He tamed a section of hair behind her ear. She brushed her lips against his hand.

'Please try. In French?'

He shook his head.

'It doesn't matter if you've been with other girls. I mean you're eighteen. You work here and...'

'*Non*. It is... I have. But it was *pas le même. Pas comme nous*,' he said.

'Not... not like us,' Emma translated.

'I want to say so much but... *je ne sais pas les mots*,' he continued.

He rubbed his thumb over her hand, back and forth.

'You don't have the words?' Emma guessed.

He nodded.

'You are different. We are… *spécial*,' he continued.

His answer made her heart swell. He had felt it too. Although she had tried to put everything she felt down to it being her first time, her first time with someone she cared so much for, it wasn't just her own romanticism. It had meant something to him too. Perhaps when he'd said *amour* he'd really meant it.

She caught sight of her watch. It was a minute to eleven. She let him go, leaping up.

'I have to go.'

'You have to leave me here. I told my dad I was with Sally. If he sees you then…' she began.

He silenced her with a kiss. His lips smothered hers and he drew her towards him. She folded her arms behind his neck and played with the hair at the nape. Closing her eyes, she sucked in his scent and tried to imprint it on her memory. This night had meant everything.

'Can I… see you tomorrow?' Guy asked, adjusting the strap of her dress and leaving his fingers on her bare shoulder.

'After your trial?'

'In the morning… for *bonne chance*,' he suggested.

'You won't need good luck,' she assured.

He hugged her close, brushing his hand down her hair.

'I'll meet you by the back gate again? At ten? *Dix heures*,' she said.

'Emma? Is that you?'

Mike's voice came through the canvas of their tent just a few yards in front of them. Had he heard them talking? She didn't want him to know she was with Guy.

'I have to go,' she whispered to Guy.

'*À tout!*'

He kissed her cheek and she held on to his hand as he went to walk away. He smiled at her and finally, reluctantly, she let go.

She unzipped the tent and parted the way to go in. Mike was sat in a camping chair, reading a caravanning magazine. He put it down as she entered.

'Did you have a nice time, love?'

'Yeah. It was good. Sally had some great music,' Emma responded. She had to stop her face flaming or the game would be up. She needed her dad to believe in Sally so she could arrange more dates with Guy.

'Was that a boy I heard you talking to?' Mike asked. He looked straight at her.

'Yes. It was Sally's brother, Kevin. He insisted on walking me back to the tent because it was dark…'

'Sensible lad. Thank him for me will you,' Mike said.

Emma nodded. 'I'm just going to go the toilet and then—'

'Sit down a minute, love.' He indicated the other chair by the table.

This wasn't good. The last time he'd ordered her to sit down like that was when he gave her her mother's cancer diagnosis. She sank down into the portable chair and held her breath.

'So, how are things, love? How are you feeling?' Mike began.

Oh no. He was starting to sound like the Macmillan nurse. Why was he asking her this now?

'I'm fine, Dad.' *Actually I've just had sex* the voice in her head said. Did she look like she'd had sex? She certainly felt at least five years older and far more experienced. Did it show? She was quite sure she didn't want her dad sensing from a flush how much her thighs ached.

'Really?'

'Really.'

'I know things are tough, love. We've had it hard for a long time, haven't we?'

She didn't know what to say. For whose benefit was this conversation?

'I'm fine, Dad. Really fine,' she said with a little more insistence.

'I was just thinking maybe you'd like to talk it over with someone. Someone who knew your mum,' Mike suggested.

'I've been talking to the counsellor the hospital gave us,' Emma reminded.

'I know you have, love, I know. I just thought talking to someone who wasn't a medical professional might be more... casual. And if they knew your mum then...'

'Who do you want me to talk to, Dad?'

He needed to get to the point. She didn't like the way this conversation was going.

'Well, do you remember your mum's friend Marilyn? They used to go to knitting club together before she got sick,' Mike started.

No. No, no, no. He couldn't do this now. Not when they were on holiday together. Her mum was barely cold in her grave and although she knew something was going on between him and Marilyn, he couldn't bring her into their lives now.

'I don't remember her.' Her voice came out robotic.

'Yes you do, love. She's about your mum's height and build, with reddish hair and—'

'I don't remember her. Why would I want to talk to her?' she snapped.

He couldn't be doing this. He couldn't be. Did his wife's memory not mean anything to him? All the wonderful feelings she'd experienced with Guy that night were being drowned, dampened down and spoiled.

'Well, she's a very nice lady and we've become quite close. She's been helping me come to terms with losing your mum,' Mike continued.

Anger boiled in her stomach. If she said anything now she was sure it would be coated in flames. She just wanted him to stop talking. To shut his mouth and not say anything else. She shifted in her seat.

'I thought when we got home we might have Marilyn round for dinner. A nice roast or something.'

Oh my God! He'd gone all out. He was going to invite Marilyn into their home, into her mother's house, to sit in her mother's seat or maybe even make the same onion and herb gravy they'd always had with Sunday lunch. This couldn't be happening. She didn't want this to happen.

She clenched her teeth together. She didn't trust herself to say anything. She needed to work out how to deal with it.

'Would that be alright, love? If Marilyn came to lunch some time? You could have a talk to her then, couldn't you?' Mike carried on.

Was there no stopping him? Wasn't her silence speaking

volumes? She was trying hard to keep the murderous expression off her face but she certainly wasn't smiling and doing cartwheels.

'I really need the toilet,' Emma stated, rising from her chair.

'Right, sorry, of course you do.'

'Then I'm going to bed,' Emma added. She wanted to make it clear there would be no further discussion about this tonight. And if she had her way it would never be talked of again. Wait until she told Ally about this. She'd let her friend into her suspicions before they left for France. Wait until she told her it was true!

'Yes, love, of course it's late,' Mike said, looking at his watch.

'I won't be long,' Emma said, parting the doors of the tent.

'Don't forget the torch,' Mike said, holding it out for her.

She wished the toilet block was on the other side of the complex, not thirty-five steps away from their tent. She swished the torch from side to side, pretending it was a scythe whipping across Marilyn's neck. That woman was no friend of her mum's. That woman was trying to step into her mother's shoes by latching onto her dad. There was no way she could let that happen. She would stop it. Somehow. It wasn't right. Although her mum was gone from the world, she was still very much in her heart. Why wasn't she still in her dad's?

She wanted Guy. She wanted him to hold her and touch her and make everything better. He'd done that tonight. He'd taken her up to the stars and that's where she wanted to stay. With him. Just with him. If Marilyn was going to be at home she would just have to run in the opposite direction.

Chapter Twenty-Six

She nursed the coffee cup in her hands and offered him a smile. He smiled back and took another mouthful of the dark, rich blend. When she'd talked of Dominic she'd finally opened up. The love for the boy shone in her eyes, lightened up her whole expression. He could tell her son meant everything to her. She had put aside all her plans to focus on the boy. University had come, but later. Her life had taken a back seat. Dominic had been, and still was, centre stage.

'Does he do well at school?' Guy asked her.

'What?'

'Dominic. Does he do well at school? He is a good footballer. Sometimes children are good at one thing and not the other.'

'He's very bright. He loves English. One of his creative writing pieces won a local competition.'

The pride in her voice was evident.

'He takes after you,' Guy told her.

'Oh no, he's much brighter than I ever was,' she insisted.

She'd had a love of books and writing but she'd never been an A-grade student. She'd been average and she'd had to work hard to be average. It was her passion that had always driven her to succeed, not a natural ability.

She looked at her watch. It was half past eleven. They were the only people left in the restaurant. She needed to get home.

'It's late. I should call a taxi.'

'I can take you,' Guy offered.

'But you've been drinking. You can't drive.'

'I have a car… a driver,' he said. He picked up his iPhone and held it up as if to explain.

'Your own chauffeur. You must have made it,' she stated.

He shrugged.

'I can easily get a taxi,' she insisted.

She didn't know much about chauffeur-driven cars but one thing she was almost certain of was you usually sat in the back seat. She wasn't sure sitting in the back seat of anything with Guy was such a good idea.

'I can easily take you home,' he responded.

She let out a sigh that she hoped he didn't hear. It would be ridiculous to create a fuss. She may as well accept the lift.

He made a call on his phone, then gestured for the waiter to bring the bill.

When it arrived, Emma opened her bag. Before she could remove her wallet Guy waved her action away.

'Do not think of taking out money,' he ordered.

'But—'

'*Non,*' he interrupted.

She ignored the insistent tone and stood up as Guy got out a credit card and beckoned the waiter with the chip and pin machine.

She looked out through the restaurant windows at the front of the building and saw it was raining. It had been so hot lately thunderstorms were forecast almost every day. She wished she'd thought to bring a jacket.

'Shall we go? Sean will only be a few minutes,' Guy told her.

She nodded and followed him towards the exit.

As he pushed open the glass door a loud crack of thunder boomed from above them and Emma jumped with fright. Rain was pelting down on the ground and a bright flash lit up the night sky.

'Are you OK?' he asked, touching her arm. They'd stopped short of the street and stood in the entrance underneath the restaurant's canopy.

'Yes. I just wasn't expecting that,' she admitted. The storm had already cooled the air and her arms started to pimple.

'You have no coat,' he observed.

'I'm fine,' she lied through chattering teeth.

'Here,' he said. Before she could protest he had taken off his jacket and slipped it around her shoulders. He straightened out the collar and made sure it was comfortable. She looked up at him. He was so close to her. His fingers fastened the three buttons, just touching her blouse, making the silk graze her skin. Her resolve was close to breaking. She could feel it happening. He reached up to touch her cheek and instinctively she shut her eyes.

The sound of a car pulling to the kerb and stopping in front of them broke the moment. Emma snapped open her eyes and took a half step back.

'It's my car,' Guy said, stating the obvious.

She nodded. He stepped out into the rain and opened the back door. The rain soaked him instantly, turning his shirt translucent, flattening his dark hair against his head.

'Emma,' he called, indicating the open door.

She put her bag over her head to shield it from the rain and hurried across the pavement to the waiting vehicle.

She dived into the car and slid over the cream leather seats leaving space for him. The rain was hammering against the roof of the car like it could break through the metal at any second. She had only heard something as harsh as the sound once before.

Guy leapt into the car, pulling the door closed behind him. He shook himself, spraying drops all over the seats, the door and the floor. He was saturated.

He pressed a button for the intercom. 'Sean, we need to go to...' He stopped talking and looked to her.

'14 Windsor Avenue,' she filled in. 'It's a mile from here.' She tried not to look as Guy undid the top two buttons of his shirt and fanned the material in an attempt to remove the water.

'Wow, it is wet,' he remarked with a laugh. Emma laughed too and watched him shake his head. It sent a flurry of moisture everywhere, a few specks landing on her face.

'Stop!' she said, wiping at it.

He smoothed his hair back behind his ears and turned his body towards her.

'Do you remember that storm in La Baume?'

She nodded. 'There was no warning. One minute we were in brilliant sunshine, the next the heavens opened.'

'We ran for the barn and...'

As he spoke the memories overwhelmed her, grabbed at her heart, pounded her chest, overloaded her mind. All she could see was the boy she adored, sat next to her, dripping wet, gorgeous, just as he was.

She had no idea who moved first but their lips met and she had her first taste of him in eight years. There was nothing slow or tentative about it. Passion and desire ripped through her body as she caught his face in her hands and begged him to deepen the kiss.

She felt his fingers brush the skin on her shoulder as he ran a trail down to her elbow, skimming the flesh so lightly. That scent, that same scent of citrus and Merlot and the freshness of the rain filled her senses. It was carrying her away, back to a time when she'd been able to let loose, when she hadn't been a mother, when she'd been a teenage girl falling in love for the very first time. But that wasn't who she was now. And she was with Chris.

A thump of realisation wrenched her back into her seat and away from Guy.

'Oh my God. I'm sorry. I'm so sorry. I shouldn't have...'

'Don't be sorry,' he said. He moved to take her hand but she withdrew it. The car came to a halt.

'I have to go.' She picked up her bag and opened the door.

'Emma, wait,' he begged.

She shut the door of the car and rushed up the path to her house. She didn't look back.

★

He tried to compose himself but his heart was still racing. He hadn't felt that way in so long. He'd kissed her. She'd kissed him. It had been sweeter than he remembered. He put a finger to his lips, hoping to feel her still on him.

He pressed the intercom. 'Just give me a minute, Sean.'

He couldn't leave things this way.

She rushed into the house almost unable to breathe. What had she done? How could she have been so stupid? He had led her on again. He had reminded her of their past and taken advantage of the situation. She had kissed him. *Kissed* him. She had cheated on Chris! She closed her eyes and leaned against the front door. She hated herself.

'Is that you, love?' Mike's voice called from the living room.

She opened her eyes quickly and tried to calm down. She needed to get a grip and quickly. No one had to know about this. It was a mistake. A big mistake but a mistake none the less. She'd made mistakes before and put them behind her. This would be no different.

'Yes… yes, Dad, it's me,' she answered, moving towards the lounge.

She blew a breath out and put her hand on the door. Smiling, she greeted Mike.

'Hey, Dad.'

'Hello, love. How's Ally?' Mike asked, turning off the television.

Ally. Of course. She told him she was going to Ally's.

'Oh, you know, she's a bit upset but she's getting there.

A couple of bottles of wine and some chocolates and the world seemed slightly better.' She began to undo the buttons of the jacket and it was then she realised it was Guy's.

'Whose is the jacket?' Mike asked as Emma fought to get it off.

'Jonty's. The pilot. Ally's ex-boyfriend. I went out without a coat and she insisted I took it so I didn't get wet getting in and out of the cab,' she said.

'Looks expensive. I always thought those pilots earned good money,' Mike said. He stood up from the sofa.

'Dom OK?' Emma asked.

'Oh yes he's fine. Ran me ragged on the Wii despite that ankle injury. We snowboarded and kick-boxed and every other punching sport under the sun. He went up about half eight and I checked on him about ten and he was out for the count,' Mike informed her.

'Thanks, Dad. Thanks for babysitting,' Emma said.

'Anytime, love. You know that.' He picked his anorak up from the chair and headed out of the room.

'I'll give you a ring in the week. You can tell me how your search for the perfect woman's going,' Emma joked.

'You may mock, but I'm finding the internet dating to be an eye-opener... what's this?' Mike asked. He stooped down and picked something up from the doormat.

Emma's heart stopped as she watched her dad pick up a piece of paper.

'It's got your name on it, love. Didn't you see it when you came in?' Mike asked. He passed the note to her. She took it and held it in her hand. She didn't need to look at the writing to know who it was from.

'I… didn't put the hall light on,' she answered.

'Right, well, I'll get off then. I'll see you, love,' Mike said. He opened the door.

'Bye, Dad. Thanks again,' Emma said.

Mike waved his hand. She made sure he made it to his car and then she shut the door. She flipped open the note.

My phone is in the jacket. I'll call in at the school tomorrow.

She closed her eyes and squeezed them up tight.

Chapter Twenty-Seven

August 2005

'Is everything OK, love?'

She needed to leave to meet Guy but her dad was taking ages to eat breakfast and it was her turn to wash up. She looked at her watch again. She had ten minutes. It wasn't going to be enough time. She would have to make an excuse and go.

'Emma, is something wrong?' Mike asked again.

'No. I just… I promised to meet Sally in ten minutes. But I know it's my turn to wash up and…'

'Where you off to this time? I don't know! You girls,' Mike said. He shook his head and laughed.

'We were just going to hang out at the arcade and then maybe go for a walk. I'd be back for lunch,' Emma stated. After seeing Guy she thought she might take a walk. She could find somewhere peaceful to read her books and make notes. If she stayed around the campsite her dad would have her entering bingo or boules.

'I can wash up! You go and enjoy yourself. That's what this holiday's for,' Mike insisted.

'You don't mind? You'll be OK?' Emma checked.

''Course I will. Go on. Off you go,' he urged.

Guilt. That's why he wasn't asking many questions and was giving in to her without a discussion. He knew seeing Marilyn was wrong and this was how he was trying to get out of it. If he knew dating another woman was wrong then he must still feel something for her mother. Maybe the situation wasn't completely hopeless. She had to take advantage of it though, if it meant slipping away to see Guy.

She grabbed her books, a notepad and pen and smiled at her dad.

'Thanks, Dad,' she said, backing out of the tent.

As she emerged the heat hit her. The sun was already high in a cloudless blue sky. Looking up at it a feeling of serenity flooded through her, appreciation for this beautiful place and the man who had held her here last night. Despite everything that happened at home she had so much to be thankful for. And so much to look forward to. She hadn't wanted this holiday but now the thought of going home was making her ache.

She checked her watch again and raced off towards the campsite gate.

He was holding an old-fashioned pram, rocking it backwards and forwards. Emma heard a baby crying. He looked up, meeting her gaze as she approached him.

'*Salut*,' he greeted her.

'Hi. What's going on? Don't you have your trial?' Emma asked him.

'*Oui*. Yes. Emma… this is my brother. I cannot leave him,' Guy started.

There was deep concern written all over his face and the sadness in his eyes made her heart buckle. Something had happened at home. Instinctively she knew it.

'What's happened?' she asked again.

'*Ma mère est ivre.*'

Est ivre. She had no idea what that meant. Why didn't she bring the phrasebook? She shook her head at Guy.

'I don't know what that means.'

'Wine… beer… she drink… very a lot,' he explained.

'She's drunk!' Emma exclaimed. 'In the morning!'

'Sshh, please,' he begged.

He was ashamed and embarrassed. He looked into the pram at the baby and she touched his shoulder. He flinched and moved away.

He was going to end things with her. That was what was going on. He'd got what he wanted from her and now he was going to dump her. Ally had told her all about this and she never believed it would happen to her. She wasn't naïve. Last night there had been a special connection between them. She had felt it.

'Are you going to finish with me?' Emma blurted out. She wouldn't cry. She would hold her head up high and make him say the words.

'What? Finish?' He looked confused now.

'After last night… are you going to find someone else?'

'No! *Non*. Why you think this?' He kissed her then. He leaned forward and pressed his lips to hers, bringing her head close and breathing into her hair.

'I need you,' he whispered.

The baby let out a wail of discontent as the pram stopped moving and both of them were shocked back into taking action.

'I have to go to OGC Nice for the... trial,' he reminded her.

'I know.'

'I have no one... no person to be with Luc,' he told her.

Emma looked at the baby. He couldn't be more than a couple of weeks old, as small as a newborn. His tiny hands were screwed up into fists and his red face was contorted, ready to squawk again. Poor little thing.

'You need to get to the football club. Have you got someone taking you?' Emma asked.

'*Oui*. Jean.'

'Then get going,' she ordered.

'Luc?'

'I'll look after him. Do you have his milk? That's all they have, isn't it? And I'll need some nappies, won't I?' She wasn't really sure what she needed but milk and nappies seemed the two most obvious things to ask for. Something to input and something to catch the output. Anything else she could improvise.

'There are... *couches dans le sac et le lait dans la kitchen principale. J'ai fait des bouteilles. Demandez Monique*,' he explained quickly.

'Nappies in the bag and milk in the main kitchen. Monique knows where,' Emma translated.

'Thank you,' he said.

She put her arms around him and held him close.

'Don't worry about Luc. I'll look after him. We'll go for a

walk. I'll keep him out of the sun and I won't read him too much Chaucer,' Emma promised.

'I have to go,' Guy told her.

'Go! Go and get a place on the team! Good luck! *Bonne chance*!' Emma said.

He picked up his rucksack and waving, hurried past the gate and out of the campsite.

'So then, Luc. I hope you're going to be good because I know less than nothing about babies. And I don't have one in my life plan until at least 2013,' she said, looking in at the wriggling infant.

She pushed the pram back and forth and looked at the little boy. Thick dark hair and innocent eyes gazed up at her. How could a mother of such a beautiful baby not make herself capable to look after him? How could she expect her teenage son to do it for her?

'I don't think Bram Stoker's going to be your thing, Luc. How about a bit of Jane Austen?' she said, smiling down at him.

A bubble of sound from his bottom gave her the answer.

Chapter Twenty-Eight

'Good morning,' Madeleine greeted as Guy entered the kitchen.

He'd hoped she wouldn't be there when he came down. He was certain she had an appointment at the beauty salon. He'd actually paid attention to something she said. Had he really not listened properly?

'Good morning,' he responded. He opened the fridge and took out the orange juice.

'You didn't come to bed last night,' she remarked. She didn't lift her head from the magazine she was reading.

'No. I was late. I didn't want to disturb you,' he lied.

He couldn't bear to be in bed beside her when all he could think of was his kiss with Emma. He had slept in one of the guest rooms and let all the memories wave over him as he drifted off to sleep. He wouldn't let this end like before. Even if he was not Dominic's father, even if she had lied to him in the past, the connection they had together was undeniable.

'You are going to training?' she asked.

'Yes.'

'I will be out all day.'

'OK,' he responded.

'Please be back before four. The dry cleaning is arriving.'

The very worst thing about the note was he hadn't said a time. This would impact on her whole day. She would be on edge, waiting for him to arrive from the moment the school day started until it came to an end. She almost combusted in front of her class when the receptionist came into the room and informed her someone was waiting for her. The bell for morning break had gone and her stomach had sunk to the floor. Even the iced bun Ally had brought with her didn't make up for the unneeded shock.

'You should know you can't call me and ask for an alibi without giving me the full story. Are we still fighting by the way? Because I'd rather not.'

Emma ushered her into an empty classroom and closed the door.

'Coffee? Machine's all fixed and it only took me six minutes to drive here so it's still hot,' Ally said, holding the cup out to her.

'Thanks. Listen, I'm sorry about what I said on the phone before. My head's all over the place,' she said.

'Tell me what's going on? Why did I have to split up with Jonty? I haven't yet by the way. He's taking me to Amsterdam for the weekend.'

'I went for the dinner with Guy. I couldn't tell anyone that, could I?'

'You could tell people that if it was just two ex-lovers meeting up to catch up. You couldn't say that if it was two ex-lovers meeting up to reengage in the loving bit,' Ally replied.

'I had no intention of anything happening…' she started.

'But something did?!'

'I'm so ashamed. I've left everyone down. I've let myself down. And Chris…'

'What happened?'

'I don't want to talk about it really. I just want to forget it. It was one moment. A stupid moment when my brain wasn't switched on properly. We kissed,' she admitted.

'Wow! I mean… wow on skis,' Ally stated, slurping at her drink.

'And he gave me his jacket and it had his phone in and now he's coming here to collect it. It could be any time.'

'And you're in a state because…?'

'Because I don't want to see him again.'

'Or rather you *do* want to see him again.'

'I'm not myself when he's around,' Emma tried to explain.

'You mean you're the you you were when you were with him, not the you you are with Chris.'

'Ally, please, don't start this again.'

'Well, it's the excitement and the adventure, isn't it? This Gallic hunk's come back out of the woodwork to woo you and boy, does he have all the moves. He's gorgeous, he's rich and successful. I can see your dilemma I really can.'

'No. I don't think you can. I don't think you can at all,' Emma spoke, drinking the coffee.

'Tell me then. Tell me what's going on,' Ally suggested.

'It's nothing to do with his fame or his money. It's to

do with me. I did something stupid all those years ago, something I've had to live with ever since. He cheated on me and I hated him for it but I was seventeen. He was eighteen. We were too young to make proper decisions. Maybe I made two mistakes that day. I never stopped to listen,' Emma told her.

'You're thinking if you'd hung around to let him explain, you'd be living a loved-up life with him in France? What exactly happened back then? What did he do?' Ally asked.

Emma let out a sigh. She didn't want to explain. It still hurt. Yes, she'd been seventeen but she'd been in love… for the first time. She'd had plans. They both had. And he'd ruined everything.

'He cheated on me. I found him in bed with another girl.'

She hurried the words out. It didn't make it sound any better and it still made her wince with the recollection.

'Scumbag,' Ally stated.

'But was he? There could have been an explanation. And if there was I didn't let him explain it. There were lots of things going on back then, with him, his family. I was missing my mum, my dad was starting a relationship with Marilyn and—'

'You're making excuses for him.'

'I'm not. Not really. I'm just saying perhaps he isn't the person I ended up thinking he was. Maybe I broke my own heart by not giving him a chance to tell me what happened,' Emma concluded.

'And why does it matter what happened? You said it yourself. You were seventeen, he was a holiday romance. You've grown up and moved on, so has he. This shouldn't be about what happened then. This should be about now.

Take the past out of the equation. Forget the French Riviera. If you hadn't known him before he walked into the fitness centre would we be having this conversation?' Ally asked. She raised an eyebrow.

'No, but—'

'Because you're happy with Chris. Because you're making a life with Chris. As gorgeous as Guy is, you might have checked out his arse like any normal red-blooded woman, but that's where it would've stopped.'

'But you can't look at things like that. I know him. I *knew* him. What am I supposed to do? Wipe everything from my memory?' Emma questioned.

'You need to decide what you want *now*, not based on anything from 2005,' Ally told her.

'How do I do that?'

'Don't ask me! I can't manage my own love life, let alone anyone else's!'

Emma put her hands to her head and tried to soothe the ache that was beginning to tighten.

'But I will listen, Em. Whatever you decide, whatever you want to do, I'm there, here, whatever,' Ally assured her.

'Thank you,' she mouthed.

Chapter Twenty-Nine

He'd called the school earlier to check what time lunch was. He didn't want to disturb Emma's day by barging into a class or causing her any inconvenience. He could see the children coming out of the main building. Some were walking towards a smaller building across the yard, others were sat down on benches eating from lunchboxes and a dozen or so boys had started a football game.

He ran his hands through his hair and looked in the rear-view mirror of the Range Rover. He was nervous. This wasn't just about picking up his jacket and phone. He *wanted* it to be so much more. But what happened next was really up to Emma. She needed to decide if they still had a chance. And he would respect her decision no matter what it was. Even if it killed him.

She was heading through reception towards the staff room when she saw him. He was immaculately dressed in dark jeans and a fitted navy T-shirt that skimmed his chest. She stopped, watched and realised this was what she'd been waiting for all day. He pushed open the glass door to enter and smiled.

'Hi,' he greeted.

'Hello. I left your jacket and phone in the car. I'm so sorry I kept it. I didn't realise until later and—'

'It's fine. Apparently I have five text messages and four missed calls from Madeleine about a couple's massage.' He smiled again but this time his heart didn't seem to be committed.

'I hope you didn't miss it.'

'I'm hoping I did.'

There was an awkward pause.

'The car's this way. Do you want to…' she began, stepping towards the door.

'Sure.'

She led the way across the tarmac at a ferocious pace, trying to ignore the fact her body had turned into a pulsating ball of need. Why did he have the ability to move her like that? All sense seemed to disappear, she couldn't concentrate and all the memories, including their kiss of the previous night, flooded her mind. It wasn't fair.

'How is your day?' he asked, breaking into her thoughts.

'Fine. Yes, today's been fine. How about you?'

'Fine, also. I had training. It was hard. It is still hot,' he said, indicating the scorching sun above them.

'We're expecting another storm tonight. They said on the weather.'

The weather! Now she was scraping the barrel for polite conversation. She stopped in the middle of the car park, frustrated with herself. She grabbed him by the hand and began marching him to her car. Whatever she was going to say she didn't want to say it in front of any of the schoolchildren. Kids loved gossip, especially gossip involving teachers.

'Get in,' she said, pulling open the door.

He did as instructed and by the time she'd navigated the back of the vehicle he was already sitting in the passenger seat. She got in beside him, shutting the door. As it clunked closed the silence enveloped them. A moment passed and she turned in her seat to look at him.

'I don't know what to do, Guy,' she admitted.

He didn't respond but reached for her hand. She let him take it.

'No,' he said. The words fell so quietly from his lips.

He was stroking her fingers lazily, seductively and the movements were giving her delicious chills over her entire body. She ought to pull away. She shouldn't be this close, but she knew she was fighting a losing battle. What was the best thing to do? Keep fighting? Or give in and see where it took them? A rush flew through her, an excited feeling, a glimpse of something different. Was this what she wanted? Was *he* what she wanted?

'The past is the past...' she started. She wet her lips to continue.

'Emma,' he broke in.

'Wait. You don't know what I'm going to say.'

'I do know. You will say I am too late. You will say there is no chance for us.' He shifted in his seat, let go of one of her hands and swept back his hair. She could see his eyes moisten. He looked like his world was about to end.

'We have to forget what happened before. We have to put those times behind us. Whatever happened, whatever you did, whatever I did... we have to put it aside,' she told him.

All at once his eyes brightened and he held on to both her hands again.

'I don't know what I'm doing but… I can't ignore it.'

A thrilling feeling, something like adrenaline was coursing through her. Looking at him, having him close *was* what she wanted. It was what she'd always wanted. What he'd done back in La Baume didn't matter. He was here. He wanted her. And she knew, deep down, her reluctance to accept any type of commitment from Chris was because her heart had been lost a long time ago.

'We have to do this right, Guy. By everyone in our lives. And we start from the beginning. We start slowly. I have Dominic and…'

Dominic. She had to think about Dominic. Could she really do this? Was it right for Dominic? What was she talking about? Leaving Chris? Guy splitting with Madeleine? Was it too much? Was she pinning her hopes on something that might not work? Even if they tried to put the past behind them could it really be done? She needed to be sure for Dominic.

Before she'd met with Ally she was convinced she couldn't see him again but now, with him in front of her, every ion of her just wanted to try. The connection was there, the heart-bursting passion built up inside her whenever they connected. If she felt that for Guy she couldn't possibly stay with Chris. She needed to see if this was where her future was. And if it wasn't, at least she would know, not spend a lifetime wondering 'what if'.

'I can't believe it. Are you sure?' he asked her.

'No. I'm not sure. I'm not sure at all… but I don't know what else to do,' she admitted.

He continued to stroke her hands and she let out an uneasy sigh. Just having him hold her hands reminded her of the depth of feeling they'd had for each other. Their few weeks in the late summer of 2005 had felt like a lifetime. It still did.

'This is not something to be sad about. This is something to celebrate,' Guy told her.

'No. It isn't. I need to speak to Chris. God, what am I going to say to him?'

Chris was so nice. He'd done everything right for her and Dominic for the last eighteen months and now she had to tell him it was over. It was going to shatter him. Or did he know already? Deep down did he know she was never going to accept his proposal?

'Everything will be OK,' he assured. He reached across and pushed her hair behind her ears.

'I don't know,' she said, shaking her head.

'*I* know,' he said, squeezing her hands.

His reassurance was just what she needed to hear.

'I never stopped loving you,' Guy told her.

The words hit her hard as she absorbed every one, ingesting exactly what they meant. She reached for him, cupping his face with her hand and drawing it closer to her.

'I missed you so much,' she whispered.

'Emma…'

She inched forward until they were eye to eye, both breathing hard, waiting for the perfect moment. She couldn't hold off any longer. She tentatively touched his lips with hers. The response was instant. He drew her towards him, his lips luxurious against hers, deepening the kiss with every second that passed. This wasn't going slow; this was quickening her feelings with every touch. She knew they should stop but it had been so long since she had felt this way. She tried to still in the moment, memorise the way his fingers felt entwined with hers, the velvet smoothness of his lips…

From outside the bell rang, jolting her back to reality. When she broke away she was breathing hard and flushed.

'I… I have to go,' she told him.

'I know,' he responded, taking her hand.

'I don't know what happens next,' she admitted.

He nodded, straightened the collar of her blouse.

'We make things right, like you said.'

'It isn't going to be easy.'

The thought of ending her relationship with Chris and his reaction to it terrified her. He wouldn't know why and she wouldn't know what to tell him. Apart from the truth. This wasn't just about Guy. This was about everything that had happened to her. Chris was a good, straight, honest person and she just… wasn't.

'I know,' Guy responded.

He had no idea what he was going to say to Madeleine or even how to start that conversation. He had to concentrate on the fact Emma was going to give him a second chance and they were going to put the past behind them. A second chance was all he wanted, all he'd thought about since he saw her again. The past wasn't important; it was the future that mattered. And his was with Emma, he was positive of that.

But he couldn't deny the voice inside his head telling him that when he broke the news to Madeleine she wasn't going to accept it. She never gave up anything without a fight.

Chapter Thirty

August 2005

'Please, Luc, please stop crying!'
She'd fed him again, changed his nappy, rubbed his back, sang to him and shaken some daft toy elephant at him. Nothing was working. He was red in the face and his little fists kept pumping up and down as he wriggled in his pram. He wasn't too hot – she'd kept him out of the sun. He wasn't too cold – that was impossible in almost thirty-degree heat. What else could be wrong with babies? He was so so small, weighed hardly anything at all. Was he ill?

It was after lunchtime. Guy had been gone for over three hours and if she didn't get back to her dad soon he'd be getting her name announced over the camp sound system like a lost child.

She pushed the pram forward and meandered along the lane back to the campsite. For the majority of the time Luc had been well-behaved. He'd gurgled, she'd fed him, he fell asleep, she read. It was only in the last hour he'd started to get grumpy and loud.

She was about to look at her watch again but a figure moving up ahead caught her eye. She squinted her eyes and saw it was Guy.

Stepping up the pace with the pram, she waved a hand. She was so looking forward to seeing him. The trial was bound to have gone well. He was such a talented player, the team would see that.

'Hey!' she greeted, approaching him. The expression on his face made her pull up to a stop. It told her everything she needed to know. She didn't know what to do or say but she knew she had to say something. She needed to know for sure.

'What happened?' she asked tentatively.

'They say *non*,' he stated.

There was a sharp intake of breath and it took Emma a while to realise it was hers. It was a shock. She had taken Guy getting into the team as a safe bet. She hadn't even considered he wouldn't. He had pinned everything on it. It was his dream. He loved football. He was brilliant at it and he wanted to make money from it. OGC Nice was the nearest, best team. But it surely wasn't his only option. She wanted to study at Portsmouth, stay near to her dad, but she was also considering Cardiff and York. That was it! He could just try somewhere else, like she was.

'Well, never mind. They aren't the only team, are they? I don't know anything about football but back home there are loads of teams in the Premiership, at least five or something around London. There must be other teams you can try out for,' Emma said. She kept her voice upbeat. She would make him realise this wasn't the end of the road.

He shook his head and Luc continued to cry.

'What? You can try other teams. They are bound to be looking out for talented new players. It will be Nice's loss,' she continued.

'You do not… *tu ne sais pas*.'

He put his arms into the pram and lifted up his brother. Emma watched as he began to sing in French, a low, sing-song tune she'd never heard. Within seconds, Luc was contented. His eyes were drooping closed and when Guy put him back down he was verging on sleep. He rocked the pram back and forth to make sure.

'I want to understand,' Emma told him.

Again he shook his head. Now she was worried. Why wouldn't he tell her? What on earth had happened at the football club to make him think his whole idea of a career was over?

And then it was like someone had turned out all the lights. The sky blackened, the clouds converged and with the loudest crack of thunder Emma had ever heard, a storm broke, sending shafts of rain sheeting from the sky.

Their skin already soaked, Guy pointed to a barn just across the field. It was their nearest form of shelter. He set off, sprinting with the pram and Emma struggled to keep up. The ferocity of the rain was tearing into her, making it almost impossible to run. Her hair clung to her face as she tried to duck the elements. Hailstones battered her thighs, her sandals slipped, her feet squelching as she hurried along. The barn was less than a hundred yards away but it felt like a hundred miles. Every step seemed to take all her strength. The corn that had been so light and soft against her skin on their picnic was now scratchy and sharp. It irritated her calves and scraped her thighs. Finally, with stones slipping in and out of her shoes, she ran into the barn behind Guy and Luc.

She was out of breath, her legs covered in scratches and her dress practically transparent. She watched Guy rock Luc's pram back and forth, lulling him off to sleep. The baby hushed again as Guy repeated the French song.

The rain outside looked like a sheet of moving opaque glass. It teemed down, unstopping, crushing the ground, moving field and path, relentless.

'I want to… *Je veux casser quelque chose,*' he shouted. He let out a roar, kicking a bale, then turning to assault another.

'Guy,' she started.

He picked up one of the bales and threw it across the barn. It hit the corrugated wall and broke apart, sending strands of hay to the floor. He sank to the floor, pulling his knees into his chest and began to sob.

She hadn't expected anything like that and she wasn't sure how to react. Boys didn't cry. Not the sort of boys from her school. They didn't show emotion at all if they could help it. Should she try and comfort him? Would he want that? It sounded as if his heart was breaking. She stepped slowly towards him, thinking if her attention wasn't wanted he would let her know in time, before she made an idiot of herself.

She got all the way over to him, not knowing if he'd even noticed her move. He had his head buried in his knees and he was rocking backward and forward. She put her arms lightly on his shoulders, still trying to gauge his reaction. The instant he felt her touch him he clung to her. He pulled her into him and wept on her shoulder. He was shivering.

Their clothes were saturated, their hair dripping and Guy's hands were like ice on her back.

'What is it, Guy? This isn't just the trial, is it? This is something else,' Emma said, brushing her hand down his hair and letting the water fall away with every stroke.

He shook his head, still continued to sob.

'Please, Guy, you're scaring me. I want to help. Let me help,' Emma begged.

'I cannot...' he started, lifting his head and wiping at his eyes with his fingers.

'You have to! If I'm special to you you'll tell me,' she urged.

He locked eyes with her and she didn't just see the sadness, she felt it.

He took hold of the bottom of his T-shirt and slowly began to pull it away from his body, towards his head. Emma could see it was wet and clinging but that wasn't why he was going slow. As he pulled it over his head she let out a gasp. His chest and abdomen were covered in a patchwork of bruises, scratches and marks. She cried out and reached for him. This time he shifted back.

'What's happened to you? Who did this?' Emma questioned, biting her nails. She was shivering now, both from the cold of her clothes and from what she'd seen.

'I have to... *C'est pourquoi que je dois a quitter. C'est pourquoi que je dois améliorer pour moi et pour Luc,*' he told her.

'This... is why... *sortir*... leave. This is why you have to leave, for you and for Luc,' Emma translated. Once she finished the sentence the reality of what he was telling her hit her like a bullet.

'Your mother… she did this?'

She couldn't believe it. A woman. A mother. Guy's mother had done… what? Beaten him? Why? What for? It was sickening. She started to shake.

'No,' she said, shaking her head. Guy gave no response, just pulled his T-shirt back down and wiped at his wet face with his hands.

'She couldn't… you're her son…'

Guy nodded. 'At the football… we had to see the doctor… *test d'aptitude*. He see this. I have to make a lie.'

'They didn't let you into the team because of what she did to you? Why didn't you tell them the truth?' Emma urged him. She reached for his hands and held them tightly in hers.

'I cannot.'

'This isn't the first time she's done this, is it?' Emma asked. She could feel herself boiling with anger, just like she had when her mother passed away. She'd been so angry then, Mike had feared for her sanity as well as the breakables in the house. None of it had been just or fair. The same was happening here with Guy. What had he done to deserve this?

'I have to stay… a little bit. When I have money, *assez d'argent* and the job, I will take Luc and we will go,' he explained.

'That's why today was so important,' Emma said, understanding.

'*C'est l'alcool et la façon dont mon père a quitté,*' Guy told her.

'No. Don't make excuses for her. What she's done to you is not OK. It's not,' Emma insisted.

'I have to look after Luc,' Guy said. His eyes went to the pram.

'Come here,' Emma beckoned, opening her arms to him.

He shook his head, folded his arms across his chest. It was if he was ashamed of what had happened to him.

'Guy, please. I can help you... we can sort something out. I could... I could talk to my dad,' Emma suggested. He might not be her favourite person at the moment but he was all she had. Her gran said he'd been born sensible. He would know what to do.

'*Non*!' Guy exclaimed. His horror at that suggestion was evident.

'OK, stupid idea. You're right,' she backtracked.

'*Je me déteste*,' he spat.

'No, don't say that,' she begged.

'*J'ai mériter cela*!' He punched the bale next to him.

'I don't know what that means. Please, Guy,' she said, taking hold of his arms.

He broke again. Sobs racked his shoulders and this time he let her gather him into her arms.

'Sshh, it's OK. It's going to be OK. I promise,' she whispered, stroking his hair.

Chapter Thirty-One

'Guy? Is that you?'

He'd been surprised to see Madeleine's car in the driveway when he'd parked. He'd hoped to have the rest of the afternoon alone to go through his schedule. He wanted to spend some time with Emma. Proper time. But first he had to tell Madeleine it was over. He swallowed at that thought. He needed to do it quickly for both their sakes.

He entered the kitchen, found Madeleine sitting at the central island leafing through a magazine.

'Hi. I thought you were out for the day. I am back in time for the dry cleaning,' he said, looking at his watch.

'Something amazing has happened!' Her eyes were animated, her expression almost manic with excitement.

'What is it?' he asked. What was it? This could be very bad. She was behaving as if something life-changing was about to occur. It couldn't be…

'We have been invited to Suzanna Okino's fashion showcase tonight! All the major labels will be there and the press. Gabriella's even got us five minutes with a lingerie manufacturer about developing our line,' Madeleine bubbled. She got down off the chair and moved towards him.

'This could be the launch of my career as a fashion designer, Guy! Lingerie to start and then a whole clothing line,' she said, placing her hands on the lapels of his jacket.

'That is…' He didn't really know how to react. He had never seen her so enthusiastic about anything. She was glowing. She was glowing *and* smiling. He wasn't used to it. These days he mostly got sneers and orders.

'It's the best thing that has happened to me. I cannot wait to go. We should get there early. Gabriella wants us to run through our pitch. It's only five minutes with the manufacturer but he's well thought of and… we just need to get a start with someone,' she continued. She kissed his cheek and then his mouth, linking her arms around his neck.

He held her back. The closeness felt so wrong.

'What is it? Is everything OK?' she asked. She stepped back, observed him more closely.

'Yes… of course,' he said, putting a more upbeat expression on his face.

'This is what I wanted so much, Guy. The chance to own something, build something. I know you think I exist only to shop but every moment spent in boutiques was research. Perhaps maybe not the Vivienne Westwood but the rest…'

'I'm pleased for you,' Guy told her. He took her hand and held it in his.

He was pleased for her. This was a good thing. When he told her they needed to break up, she would have a focus now. It would not be so hard for her.

'What shall I wear?' she asked him, holding his hand in the air and spinning a circle.

'I don't know... you are the fashion expert,' he responded.

He couldn't tell her tonight.

'How's your steak?' Emma asked.

Chris looked up from his meal, horseradish sauce at the corner of his mouth. 'Great. Gorgeous, just like you.' He laughed then and poked in a couple of chips.

This was awful. She'd barely touched her meal. Her stomach was too full of guilt, regret and worry to add food to the mix. She poured some more water into her glass.

'How was work?'

'Work? Taxi-driving the world around? It was same as. Mrs Bootle paid me fifty quid again to drive her around for an hour passing all the places she used to visit with Mr Bootle when he was alive.'

'Again? Oh ,that's really sad,' Emma said.

'I thought that at first, but it makes her happy. When I look in that rear-view mirror, she's there, smiling away in the back. God knows what those two got up to at these places. We went past the library, which is innocent enough, but then she had me up that dirt track to the side of the recreation ground.'

'Perhaps they had a dog and used to go for walks,' Emma offered.

'She had a right twinkle in her eye,' Chris said, grinning.

Just like he had at that very moment. She swallowed. How did you start a conversation like this? She wasn't sure she could even open her mouth to begin.

'Listen, Em, I've been thinking...' he started.

He was going to propose. He thought the sirloin steak and the wine was a sign for him to try again. Why hadn't she thought of that? He would have no idea the real reason behind buying his favourite food. She couldn't let it happen.

'I've got some pudding. I got treacle sponge. I'll get it,' she said, rising from her seat.

'What? But I haven't finished and you... you haven't started,' Chris said. He indicated her plate, hardly a mouthful missing.

'I'm not very hungry. I had one of those huge macaroni cheese things at the school canteen,' she lied.

'Sit down, Em,' Chris urged.

She didn't want to sit down. She wanted to stand up and do something, anything to make this feeling leave her. Now she wasn't only worried about what she had to say, she was also concerned about what Chris wanted to talk about.

'Please,' he urged.

She had no choice. She sunk back down into the chair, setting her eyes on the meal rather than him.

'I know why you've been down lately.'

No. He couldn't know. He just couldn't. His statement was enough to make her raise her head and look at him.

'You've been a bit out of sorts since the beginning of August. Since the anniversary of your mum dying,' Chris spoke.

Her throat tightened and she felt that familiar lurch inside. Thoughts and memories still triggered that surge of loss so easily.

'I just want you to know... I understand. You can talk to me about it. You know I was ten when I lost my dad. I've been there and I still miss him. There's times – birthdays, Christmas, anniversaries – when it still feels fresh,' he continued.

Why was he doing this? Why was he doing this now? She almost wished he'd propose. This was worse. He was feeling sorry for her, showing empathy, bearing his soul, talking about his dad. She didn't deserve his compassion. She didn't deserve anything.

'I...'

'You don't have to say anything, Em. I just want you to know I'm here. I'm here and there's no pressure,' he said. He reached across the table and took one of her hands in his.

She was despicable. He was a wonderful, wonderful man and she was so lucky to have him. What was she doing pretending she could go back to being a teenager with Guy? It was impulsive, impossible, irresponsible love. There was no place for that in her life. Her life was with Chris. It *should* be with Chris. He was stable. Dominic needed stability.

'No pressure?' she queried, wiping a lone tear from her cheek.

'Yeah, I mean the proposing thing. I knew the other day, when I said it; you weren't going to say yes. But that's OK. I want you to know that's OK,' he carried on. He was rubbing her fingers, just like Guy had, but the feeling couldn't have been more different. It was comforting. She felt content. But that was *all* she felt. Nothing stirred within her. There was no passion, no rise in body temperature or blood pressure, just the sensation that he cared for her. Was that enough? Could that be enough? It should be, shouldn't it?

'It isn't OK though, is it?' she mumbled, half to him, half to herself.

'Hey, I know I'm punching above my weight with you. I mean look at you! Beautiful and clever and me, well… I'm nothing special,' he said. He shrugged.

'You *are* special,' Emma jumped in.

'What I am is lucky. Lucky to have you and Dom and I'll take that. Marriage or no marriage, I'll take it,' he told her, squeezing her hand.

She couldn't speak. She didn't know what to say. He *was* a special person. He was funny, hard-working, honest, caring and fantastic with Dominic. The list went on and on. But what the list didn't cover was heat, passion, that intense connection on every level. She had never had that with Chris. Chris was the favourite little black dress you could always rely on. Guy was the bright red expensive frock you could only just fasten up but when you did, it made you feel alive.

She nodded. That was all she could do. Now wasn't the time. She couldn't do it. She didn't know if she really *should* do it. There was so much at stake. Chris had been a constant; Guy had been back a few days. She couldn't make any decision based on that.

'Did you mention treacle sponge?' Chris asked, letting go of her hand and picking his knife and fork back up.

'Yes.' She stood up, glad the atmosphere was broken.

'Dom's going to be buzzing in the morning by the way,' Chris remarked, before Emma moved to the kitchen.

She looked at him, waiting for an explanation.

'Put tickets to Finnerham's next game under his pillow.

Mate of my boss only has a box there! Me, you and Dom in executive seats, food, drink, the lot – next Saturday.'

Guy's team. Watching Guy's team. Watching Guy – with Chris and Dominic. She couldn't think of anything worse.

'Oh, well, I don't know whether I'll be able to come. We're going to need some extra rehearsal time for *Copacabana* and I was thinking of getting the students in on Saturdays,' she said as fast as she could.

'Come on, Em! It's free food and drink and sitting in the warm if you want. I know you're not a football fan but there'll be other wives there… well, partners… you know, girlfriends you can talk to. Dom would want you to come,' Chris urged.

Yes, when Dominic saw the tickets, Chris was going to move even further up to hero status and nothing else would be talked about for the rest of the week. She couldn't get out of it. Not even the school production was going to cut it when Chris had obviously pulled strings to get the opportunity.

'I'll work something out. Maybe we can start the week after,' she said. She smiled at him, then turned away.

'Magic! I can't wait to see that Guy Duval in action. If they've really paid all that money for him like it said in the papers, I'm expecting him to score at least once,' Chris commented.

She left the room and closed the door. Resting her body against the back of it she closed her eyes. What was she going to do?

Chapter Thirty-Two

She had fidgeted in the car the whole way to London. Fingers in her hair, powder compact open, re-touching her make-up and straightening her clothes. He'd never seen her like that before. It was usual for her to take care of her appearance, but this was different. She was jittery, with what seemed like a mixture of nerves and excitement. Now, as they prepared to leave the car, she was toying with her hands, wringing them together.

'Madeleine,' Guy said, taking one of her hands.

'Don't touch me, Guy, I've just straightened my jewellery,' she gasped, snatching back her hand.

The driver opened the back door and Madeleine was out, surging up from the back seat like a breaking wave hitting its crest.

Guy let out a breath and smoothed his hair back. He didn't want to be here. All this pomp and circumstance over fashion labels. He might have the means to afford whatever he wanted but he was happiest in his oldest jeans and a worn, faded T-shirt.

He stepped out of the car, joining Madeleine in front of a small number of photographers. She was turning to them, showing off a dress she was wearing that he definitely hadn't seen before.

'Guy, this way!'

'Guy, are you looking forward to the match on Saturday?'

'Guy, any truth in the rumour you've been approached by Calvin Klein?'

Madeleine turned to him, an infuriated look on her face.

'Why do they always ask so much about you? I've been in three motion pictures,' she stated.

Not to be outdone, she coiled her arms around his neck and pouted a kiss towards his cheek.

Chris hadn't stopped talking about the upcoming match. Although they were supposed to be catching up on past episodes of *The Glades* he couldn't stop interrupting with information about match days and talk of how thrilled Dominic would be.

She couldn't concentrate on the TV either. Her brain was working overtime, everything converging together, in one massive problem she didn't know how to start sorting out.

'I'll wash up,' Chris said. He bounded up from the sofa and flicked off the television.

'No. You don't have to do that.' She leapt up after him.

'Don't be daft. You made the dinner, I'm washing up,' he insisted. He started to run the water to fill the bowl.

'Don't Chris, please. I want to do it,' Emma begged.

He turned the tap off and looked at her.

'You *want* to wash up?' he queried.

He didn't understand. She just wanted to be alone. Alone with the million thoughts she needed to unscramble.

'I… well, to be honest I have marking to do and…'

'Ah, I see. You want me to go,' Chris guessed.

'No. I mean, yes. But…' No matter how she wrapped it up it sounded mean. But she *was* mean. Everything she was doing lately was mean.

'It's alright, Em. I know you're busy and I've got an early start in the morning anyway,' Chris said, picking his coat up from the back of the chair.

'Sorry, I didn't mean to sound… I just…' What was she trying to say? She hated this. Everything was off-kilter and it was unsettling. She didn't want it to be like this.

'What are you apologising for? I've come here, I've had my favourite dinner and wine *and* on a weeknight! I'm a lucky man,' Chris said, grinning.

She tried to grin back but the expression didn't really work like it should.

'Listen, give me a call tomorrow. Let me know what Dom says about the tickets,' he said.

She nodded. 'I will.'

'Right, well I'll be off.' He put his arms around her and she held on. Good, solid, salt of the earth, Chris. She closed her eyes and tried to make the world still.

'Night,' he said, kissing her on the lips.

'Night.'

They'd been sat in the second row to the right of the catwalk. Madeleine had been miffed to begin with. She'd wanted to be the centre of attention, recognised by someone, anyone. But she'd been appeased when she realised Victoria Beckham was positioned just four places away.

'She has her own fashion label you know,' Madeleine whispered. Victoria Beckham was causing quite a stir in the after-party. Everyone wanted to chat to her, including Madeleine.

'She's already done knickers,' Gabriella announced, guzzling down an oyster.

Guy wondered why Daniel wasn't here. What excuse had he used to escape this?

'Guy, please get us some more champagne,' Madeleine ordered.

'Yes. I won't be able to pitch anything with a dry throat. Are you nervous? I haven't been able to eat a thing all day,' Gabriella stated, smoothing the fabric of her dress over her ribs.

Guy headed towards one of the waiters, circling the room with champagne flutes on trays. He needed an opportunity to duck out and call Emma. He wanted to hear her voice, needed to know there was a new future waiting for him, waiting for them both.

'It *is* you! I knew it! Well, look at you!'

The woman's voice addressing him had him turning around. Facing him was a tall, slim woman, mid-twenties, wearing a midnight-blue, full-length gown. Her blonde hair was twirled up into a chignon.

She laughed. 'You don't recognise me, do you?'

'I'm sorry. Have we met before?' he asked, unsure.

'We certainly have. Although it didn't last as long as I'd hoped. You were the campsite hottie. Summers in La Baume just haven't been the same since you left.'

Guy looked at the woman, trying to think back. It took him less than ten seconds to realise who it was.

'Tasha,' he said.

'Yes, that's right! See, you do remember me! I've changed a bit, I suppose. Better clothes and I know what I'm doing with my make-up these days.' She laughed.

He smiled.

'So, look at you! Gorgeous as ever and at the top of your game. I hate football but the players who make it into the glossies always tend to catch my eye,' Tasha continued.

Although she was dressed in something obviously expensive, all he could see was the teenage girl from the clubhouse discos wearing mini-skirts and neon. That vision brought back the memories he was so ashamed of.

'So, were you invited here because you model? I haven't stalked you or anything but I did see *that* billboard. You could hardly miss it. It was right outside Waterloo. I told people I knew you but I don't think they believed me,' Tasha continued.

'*Non.* My girlfriend, Madeleine, she was invited. She has a meeting with a lingerie manufacturer,' he informed, taking a sip from one of the drinks he was holding.

'Ooo that's exciting. Which one?'

'I… I don't remember the name.'

'Was it Soft Touch?'

'I don't…'

'Because that's my father's company. You remember my father, don't you? Always drank too much and laughed too loudly,' Tasha continued.

The glasses fell from Guy's hands.

Chapter Thirty-Three

She wasn't sure this was the right thing to do but she had to do it. The box was heavy and covered in dust, despite having been underneath a child's car seat she no longer used and at least fifty CDs she never listened to.

This was everything that meant anything to her from her past. She knew most of what was in there, knew the items would spark emotion, but she had to open it. She had to put herself back there to try and resolve what was happening now.

She placed the container on the table and braced herself. There was a reason it had been in a cupboard under the stairs for so long. It was full of the person she used to be. There were items in it that held little meaning to anyone else but they all told a story. Her story.

She took off the lid and put it to one side. There on top was a patterned blanket. Just disturbing it slightly brought a scent to Emma's nose. It was her mother's. It was something Emma had made at school out of squares of knitting sewn together. That had been the blanket of choice to wrap around her mother's frame when she was ill.

Lifting it out carefully, she brought it to her face. Inhaling, she pressed the material to her cheeks, flattening her nose against the wool. It was still there, the very essence of her mum.

Clean cotton with notes of hardback books and soap. She was drawn right back to the time she'd had to say goodbye. The tears were brimming but she wasn't going to let them fall. That wasn't what this task was about. This exercise wasn't about falling apart it was about putting things back together.

She put the blanket on top of the table and looked back into the box. She dipped her hand in and pulled out a stuffed toy. This time she let the tears fall.

It was so worn and threadbare it was almost impossible to tell what animal it was supposed to be. Dominic hadn't gone anywhere without it when he was small. One of its eyes was loose and the line of stitching that represented its mouth was coming apart. She'd never known what it was called. She wasn't sure it had a name. She just knew it had been loved.

She put it on the blanket and reached in for something else. She brought out a small black velvet box and this time her hand shook. Why had she kept it? Why had it found its way into this collection of precious treasures?

She chewed her lip, strengthened her resolve and snapped open the lid. There it was. It looked just the same as the picture she had in her head. Why would it have changed? She'd worn it for just a few hours and then it had been consigned to the box for all time. With an unsteady hand, she loosened the ring from the cushioned surround and took it out.

The light caught the almond-shaped sapphire as she held it between her fingers, remembering the moment she'd received it. It had held so much hope, so much love and so many dreams. Why had it gone wrong? Why hadn't their bond been enough for him? Or was it more than that? Were they both just too young to say yes for a lifetime?

★

The sound of smashing glass had brought gasps and attention to him. Champagne had licked Tasha's ankles and shards had scattered across the wood floor. In his state of shock he'd grabbed the arm of the nearest wine waiter and indicated the mess before fleeing. Now, hunched over the sink in the gents, he was still struggling to get his breathing under control.

He ran some water, wetting his hands under the tap. He flicked it up with his fingers, ran them through his hair. He was sweating and his hands were trembling. It was his worst nightmare. That man was here.

He studied his reflection in the mirror and all he saw was the person he'd been back then. Young, weak, trapped. That essence hadn't left him. It haunted him. He was tainted by what had happened, forever dragged back there in mind if not in body. He couldn't move on. Even now, after eight years.

The door to the toilets opened and he tried to pull himself together. Sucking in a breath he straightened his expression, pulled his shoulders back and turned the tap on again.

'Hello, Guy.'

Hearing his voice sent him into a panic. He turned off the tap and reached across for the paper towels, not daring to look his way, let alone greet him. He wasn't here. It was his imagination. He couldn't be here in the present. He belonged in the past.

'How are you? Long time no see,' the voice continued.

Guy put the used paper towel into the bin and raised his head.

'I'm sorry. Have we met before?'

His voice hadn't come out convincing at all. It had sounded faint and uncontrolled.

Tasha's father, Keith Crone, let out a raucous laugh, holding his sides for effect. He looked no different. Dyed blond hair, thick black designer glasses and his rotund form squeezed into a fashion that made him look like a cross between Humpty Dumpty and Elton John.

Bile was rising in Guy's throat as the man continued to laugh. He needed to get out of here.

Keith stopped laughing, took off his glasses and studied Guy. His scrutiny made him turn away.

'You've turned into quite the young man, haven't you?' Keith remarked.

'Where have we met before? If you just remind me then…'

He didn't know how to handle this. He wanted to wipe his memory of everything and perhaps he could. Maybe if he just didn't acknowledge it, it would disappear.

'You need reminding, do you? I'm disappointed by that,' he responded, putting his glasses back on his face.

He didn't know what to say so he just stood there, stock still, waiting for something to happen. Silence descended and all he could hear was Keith's breathing.

'Still got my lodge in La Baume, you know. Had it modernised just last year. I was sorry to hear about your mother. Lovely lady,' Keith said. He nodded as if to indicate reverence.

He was so close to retching he could taste it in his mouth. His stomach contracted over and over and beads of sweat were forming on his brow.

'Listen, I think you and me could have quite a lot to talk

about, don't you?' Keith said. He pulled his jacket aside and reached into the inside pocket.

Guy stepped back, pressed his body against the porcelain of the basin.

'I'd like to have lunch. My treat. Call my secretary to arrange something,' he said. He held out a business card.

Guy just looked at it. He might as well have been holding out a poisoned apple. His eyes were focused on the card but he couldn't move.

Keith stepped forward and pressed the card to Guy's chest. At once, Guy cowered, lifted his hands to shield his head.

'What you doing? I'm not going to hurt you. Keith wouldn't do that,' he said in soft tones.

Guy pushed past him and made for the door, every inch of him screaming out for escape.

Marry me. Just two little words but they meant so much. They had meant so much back then. Back then they had actually meant everything. She toyed with the ring, rolling it around her fingers, letting the light dance off the stone and the slim golden band. What would have happened if she'd stayed? How would things have turned out? Would they still be together? Would there be more children? Or would their love have died out? Were the feelings she was having now just because she'd backed out too soon? Was it a case of getting the passion out of her system?

Her mobile phone began to ring. Emma checked her watch. It was almost eleven. She stood up and picked it up off the side. Guy.

'Hello.'

There was no greeting back, just the sound of background noise. There was laughing and shuffling and what sounded like bar room conversation.

'Guy? Are you OK?'

Still there was no response. Maybe it wasn't him. Maybe it was his girlfriend, Madeleine Courtier, wondering who 'Emma' was in his list of contacts. She swallowed and braced herself for an onslaught and accusations.

'Guy,' she tried again.

Someone was definitely there. She could detect breathing in the foreground.

'Guy, please. Are you OK? Has something happened?' Now she was worried.

'I love you, Emma.'

The words were barely out before an anguished sob took over. Her chest heaved and she pushed the phone closer to her ear.

'Guy, are you hurt? Where are you? I can come to you if you want me to.'

She would have to call her dad or Ally to be with Dominic but whatever this was it was serious.

Still he cried and her heart started to fall apart. She wanted to reach down the phone to him, to put her arms around him and make whatever this was, better.

'Guy, you're frightening me. Tell me what's happened,' she begged.

'I have to go,' he whispered through the tears she could hear were there.

'No, please, don't go. Talk to me... Guy...'

The call ended and she put her hand to her chest, taking a much-needed breath. What had happened?

Chapter Thirty-Four

August 2005

'Whose is the baby? Is it yours?'

Melody cackled at Tasha's wisecrack and both of them moved their jaws up and down, crushing the chewing gum against their teeth.

'Crying a lot isn't it? Is it sick?' Tasha continued.

Guy's mother was again drunk and incapable of looking after her infant son and Guy had to work teaching football skills at the campsite. Emma had offered to have Luc for a couple of hours. Apart from the screaming she quite liked having something to do. She could snatch half an hour to read and revise while he napped and it meant she had an excuse not to join in with the lame campsite games. This afternoon her dad was going to be competing in a raft race in the lagoon pool so this morning he had gone off to practise.

She ignored Tasha's comment and parked the pram next to a picnic bench, across from where Guy was teaching football. She put Luc's bag on the table and took her books out of it.

'What you reading?' Tasha asked, picking up *The Canterbury Tales*.

'Give it back,' Emma ordered. Tasha began to leaf through the pages.

'Looks crap to me. It's not even English,' she said, making exaggerated facials at Melody.

'Not the type of English you speak, no,' Emma responded.

'What's that supposed to mean? D'you think you're better than us just because you've got some posh accent going on?' Tasha questioned, pushing her face into Emma's personal space.

'You said it, not me.' She stood her ground.

'You cow!' Tasha exclaimed, raising her hand.

'Tasha! What d'you think you're doing?'

A loud male voice cracked through the situation.

Tasha dropped her hand down as quickly as she'd raised it.

A plump man with spiky blond hair and dark sunglasses, dressed in white trousers and a red and white striped short-sleeved shirt arrived on the scene.

'What you doing? It didn't look like you were making friends and influencing people, Natasha,' he said, glaring at Tasha.

The girl didn't speak and Emma used this as her opportunity to grab her book back.

'Apologise, Natasha,' the man ordered.

'I didn't do anything, Dad,' she insisted, scowling.

'Apologise,' he repeated.

Tasha looked at Emma; her eyes narrowed, her shoulders back, looking defiant.

'Sorry,' she said almost inaudibly.

'Good. Now I want you to go and help your mother get the picnic organised. We're going out on the boat in an hour,' the man told her.

'D'you want to come, Melody? Melody can come, can't she, Dad?'

'You'll have to ask your parents.'

'Come on, let's go,' Tasha said, pulling Melody by the arm.

Luc's cries seemed to intensify as Tasha and Melody left and Emma reached into the pram to lift him out. She hugged him to her chest and whispered in his ear like she'd seen Guy do. Sweet, tiny little thing.

'Now, he's a handsome chap, isn't he?'

The man admired Luc and put his pinky finger into the baby's hand. Luc clung on tight and stilled slightly.

'He's almost due a bottle,' Emma informed.

'Keith Crone,' he introduced himself, holding his free hand out to her.

'Emma, Emma Barron.'

'I'm Natasha's dad and I have to apologise for her. She's been spoilt – totally my fault –but I did bring her up to have some manners. Any more trouble from her or her sidekick and you let me know,' he said.

'They weren't really trouble just...' Emma began.

'I'll leave you to this little one. Handsome boy,' Keith said. He let go of Luc and waved a hand at Emma before strolling off with a confident gait.

She'd barely had time to look in Luc's bag for his bottle before Guy was at her side.

'*Que voulait-il?*'

'What?' Emma asked.

'The man… what did he want?' Guy wanted to know.

'Oh, he's Tarty Tasha's dad. Can you believe she took a swing at me? I actually had the Oxford English Dictionary in my bag. If she'd slapped me she wouldn't have liked a wallop with that,' Emma said, smiling.

Guy winced and held his left side.

'Are you OK? Is it still your ribs?'

'I'm OK,' he insisted.

'I still think you should go to the hospital.'

'I am fine.'

'This can't go on and as much as I like Luc, I can't look after him all the time because your mother's too drunk to. What happens when I have to go home?' she asked.

She looked at Guy, watched his expression dull, the light in his eyes dim. They hadn't talked about what would happen to them when she left. She only had one more week. Then it was back to Wiltshire, back to the house her mother had died in and to her dad's blossoming relationship with Marilyn, the woman who was basically dancing on her mother's grave.

'Can we meet tonight?' he asked her, lacing his fingers through her free hand.

'I don't know. It's difficult to get my dad to believe I'm spending all this time with a friend I made up who he hasn't seen. He's going to start asking questions sooner or later.'

'*S'il tu plait*,' Guy said, rubbing his finger against Luc's cheek and watching him gurgle.

She wanted to meet him. Should she really be worried about what her dad thought? At the moment he was quite content to live his life to the full. He didn't really have the time to worry about what she was getting up to. He had raft races and Marilyn.

'OK,' Emma agreed.

'Thank you,' Guy said. He leaned forward, kissing her lips and making her sway with the feeling that gave her.

'You'd better go back to the football. We'll be right here,' Emma said, nodding her head in indication of her planned reading.

He kissed Luc's tiny face and squeezed her hand before hurrying back to his pupils.

Chapter Thirty-Five

Present Day

'There's a distinct lack of tuna in this tuna roll. I'm going to have to have a word. I know we're not supposed to be serving stuff like Heston, but it is meant to rival the sandwich shop on the corner. I thought we might be able to steal some of their custom. We won't be if our tuna rolls are just bread that was shown the fish but didn't quite start a relationship.'

Ally placed the offending item back on its plate and reached for her pastry. She raised her eyes from her food to Emma and shook her head at her.

'You look pasty and sleep-deprived. What's been happening?' she asked.

'Guy and I… oh I don't know.'

'You do know and you're meant to tell me. That's how the whole best friend thing is supposed to work.'

'We want to try. *I* want to try,' she began.

'Things have moved on. Tell me more,' Ally encouraged.

'It's all such a mess. I don't really know what's going on.

We met, we decided we had to see if our feelings were going to lead anywhere but I said we must make sure we do the right thing. He has a partner, I have Chris.'

Ally didn't speak.

'I was supposed to tell Chris. Not about Guy necessarily, but end things, make a clean break...'

'You couldn't do it,' Ally guessed.

Emma shook her head.

'Well, maybe that's telling you something in itself,' Ally suggested.

'You don't understand,' Emma said, reaching for her coffee.

'Listen, I know you say the bond the two of you had eons ago in France was tight, but we're in 2013 now. You're judging the situation on that first flush of romance suddenly being rekindled...'

'He phoned me. Something's happened to him but I don't know what. He was crying and I haven't heard from him since,' Emma carried on.

'Second thoughts. He's had a change of heart. He's realised what I'm saying. Sometimes you have to count the chicken that's keeping your bed warm at night, not the one who frantically ruffled your feathers when you were seventeen, no matter how great it was at the time.'

'You're doing it again. You're trying to make me stay with Chris. Why?' Emma queried, her eyes meeting Ally's.

'Because he's been there for you and Dominic and before him, the longest you'd ever been with anyone was four months.'

Ally held her gaze until Emma was forced to look away. Of course, Ally was right. Chris had been there. He seemed to be able to take the rough with the smooth. He was a rock in so many ways but... he wasn't Guy.

'Now we're going to this football match in an hour and I'm not going to be able to avoid him. After the game there are sandwiches and tea with the team and Chris and Dom will be there. It's going to be so awkward,' Emma explained.

'I can't help you if you're not going to be honest with me,' Ally stated. She pulled a raisin out of her cake.

'What d'you mean? I am being honest with you. You're the only one I am being honest with!'

'Who's Dominic's father?'

'I told you I don't know.'

'No, you fed me a story about turning into some sort of teenage nymphomaniac and having it away with half our year. I was around at the time. And I wasn't permanently drunk on cider,' Ally continued.

She was starting to shake and she tried to hide it. She put her coffee cup down.

'He *is* Dominic's father, isn't he?' Ally stated.

Emma shook her head. There was no way she could tell Ally any more. She had told her too much already.

'Tuna rolls, my favourite!' Chris enthused as he and Dominic approached the table.

'Don't,' Emma warned her friend. She was rescued from having to answer by Dominic bundling into her.

'Hey, Aunty Ally!' he greeted, hugging her.

'Hello, Dom. How's your ankle?' she asked, ruffling his hair up.

'It's fine now. I played football at school yesterday and scored two goals,' he said proudly.

'That's my boy. Super stuff – on skis,' Ally replied.

'We're going to watch Finnerham later. Guy's going to be playing,' Dominic said.

'He might not be, Dom, you don't know. He might be injured,' Emma interjected.

'Is he? Did you hear the team news?' Chris piped up.

'No. I just... well, we don't know the team yet, do we?' She stopped herself from saying any more.

'How's your dad's internet dating going?' Ally asked, swiftly changing the subject.

'Oh he's done with all that. He's back with an old flame,' Chris said. He winked at Emma. Her stomach turned. Her dad was back with Marilyn. They'd bumped into each other again. That had led to dinner and now there was talk of joining a darts team. All that in a few days.

'Well, good for him. Is it good for him?' Ally asked, looking to Emma.

She shrugged. It was all she was capable of.

'We'll find out tomorrow. He's invited us to dinner,' Chris told.

'But we haven't said yes yet. I might be—'

'Not more marking.'

'Well, I *am* a teacher.' She couldn't keep the harshness from her tone. She followed it up quickly. 'Sorry.'

'Jonty's promised me Italian tonight, no expense spared,' Ally told the group.

'I thought you'd broken up with him. Didn't he like someone else?' Dominic butted in.

'Dom!' Emma exclaimed.

'You said!'

'I'm sorry, Ally,' Emma said.

'That's OK. He's still in the dog house. I'll make sure his credit card takes a real pounding on tiramisu.'

He hadn't slept since the night of the fashion show. He was back to prowling the house, working out at three in the morning, anything to get out of lying down and closing his eyes. He'd never in a million years thought he'd see Keith Crone again – anywhere but in his nightmares.

He'd never known his occupation; just that he had money and lots of it. Knowing that Madeleine and Gabriella were going to be working with him on their lingerie label made him nauseous. This was where it was going to start all over again. He'd never be free.

'Hey, Guy... you want something? Big game today,' Daniel asked, standing in front of him.

Guy put his boots down and faced his teammate.

'*Non.*' He shook his head.

'You sure?' Daniel checked.

'I said no,' Guy barked, standing up and squaring himself towards Daniel.

'Alright, man, chill out. You know where I am if you change your mind.' Daniel backed off and Guy turned his attention to the number eight shirt hanging on the hook above the bench. It was his. Finally he had what he wanted and he couldn't enjoy any of it.

Chapter Thirty-Six

Today *was* a big game. It was at home against the top of the league team, Irwell Rovers. He needed to perform. He needed this to be his best game yet. So far, although he hadn't played badly, he was yet to score a goal for his new team. And he knew Emma would be watching.

She'd called and texted and he hadn't answered. He couldn't. There was so much he wanted to say but he just didn't know how to say it. As much as he wanted a fresh start, as much as he longed to be with her, he didn't want to bring pain back into her life. And that's what would happen. He'd hurt her before. He didn't want to do it again.

'This is it, Dom. This is how the rich and famous watch football. From a glass-fronted box,' Chris announced, leading the way into the private suite.

Emma had shrunk into herself from the moment they left the car and entered the huge stadium. She wasn't overawed by the size of the building or the number of people working there who seemed to accumulate the further they moved into the inner sanctum, she was just wary, on guard. She didn't want to bump into Guy. She was concerned for him.

She wished he would just send her a message to let her know he was OK, but she didn't want to see him today. Not now.

The suite was as luxurious as Chris had promised. A manned bar at the back of the room where they had entered, leather sofas, chrome and glass coffee tables adorned with magazines to suit every taste and a spread of food laid out at one side.

'We don't have to actually watch the game here though, do we? Don't we have seats out there?' Dominic asked. He moved through the suite, bypassed the luxury and headed straight towards the wall of glass at the other end of the room. There were the stands, so many seats, in white and royal blue, matching the Finnerham colours. And then there was the pitch itself. So lush and green despite the hot conditions they were experiencing. It was a grassy oasis that would soon be scuffed up by more than a score of football boots.

'Nah, mate, of course we have seats! Can't exactly cheer them on from here, can we? They'd never hear us,' Chris said, laughing.

Emma stood in front of the glass, looking down at the pitch. She'd never seen Guy play a full game of football. Not a proper one. Ever. He'd been good at the campsite but what did she know? To be where he was today, a star at Finnerham and playing for his country, he had to be better than good. He had to be one of the best.

'Want a drink?' Chris offered, putting his arm around her shoulders.

'No. I'm fine,' she said, moving out of his embrace and approaching Dominic.

'D'you think I'll play for Finnerham when I'm older,

Mum?' Dominic asked. He looked up at her, waiting with bated breath for her response.

'Is that what you want?'

'Footballers earn loads of money. I could buy you and Chris a bigger house and some new cars,' he said, grinning.

'Money isn't everything, Dom. It's more important to be happy,' Emma replied.

'Wouldn't a new car make you happy?' He smirked.

'She's too attached to the old one, Dom. That's the thing with women. They get emotionally attached to everything. I'd have a new car though and a holiday villa... Italy I reckon. You could actually set your sights on Inter Milan,' Chris suggested.

Emma turned away. Today was going to kill her.

Despite telling Daniel he didn't need anything to see him through the game; he'd taken on board three energy drinks. Now he was buzzing. This would be the game where everything came together. He would earn the respect of the team and the fans, justifying the price Finnerham had paid. He had to focus. He had to clear everything else from his mind and concentrate on the match.

'Right! Listen up!' The manager prepared to give his team talk and Guy was all ears. He'd listen to everything that was said and he'd replicate that and more. He was going to end the day a winner if it killed him.

'All that food in the suite and he wants a pie,' Chris said. He shook his head and nudged Emma's shoulder. Dominic was digging into a meat and potato pie with brown sauce using a flimsy plastic fork.

'It's the experience. Dad took him to the greyhounds once. He ate three hotdogs, a tray of chips and a bag of pick and mix,' Emma replied.

'Pick and mix. That brings back memories,' Chris said, nodding.

'They're coming out!' Dominic announced, his excitement clear for all to see.

Emma looked to the tunnel and both teams, led by the referee and his assistants, began to emerge onto the pitch. The roar of the fifty thousand plus crowd started to heighten until it turned into a frenzy of excited cheering, clapping and singing along to the tune they'd started running out to this season, 'Hall of Fame' by The Script.

Dominic was juggling with his pie, desperate to get his scarf in the air. He was out of his seat, jumping up and down as the Finnerham players ran onto the grass, applauding their fans and warming up.

Emma didn't see anyone but Guy. He was in the middle of the line of Finnerham players running out, clapping the crowd's vocal appreciation. Her heart soared to see him. She didn't know exactly what was going on but he was here and he was OK enough to play. Something in her settled slightly and she realised just how worried she'd been. They were three rows back, not close enough to jump the barrier but near enough to feel connected. The game was a sell-out. So many other people in the stadium, it would be impossible for them to share anything. And they shouldn't.

Just as that thought passed through her mind, Dominic started calling.

'Guy! Guy!'

'Dom, he won't be able to hear you,' Emma said, touching his arm.

'Yes he will! Guy!' Dominic carried on.

He thought he could hear his name being called. It wasn't unusual. Fans called for photos and attention all the time, but this voice he recognised. He turned to the stands and saw Dominic. The boy was leaping up and down, swirling a scarf in the air and waving, his other hand holding a cardboard container. He was yelling his name.

Then he saw Emma. She was wearing a pretty pale pink T-shirt, her hair pushed back behind her ears. He felt his chest contract at the sight of her and the guilt that he hadn't responded to her messages coursed through him. Dominic yelled again and he raised his hand, waving with enthusiasm.

The referee blew his whistle, indicating which way the teams were kicking and Guy gave a final wave at Dominic before he jogged off to get into position. Seeing the boy so animated gave him another boost. Dominic was another reason to get things right.

Despite not being a football fan, being so close, Emma couldn't help but get involved with every second of the match. Within ten minutes, Finnerham had gone one goal down. A free-kick just outside the box had resulted in the Irwell winger delivering a powerful shot that flew into the top corner. But the shock of losing the lead so early had spurred Finnerham into action. Just before half-time they had drawn level thanks to a penalty Daniel had slotted home.

Dominic had been a ball of energy the whole way through. He had drunk two bottles of Coke and had another meat pie and now, just five minutes before the end, he was asking for more sweets.

'Chris,' he begged.

'No, Dom, there's five minutes left. I know what will happen, I'll get to the counter and I'll miss a goal. Shit! That was close!' Chris exclaimed as a Finnerham shot fizzed past the post.

'Language,' Emma told off.

'Sorry. Sorry, Dom, don't repeat that,' Chris said, putting his fingers to his mouth and chewing his nails.

'I can't watch,' Dominic said. He hid his eyes in his scarf as Irwell set about an attack.

He knew time was running out. He'd clocked the scoreboard. Four minutes remaining, plus perhaps two minutes added time for injuries. There'd been a slight delay when one of the Irwell players was treated after a heavy tackle. It was now or never and the team were getting tired. They'd played well but Irwell were strong. That was why they were top of the league.

Josh made a run and Guy saw nothing but space in front of him. Screaming from the bottom of his lungs he sprinted off, heading for the penalty area.

The cross came over and he leapt up into the air. His head made contact with the ball first then the elbow of the Irwell defender. As the crowd screamed with joy and the ball shot over the line, past the stranded goalkeeper, everything in Guy's world went black.

Chapter Thirty-Seven

Dominic and Chris' cheers were echoing in her ears but her heart was throbbing. She'd seen what had happened, seen the blow to the side of his head and then him falling, landing like a dead weight on the grass. She watched as the physios from both teams raced onto the pitch, armed with their medical bags to assist. He was unconscious. He was injured. She didn't know what to do.

'What's going on? Is he hurt?' Chris inquired. Most people had been too elated at Guy scoring the winning goal; they had taken a minute to realise their new number eight was lying on the floor knocked out cold.

'He isn't moving,' Dominic stated.

Emma's insides lurched at his explanation and she wrung her hands together, feeling so useless. *Just get up. Just come to and get up. Let me know you're OK.*

'Well, this isn't such a great end to the game, is it? Cracking goal though,' Chris said cheerily.

'He is going to be OK, isn't he, Mum?' Dominic asked, looking up at Emma.

'Yes. Yes, of course he is,' she said immediately. What else did you say to a child, even if you weren't really convinced?

The seconds seemed to tick by. More and more of them

passed. The wait felt endless but finally there was movement. Guy was moving his upper torso and seemed to be coming round. As quickly as they could, the physios got him onto the stretcher and began to take him from the field.

Both sets of supporters began to cheer his departure from the game, clapping to acknowledge the goal and his whole eighty-six-minute performance. Before she really thought about what she was doing she was moving.

'Emma?' Chris noticed her as she moved to leave her seat and the stands.

'I'm desperate for the loo. Can't wait. I'll meet you back in the suite,' she called as she shifted past other fans towards the steps.

'Can you get sweets, Mum?'

She was quite certain that at any moment she would be collared by a member of staff and put in a room wherever they kept football-player stalkers. She had no idea where she was going. The place was a labyrinth of corridors and rooms, but she just kept following signs mentioning 'players and officials' and 'restricted area'.

She turned a corner and caught sight of the group. Half a dozen people were making their way down the corridor carrying a stretcher.

'Guy!' she called. How desperate she must sound but then wasn't she desperate? Absolutely desperate, and needing to find out for herself if he was really alright.

Two men dressed in polo shirts in the Finnerham colours turned their attention to her.

'You can't come down here. It's team officials only,' the first man said.

'I...' she started, taking another step forward.

'Are you lost?' the other official asked.

'No. I need to see Guy. Guy!' she shouted. Now she was sounding close to deranged. Soon they'd be calling security.

'Emma? Please, let her through.'

Guy's voice calling for her soothed her panic. The two men in her way looked at each other then parted like the Red Sea. The stretcher moved on, turning at the bottom of the corridor, Emma in pursuit.

'Emma,' Guy said, trying to sit up.

'I'm here,' she assured, rushing forward.

'You must lie back, Guy,' the physio said, guiding the stretcher-bearers into a clinical-looking room.

'Emma, stay. Please,' Guy begged.

'I will. Of course I will,' she responded.

What started out as half a dozen people in the room soon became whittled down to just the three of them. Guy, Emma and the club doctor, Colin.

'I'll be back to take your blood pressure in half an hour. You sit quietly and if you start to get any headaches or if you feel faint, you press the button,' Colin told him.

'I am fine now,' he responded.

The surly-looking Scotsman didn't look convinced but went towards the door anyway and left.

Emma reached for Guy's hands and held them in hers.

'I saw you go down on the ground and I was terrified,' she said, the tears falling fast.

'I'm OK. I was unconscious only a few minutes,' he assured. He brought her hands to his lips, grazing the skin with them.

'What's going on, Guy? You called me. You were crying...

then nothing,' Emma began, brushing his damp hair with her hands.

He shook his head, let go of her and began toying with the blanket covering his legs.

Emma took a moment and watched him. He couldn't meet her eyes now. He had dropped them to the blanket, his long, tanned fingers picking at the polyester.

'I couldn't tell Chris.'

The words sliced through the atmosphere, acting as another barrier between their emotions.

He nodded, as if he had been expecting it.

'I wanted to... I tried but...' Emma started. She felt pathetic and seventeen again. She always made decisions quickly, decisively, why was this so different?

'I have not told Madeleine.'

Emma closed her eyes as her stomach dropped. She wasn't the only one who hadn't kept a promise.

'I wanted to but... something happened and...'

'You don't have to explain. I understand,' Emma said. She *did* understand. They were both in an impossible situation. Whatever they did was going to have an impact, either on them or the people they cared about.

Guy made a frustrated noise and tossed the blanket to the floor.

'I cannot go on like this... without you. Now I've found you,' he stated.

'I know,' she whispered.

'I do not know what to do,' he admitted.

He looked at her at last. Those bottle-green eyes radiating frailty. He appeared frightened and vulnerable, just as he had that day in France, in the barn, covered in bruises. That was a memory she would never forget.

She took his hand and brought it to her mouth, echoing his earlier gesture. Her pulse was racing, watching his reaction, wanting to convey the depth of her feelings for him. He closed his eyes, giving in to her caress and everything it meant.

'I love you, Guy. I never stopped loving you,' she blurted out. She was admitting that to him and to herself for the very first time. Yes, he had hurt her, torn her heart in two. But even while broken, her heart hadn't let her forget. She'd tried to hide her feelings away like the special items in the box under the stairs, but love didn't always let you put a lid on it.

He kissed her then, furiously, desperately. She felt his eagerness to share the closeness, how keen he was to express everything he felt. She wrapped her arms around him, tracing her hands along the contours of his back. She longed to touch his skin, remember the velvety smooth texture.

He broke away, holding her face in his hands.

'Come away with me.'

'What?'

'Come to France with me. I have a game, an international game next weekend. It's one match. We have the rest of the time together,' he elaborated.

'Guy, I can't. I have Dominic and there's Chris and...'

She needed excuses. She needed hundreds of them because her heart was in danger of skipping out of her chest just from the idea of it.

'We can stay at my house. We can take the train,' he continued, gesturing, animated.

'I can't,' she said again, ignoring all the things her body was telling her.

'We can be together there. Like before.' He kissed her lips, pressing her mouth with desire.

'I have to go,' she said, looking at her watch.

'Back to him,' Guy said harshly.

'That's not fair,' Emma responded.

'*This* is not fair. We are meant to be together. *You* know that. *I* know that – we've always known that.'.

She was crying again. These days it wasn't taking much. She needed to be strong. She could be strong. She'd done it before and survived and survival was what mattered.

'I have to go,' she repeated with a little more force. She let go of his hand, moved to the door and taking one last look at him she left.

As the door closed he broke. He felt as if his world was collapsing. It had come crashing down a long time ago but he had picked himself up so well and held it together so competently that no one would know he was constantly fighting an internal battle. Now he was going through it all again. He drew his arms into his chest and wrapped himself up as he sobbed. The pain in his head from the blow of the Irwell defender was nothing compared to the savagery going on inside. He was not good enough for her. He had never been good enough for her. He was a bad, dark person.

Chapter Thirty-Eight

'He's eaten at least two rounds of sandwiches and he sprayed the goalie with pastry from a sausage roll when he congratulated him on the penalty save,' Chris informed.

Emma nodded although she hadn't really heard what he'd said. She was watching Dominic and, periodically, the door to the function room they were now in. The players and officials were filtering in, all showered and changed into smart casual clothes befitting of a window of H&M.

'He's having a blast, isn't he? He's spoken to the youth manager already. I said I'd take him for a try out,' Chris continued, following Emma's gaze.

She didn't respond.

'Is everything alright?' Chris asked.

She turned to face him. He was giving her the full concerned face, complete with soulful eyes. He'd looked that way when he'd ask her out the first time.

'I'm fine.' That was becoming her stock answer for everything lately.

'Want some nosh? There's salmon on those cracker things.'

'No thanks.'

'How about a drink then? Wine?' Chris offered.

'Wine. Yes, red. A glass of red would be nice,' Emma decided. She needed something, if only to keep her hands busy.

'Coming right up,' Chris said, getting out of his seat. He headed to the bar and she couldn't help but breathe a sigh of relief. Just having him here felt stifling. There was just too much going on. And the longer the situation continued the more she felt like her whole world was going to cave in.

The door swung open and there he was. His hair damp from the shower and flicked across his forehead, he was dressed in dark trousers and a pale blue shirt. He was showing no signs of having been unconscious just a short time ago. He just looked perfect. She looked away, tried to concentrate on Chris who was doing battle at the bar. But she knew he was heading towards her. She could feel it.

Without waiting to make contact first, he pulled up a chair and sat next to her, placing a bottle of water on the table.

'You cannot keep walking away,' he stated.

'Guy, please don't do this. Not here. Chris is there and Dominic is…' Her voice came out panicked.

'There are things I have to say,' he continued. All confidence had dropped from his tone.

'Are you going to tell me what's wrong? Why you called me the other night?' she asked.

He took a breath and clasped his hands together.

'I wanted to tell you… back then but… it was easier to let go,' he admitted.

She could see he was hurting and every fibre of her being screamed for her to reach out and make a connection. But she couldn't.

'It's about the past?' she whispered.

He managed a nod and picked up the bottle of water.

'We agreed not to talk about it. We said a fresh start.'

Her heart was pumping now. Fear and adrenaline were driving through her, urging her body to work faster and harder.

'I know, but I don't want this affecting the present and... it could,' Guy spoke softly.

'No.' She shook her head.

'Emma...'

'Guy! Are you alright?' Dominic had bounded up to the table and launched himself into a chair opposite them.

'Hey, Dominic. It is nice to see you again,' Guy responded.

Tears were stinging her eyes, her breathing rapid but she had to pretend everything was OK.

'I might be joining the youth team,' he announced proudly.

'Wow. That is amazing. You will do very well. You are a good player,' Guy encouraged.

'Here we are. One glass of red wine. Well, hello, Guy. How are you? We were all a bit worried when that full-back clobbered you,' Chris said, joining the group.

'Hello, Chris. I am OK. It was more important to score the goal,' Guy responded.

'It *was* awesome,' Dominic enthused.

'Well, I'm sure you have lots of people to talk to and interviews maybe... *Match of the Day*?' Emma suggested to Guy.

'I have spoken to *Match of the Day*, just now,' Guy responded.

'Wow! Did you? Are you going to be on tonight?' Dominic wanted to know.

'Of course he is! He's the hero of the hour,' Chris reminded.

She couldn't take this anymore. All elements of her life sat around a coffee table in a function room of a football stadium. She stood up, picking up her bag and looking to the door.

'Em?' Chris queried.

'I just need to get some fresh air. I've got a headache coming on,' she stuttered.

'We'll come with you,' Chris said, urging Dominic to finish his Coke.

'No. No, it's fine. I'll just be a minute. You talk to Guy,' she said, looking to Guy.

He saw the despair in her eyes. What was he doing? What were they both doing treading this dangerous path? They'd promised to make it right but it seemed to be impossible. He knew he didn't deserve her but he wanted her. He had never wanted anyone else.

'Does your head still hurt?' Dominic asked, breaking Guy's concentration.

'A little. I have small lump here,' Guy said, putting his hand to the back of his head.

'Do you?! Gross!'

'D'you want a drink, Guy?' Chris offered.

'No. But thank you,' he responded. He gave Chris a smile. Knowing that Chris was a good man and how well he had looked after Emma and Dominic made this all even worse.

Ally's phone went to voicemail again. Emma suspected she would be either somewhere with Jonty, rekindling their relationship, or up to her eyes in registering children for swimming lessons which started next week. Either way Ally wasn't answering. Not that she would be able to help. Ally already didn't approve of the situation and who could blame her? Emma had made her tell lies to cover her infidelity and that couldn't carry on. That wasn't who she was anymore. She was better than that.

The executive box was empty now and as she looked out from the balcony, over the stud-marked pitch, she sucked in the tranquillity. Thousands of fans had screamed and shouted not more than an hour ago, filling the stadium with a cacophony of sound. Now there were half a dozen grounds men on the turf and just quiet.

She sensed and smelt him before he made it up to her. She turned around and faced him before he could open his mouth to speak.

'I don't want this anymore. It isn't good. Whatever we have, it's hurting people. It's hurting me,' she blurted out.

He said nothing, just moved towards her, his form blocking out the sun.

'No one knows anything yet and if we stop this now there's nothing *to* know,' she continued.

Her heart had stepped up a gear and was pounding in her chest and up into her ears. He wasn't listening. Just coming closer. And the nearer he got the more she shook.

He stopped only when he got alongside her, leaning on the balcony rail next to her, his eyes not leaving hers.

Involuntarily a noise escaped her lips and it rocked her. It was something between a sigh and a yelp, frightened yet excited, longing.

'I do not deserve you, Emma. But I cannot let go,' he whispered.

She gazed at him, taking in every inch of his face, the grass-green eyes, the olive complexion, the hint of stubble on his face, his full, lush lips. She couldn't fight this feeling. It was forcing her to act. This deep-rooted need she had, this connection she couldn't deny was overtaking all sense about rights and wrongs.

She only moved a centimetre but they both knew what it meant. Restraint had been overridden; passion and desperation were taking over. She drew his face to hers and their mouths met. Hungry, wet – fusing together as if time needed to be made up.

'I cannot let you go. I will not,' Guy said, kissing her lips, holding her tight.

'I know... I know,' she responded, tears spilling from her eyes.

'I want to hold you so much. To never let go,' he whispered. His hands traced the line of her shoulders as the kisses continued.

'I'll come to France,' she said. She kissed his cheek, took his hands in hers.

'What?'

'I'll come with you to France next weekend. I'll tell Chris and I'll come,' she stated again.

He looked at her, an expression she couldn't quite read

on his face. Perhaps he had changed his mind. Maybe he'd decided they shouldn't.

'*Formidable!*' he exclaimed. He picked her up and spun her around in his arms. She laughed out loud, a surge of euphoria spiralling through her as he put her back down on the ground and pressed his lips to hers again.

'A new start,' he said.

'A new start,' she echoed.

The door of the balcony closed shut.

Chapter Thirty-Nine

August 2005

'Where's the baby?'

'With his mother. Where's your lapdog?'

'Where's your books?'

'Where's your dad?'

'With my mum. At least I have one of those.'

Tasha's last remark cut deep and before she could control the rage, Emma lashed out. She hit Tasha around the head with the supermarket carrier bag she was holding. It contained a carton of wine and some brie and Tasha fell to the floor in a heap.

'What happen? What did you do?' Guy asked, suddenly appearing at her side.

'That bitch made a nasty comment about my mum,' Emma stated.

Tasha was crying. Loud, babyish crying that sounded ridiculous. She was glad she had hurt her. She wished she'd bought a bottle of wine rather than a carton.

'Emma… is she *blessé*?' Guy asked, bending down to look at the girl.

'If *blessé* means blessed then no she definitely isn't!' She was shaking and she folded her arms in disgust as Guy inspected the crying Tasha as if she were something worthwhile. He took hold of her arm, almost gently, and helped her to her feet.

'Are you OK?' he asked Tasha.

'I can't believe you're fawning over her! She's a complete cow!' Emma blasted.

'She hit me with the bag,' Tasha answered. She looked only at Guy and sniffed, blinking damp eyelashes.

'I'll hit you with it again if you don't stop faking it. If I really wanted to hurt you I wouldn't have stopped!' Emma hissed.

'I think you should… *dire pardon*,' Guy said.

'What?! You want me to apologise?! No way! She made a comment about my mum. My dead mum!' Emma shouted.

Why was he being so nice to Tasha? He said he didn't like her and Melody and now he was acting as if Tasha was important… more important than her. He was taking Tasha's side when he should be defending her.

'Emma…'

'No. I'm not apologising. Frankly, she deserved more than I gave her. Here! You can take the wine and cheese. You enjoy them… on your own!'

She launched the bag at Guy and marched in the opposite direction. She had gone four or five steps before the tears started to fall. How could Tasha have been so cruel? Bitchy banter was one thing but making a remark about her mother was below the belt. And Guy was protecting her. Why didn't he see her point of view? Well, he could eat the wine and cheese with Tasha if he wanted because she didn't care what he did. She had lied to her dad again to be able to see him and now he had ruined it.

By the time she'd left the campsite her chest was heaving with emotion. Why was this happening? She was leaving soon. She didn't want to leave like this. She didn't want it to be just a holiday romance. She loved him. He loved her. Or so she thought. They could write to one another, send emails… It was only a few months until the half-term break. She could persuade her dad to come back to La Baume.

Before she knew it she was at the barn. She didn't know why she had walked there but it was away from the campsite and it was as good a place as any to cry.

She sat down on a hay bale and curled her legs up underneath her. What was she going to do when she got home? Despite drowning in all the books Mr Devlin had recommended and more, she wasn't convinced the exams were going to go as well as they should next year. Her work and concentration had slipped. She'd let them slip because she'd needed to concentrate on her mum. Spending moments with her had been the most important thing in her life and she didn't regret that decision one bit. But would that decision cost her the life that she so badly wanted?

She looked out of the barn door at the scenery before her. Golden banks of corn, set against greener fields and the spire of a distant church. It was beautiful, it was peaceful, perhaps that's what she needed to focus on. Being at peace with how things were. Shouldering the situation she'd been placed in.

'You are here… I knew.'

He was standing at the small side door of the barn, his hands in the pockets of his trousers.

He'd come to find her. He wasn't with Tasha. But she should be angry with him. He hadn't supported her when she'd needed him too.

'We should go. We don't want to be… *en retard*,' Guy continued.

'Late? Late for what?' she asked. She tried to disguise the interest in her voice.

'For fun,' he responded, a smile on his lips.

The joy in his face was infectious and she couldn't help but mimic his expression. But then she stopped, remembered she was cross.

'Why were you so nice to Tasha? She said something really hurtful.'

Guy threw his head back and let out a tut.

'She is… *elle est agaçante*! But… her father…'

'The man I met today?'

'*Oui*. He is… he go to the hotel I work at. He knows the boss,' Guy explained.

Now she felt a bit stupid. She knew money was difficult for him. He wouldn't want his job in danger.

'Don't be… what is the word?'

'Angry?' she offered.

'Are you that?'

'A little,' she admitted.

'You cannot. We have… *Nous avons le plaisir d'avoir*.'

'A what?'

'*Musique, vin, danse, sur le bateau*,' he explained.

'A boat? Where?'

'Do you come?' he asked, holding his hand out to her.

This sounded exciting. This sounded daring and different and not safe at all.

'How do we get there?' she asked, taking his hand.

'*Voiture.*'

Chapter Forty

The 'car' turned out to be more of a delivery van Guy had borrowed from someone else he knew in the kitchens at the campsite. The seats were ripped, springs and sponge oozing out, there wasn't a panel without rust and the tyres looked like they needed serious attention. But when they pulled up at the quay in Fréjus she felt like Cinderella arriving at the ball in her golden carriage.

'This is crazy,' she said, admiring the port and all the boats moored along the edge of the water.

'You spend all this time here and you have not seen the town,' Guy remarked, taking hold of her hand.

'I don't think my dad really knows what to do with me. The campsite is safe. He gets involved in the activities and I… sneak away to see you,' she said, leaning forward and kissing his lips.

'The boat… it is there,' Guy said, pointing to a luxurious yacht moored a few feet away from where they had parked.

Emma took in the view. Pristine white and chrome with royal blue trims, the boat was more like a mini luxury liner. She could see people stood up on deck. They were laughing, glasses of wine in their hands. There were waiters with trays of food, jazz music was playing. Harry Connick Jr or someone like him. She froze when she saw what people were wearing. The women were in cocktail dresses, the men in short-sleeved shirts and smart trousers. She looked down at her tangerine-coloured sundress and her white pumps.

'Guy, I can't go to a party... that party, dressed like this. I look under-dressed... not posh enough... too casual,' she said, hoping he would understand.

'Your dress?' he asked, looking confused.

'Yes. It isn't good enough,' she said.

'You are with me... my... *mon invite*,' he told her.

'But...'

'Come on,' he urged, pulling her forward.

She let herself be tugged forward because there was nothing else she could do. This party was obviously important to him and she didn't want to ruin it just because she was self-conscious and concerned over party etiquette.

There was a walkway from the edge up onto the boat and two men dressed in dark T-shirts and trousers were checking names on a list.

'Guy, are you sure this is OK?' Emma asked as he hurried her on board.

'*Oui!* Do not worry... Guy Duval *et ceci est ma invitée*,' he greeted the men at the top of the gangplank.

The list was duly checked and there they were, on board the boat among some of the most extravagantly dressed people Emma had ever seen.

'Champagne?' a waiter offered. Emma hesitated. Guy took two glasses from the tray and gave one to her.

'What is wrong? We are here for fun?' he asked.

'I know but... who are these people? How do you know them? *Do* you know them?' she whispered, following Guy through the boat.

'The man who owns the boat. He is... *quelqu'un que je connais.*'

'Someone you know,' Emma translated.

Guy nodded and drank some champagne. He took hold of her hand and led her off down the boat towards a middle-aged man who was centre of attention.

'*Bonsoir, David*,' Guy greeted, butting right into the conversation.

The grey-haired man turned his attention to them and his face lit up like a Christmas tree.

'Guy! I'm so glad you could make it! This is Guy everyone. Another little friend of mine. Fine worker. Always punctual, always a delight,' David introduced, squeezing Guy's shoulder with affection.

'David, this is... *ma copine*, Emma,' Guy said, stepping back a little.

'Hello,' Emma greeted.

'*Petite amie*?' David queried.

'*Oui*,' Guy responded.

'Well, it's delightful to meet you, my dear! Wonderful. Help yourself to anything you like. Guy will look after you I'm sure,' David said. He smiled briefly at Emma then turned his attention back to his group of friends.

Guy smiled at her and led her to the side of the boat where there were some free seats. They sat down and Emma drank some champagne, the bubbles light on her tongue and fizzy up into her nose.

'He must be very rich,' Emma remarked, still absorbing all the decadence and luxury surrounding them.

'*Oui*, he is,' Guy said, nodding.

'So what work do you do for him?' Emma asked.

'He has parties… at the hotel I work at,' Guy explained.

'You're a waiter or something?'

'*Oui*,' he said, nodding again.

The boat's engines kicked into life and squeals of excitement rose up from the deck. Emma knelt up on the seat to look over the side at the water below. The yacht was nothing like the ferry back to England.

'But tonight I do not work. Tonight we have fun,' he said. He stood behind her and wrapped his arms around her waist as the boat left the harbour.

She'd had at least five glasses of champagne and she knew it wasn't the slight sea breeze buoying the boat along that was making her dizzy. She swayed to the left and fell into Guy's arms, giggling.

'We should dance,' she said, linking her hands behind his neck.

'We should,' he agreed, putting his hands on her hips. He rocked her back and forth in time to the music and she let herself melt into him. The alcohol was running through her, making her head spin and her heart race but, she liked the feeling. She was slightly out of control and she liked being that way when she was with him. It felt nice, doing something she shouldn't, but feeling safe because he was there.

The boat pulled back into the quay but nobody moved to disembark. Emma raised her head from Guy's shoulder and looked at the sky. It was pitch black. What time was it? She took a look at her watch. It was almost one in the morning. Normally, panic would have washed over her. Her dad would be worrying, but right now she didn't care. He had Marilyn. He would probably be in his sleeping bag on the phone to her like he was the other night. It made her want to puke. Or perhaps it was the boat motion doing that. She lurched forward, suddenly feeling as if there was no air.

'Emma,' Guy said, steadying her.

'I'm OK,' she insisted, breathing in and stabilising herself.

'We should go,' he said, letting her lean on him. He headed towards the rear of the boat and the exit off.

'Going already, Guy?' David asked as they prepared to descend to shore.

'*Oui*,' he responded.

'Work tomorrow. Don't be late,' he reminded.

He nodded in response and turned his focus back to Emma.

When they got back down onto solid ground she did feel a lot better. Why had she drunk so much? Because it was free obviously and it had been reckless and fun. She laughed and put her arm around Guy's shoulders.

'You have fun tonight?' he asked her.

'Yes. Lots of fun,' she replied, smiling at him. He smiled back at her then indicated the bench by the water. They sat down and Emma shivered. The balmy evening had turned into another chilly night.

'I don't want to stay here forever,' he began. 'You know this.'

'I don't know why. I love it here,' she responded.

'It isn't about the place. It's about the... *les gens*... the people.'

Emma looked up at him, her eyes willing him to continue.

'*Ma mère et Luc*... he needs a better life. My life, it has been difficult. I do not want this for him,' he explained.

'I know you want to leave, because of what your mother did and something should be done, but you can ask for help. There must be someone. I mean if you're on your own where will you go? What will you do? Here you know people, you have work...'

'I want to play football, Emma. I know I can do that. Very well. For a good team, for France.' His reply was passionate.

'I know you do and you will but—'

'AS Saint-Étienne are holding trials. I want to go there. Without my mother, without this place, I can make it work,' he insisted.

'You will take Luc with you? But how will you manage?' Emma asked, her eyes wide.

'I want you to come with us,' he stated.

Something happened to her at that moment, something exploded inside her and her body was filled with shock, delight, excitement, anxiety all at once. She felt nauseous, grabbing the wooden bench to stop herself from swaying.

'I do not do this well.' He put a hand into the pocket of his trousers and took out a small box. He dropped down onto both knees in front of her and opened the lid.

'*Épouse-moi?* Marry me?'

Her jaw had dropped. She couldn't believe this was happening. All this time she had been convincing herself it was just a summer romance, a wonderful love affair, frantic, deep but short-lived. And here he was proposing to her with the most gorgeous ring. A real ring. Like her mother's engagement ring they buried with her. Gold and sapphire, understated but beautiful.

'Guy...' she started. She actually didn't know what she was going to say. What did this mean? Could this really happen? Marrying him? Staying in France? Giving up school and her plans? She was only seventeen.

'*J'taime*, Emma,' he told her.

She could see how nervous he was. The box was shaking in his hands and his words were tinged with fear. What was he afraid of? What he was asking or what her answer would be?

'I love you too, Guy,' she answered, smiling.

'So...' He inched the box a little closer to her.

'Yes!' she exclaimed, putting him out of his misery. 'Yes, I'll marry you. *Je t'épouserai.* Is that right?' she asked, laughing.

He laughed and nodded his agreement, then paused. She watched him take a breath, as if he was composing himself.

'You are... sure?' he guessed at the word.

Was she sure? At the moment, seeing him on two knees, having had half a dozen glasses of champagne, wanting some adventure, wanting to be something other than the daughter of a dead person, she was sure. Right now it seemed the most straightforward decision she had ever made. He loved her. She loved him. That was all they needed, wasn't it? As for her dad, well, he had Marilyn now.

'I'm sure,' she replied, nodding.

Guy took the ring from the box and slipped it onto the correct finger. It was slightly too big but it wouldn't fall off unless she shook her hands vigorously. It looked good there. It looked right.

'You are happy?' Guy asked, looking up at her, still on his knees.

'Yes. I am. Very happy.' She pulled him towards her and kissed his lips. At that moment, she'd never been happier.

She was still looking at the ring as they drove into the campsite. Guy stopped the van and along with the engine, everything silenced.

'I have this planned before I meet you. I was going alone, then with Luc when he arrive and now…' He put his hand to her head, stroked her hair with his thumb. 'I just need this last week and I will have enough money to begin.'

She leaned across the seat and caught his lips with hers, kissing him. He deepened the kiss and she clung to him.

'I will look after you, Emma. And you must still study. I will work,' he told her.

'I don't want to leave you tonight,' she said, groaning in annoyance.

'You must. Your father, he will be concerned,' Guy said.

'I love you.'

'I love you.'

She wrapped her arms around him and held his body close, breathing in the aroma of lemon, champagne and sea breeze.

'Goodnight,' she said, opening the door of the van.

'*Bonne nuit*,' he responded.

The campsite was so quiet at this time. Just the hum of the insects in the bushes and the glow of the path-lighting lamps disturbed the night. Before she reached her tent she could hear voices and see activity. There were torches and a group of people. Was that a policeman? Oh, God! Had her dad called the police?

Her instinct was to hide and run from this awkward situation but she decided it would only make it worse. He was obviously worried about her. She should have called him.

'Emma! Oh my God, Emma! She's here! She's here!'

Mike greeted her with a bear hug usually reserved for a returning war hero. He squeezed her so tight she couldn't breathe.

'I'm sorry I'm late. I lost track of time and...' She surveyed the people looking at her. Campsite security, the woman from three tents along and the lifeguard with the tattoos. No police.

'I'm sorry everyone, for causing a panic but all's well that ends well, eh?' Mike suggested to the search party.

'I'm really tired, Dad. I'm going to go to bed,' Emma said, unzipping the door of the tent.

Listening to her father apologise again for inconveniencing everyone in the middle of the night, she looked at the ring on her left hand. What was she really going to do? She couldn't actually tell her dad, could she? He wouldn't believe her. He wouldn't understand how she felt about Guy. No, it was best to keep it a secret... and just disappear.

Chapter Forty-One

'He's asleep already. I think football, fresh air and giant portions of food have knocked him out,' Emma said, returning to the living room.

They'd stopped for more food and drinks on the way home from the football stadium. Dominic had eaten nachos followed by pasta carbonara, then ice cream.

She stopped by the door, didn't move any further into the room when she saw Chris was standing up. Usually he would have flicked on the TV, thrown his coat over a chair and be sitting on the sofa channel-hopping through the sports networks.

'Listen, Em, I'm going to head off.'

His voice sounded a bit on edge, not normal. His hands were in the pockets of his jacket. It was almost as if he didn't want to be near her.

'What's wrong, Chris?' she asked. He couldn't know. How could he know?

He made a noise in answer to her question. A strangulated

sound she'd never heard before. The next time he looked at her, his eyes had a definite sheen to them. She didn't know how to respond.

'I saw you at the football… with Guy Duval,' he stated.

What did that mean exactly? What had he seen? Could she deny it? Why did she want to deny it? She needed to end the relationship, didn't she? What should she say?

Instead of saying anything she burst into tears, overwhelmed with a feeling of desperation, humiliation and treachery. She reached for the armchair and steadied herself.

'Oh, Emma,' Chris said, moving towards her.

As she wept uncontrollably he wrapped his arms around her, rubbing her back and comforting her. She didn't deserve this. He didn't deserve this. She had cheated on him and he was holding her, soothing her tears. It wasn't right. She stepped back from his embrace, wiping her tears with her forearm.

'Why aren't you angry?' she asked him.

He shrugged. 'I don't know, Em. I guess I knew it was coming. Some time, some when.'

'Why do you say that?'

'I've told you before. You're way out of my league.' He shrugged again.

'No. It's the other way around. I don't deserve you. You're special and I'm ruined. I was ruined when we met and there was nothing you could do to change that,' she spoke.

He nodded, shuffled his feet and then locked eyes again.

'Is he Dominic's father?' The question hung in the air, silence shrouding it only slightly.

What should she say? Should she tell him the truth? Didn't he deserve something?

She nodded then and swallowed, dipping her head and avoiding his eyes. When she finally lifted her head back up, Chris was looking resigned.

'I just knew… a sixth sense or something.'

'I hadn't seen him or had any contact since Dominic. He just turned up, opening Ally's fitness centre and…'

'You're still in love with him,' Chris finished for her.

She couldn't respond. This was the hardest conversation she'd ever had. Her heart wasn't just breaking for Chris; it was breaking for the loss of the relationship. There had been nothing bad about it. Chris had been everything a boyfriend should be. He just hadn't been Guy.

'What happened with you two way back then? Before Dominic?' he asked.

Emma shut her eyes. This was the problem. You gave someone some information and it was never enough. They always wanted more. Like Ally wanting to know the names of all those boys she said she'd slept with.

'I can't, Chris.'

'Why not? I mean, I can't say this is great for me but for Dominic… he gets to meet his dad after all this time,' Chris said.

'No. No, Chris, you mustn't say anything to Dominic about this.'

Now she was petrified. She shouldn't have said anything. It was all very well trying to lessen the blow on someone's feelings but not if it was going to cost her her relationship with Dominic.

'I don't understand. You're going to get back together, aren't you? It looked very much like that from where I was standing at the stadium,' he snapped.

Now he was angry and she was glad. Having him feel sorry for her when their relationship was crumbling before his eyes was far worse than any of his rage.

She didn't say anything. She didn't know what to say now. She had said too much again.

Chris stepped closer to her and put a hand on her arm.

'You've got one amazing boy up there. Do one thing for me. Do the right thing by him.'

His voice cracked at the end of the last sentence and Emma let out an anguished sob as Chris opened the door to the hallway. He was leaving. He was leaving her. She closed her eyes, then hearing the front door open, she dashed after him.

'Chris!'

He stopped in the doorway, turned to look at her, tears streaking his cheeks.

'Take care of yourself, Emma.' He paused, took a breath. 'And take care of Dominic.'

With those words said, he left, closing the door for the last time.

He could hear laughing and voices chattering excitedly as he entered the house. Madeleine was obviously entertaining. She had done that a lot in France. Usually it was women like her, drinking too much, eating too little and discussing what was 'hot' or 'not'. He slipped off his jacket, hanging it over the banister before moving towards the kitchen.

'Guy!' Madeleine greeted in excited tones. She threw her hands in the air and teetered towards him. She was wearing her favourite pair of Blahniks. He only knew what they were because he'd bought them for her and they'd cost close to a thousand Euros.

As she kissed both his cheeks he noticed her guests. Gabriella was there and…

He stepped out of Madeleine's embrace and took another pace backwards.

'Hello, Guy. You've come at the right time. I was just telling the girls here a few stories about La Baume,' Keith greeted, raising his wine glass.

'I've just remembered. I have left something at the club. *Merde!* My phone again. I should go and get it,' he started, concentrating on Madeleine.

'What? But you've only just arrived. It can wait. Come and sit with us. We are discussing the designs. Keith has some wonderful suggestions about the trim,' Madeleine said, pulling his arm.

'It's looking gorgeous,' Gabriella commented.

How was he going to leave? It would raise questions. What was he going to do? Keith had a self-satisfied smile on his face and he was in his house. How had this happened? Why had this happened after so long? He had no choice but to let Madeleine lead him to the table. He pulled up a seat opposite Gabriella and instinctively reached for the wine bottle.

'How did the game go today, Guy? Win? Or not?' Keith asked, offering a laugh at the women.

'It is football… so boring,' Madeleine said, waving a hand in dismissal.

'You're telling me! Luckily, Daniel realises it bores the pants off me now so he doesn't talk details anymore,' Gabriella responded.

'We won,' Guy answered, picking up a wine glass and starting to pour.

'That's fantastic. Well done you. Did you know this boy was a bleeding marvel at eighteen? Best thing I've ever seen,' Keith continued.

Guy could feel he was starting to sweat and without looking he knew Keith's eyes hadn't left him. He almost spilt the wine and with haste, he put the bottle down and lifted the glass to his lips.

'Oh, Guy. You didn't say you knew Keith. It is so nice that you are old friends. We're going to work so well together,' Madeleine said, her excitement plain to see.

'It will be just like old times,' Keith said. 'Won't it, Guy?'

He sank the glass of wine in one gulp and replaced the glass quietly, unable to summon speech.

'To old friends and new beginnings,' Keith toasted, holding his glass aloft.

'Old friends and new beginnings,' the ladies chorused.

Chapter Forty-Two

He'd had to endure two hours of that man in his house. Two hours with the looks across the table, the stories about La Baume, the hidden meanings, the wrapped-up threats, with Madeleine and Gabriella giggling like schoolgirls. He'd drunk a bottle of wine on his own and now he was paying for it with another sore head. He didn't suppose the slight concussion was helping either. But despite his hangover, when he woke up he made a decision. It was time to leave Madeleine. Her involvement with that man was the final nail in the coffin of their relationship with or without what was happening between him and Emma.

He dressed quickly, knowing Madeleine was out power-walking with the aerobics instructor that lived across the road. Elite people made friends quickly if there was networking to be done. Mutually appreciative blogging would take place soon after.

He opened the walk-in wardrobe and located his battered case from the top shelf. Madeleine hated his luggage. She said it was a disgrace. She did have a point. It was old and falling apart but it had belonged to his father. In fact, it was the only thing he had to remind him he'd once had a father. And he only had it because his mother threw it at him once.

He put the case on the bed and opened it. He'd just take clothes. Fripperies were Madeleine's thing, not his.

She didn't know what to do. When she'd woken up that morning everything had felt so different. The bed was big, but then Chris hadn't stayed every night. The house was quiet, but that was nothing to do with Chris either. Despite Chris never living at the property, it was like something was missing. She'd actually felt bereft. As if someone had died. And, in a way, they had. The couple that was Emma and Chris had died, and it was never coming back.

'I thought Chris was coming with us,' Dominic remarked for the third time as they walked up the path of her family home.

She hadn't been able to tell him. She attempted over breakfast but the words wouldn't come. What was the matter with her lately? She hadn't been able to tell Chris it was over and now she couldn't tell Dominic it was over either. Weak and cowardly, that's what she was.

'He had to work,' she answered. She rang the doorbell and took a deep breath. Here she was, standing on the front doorstep of her family home where Marilyn, the woman her dad had slipped so quickly into a relationship with, was cooking them Sunday dinner.

She remembered quite vividly the last words she had spoken to Marilyn and they hadn't been nice. In fact, they'd been vile. But a lot of water had passed under the bridge. Both of them were older, wiser, moving on. Hopefully it would be forgotten. Perhaps if she apologised. As that thought rode through her mind she closed her eyes and shut it out. She wasn't quite ready for that yet.

Mike opened the door, an apron over his short-sleeved shirt and khaki trousers, a wooden spoon in his hands.

'Hello you two... oh, there's only two of you. Where's Chris? Couldn't he park the car outside?' Mike asked. He looked past Emma and Dominic to the street.

'Mum said he has to work.' Dominic pushed past Mike into the house. His tone suggested he didn't believe the lie.

'Dominic, wait,' Emma called.

'He's alright, love. Are *you* alright?' Mike asked, looking at her, concerned.

'Yes. Yes, of course. I've brought a bottle of rosé. I didn't know what meat we were having and...' Emma galloped.

'That's perfect. Come on in,' Mike said, opening the door wider for her.

The smell coming from the kitchen brought it all back. Her mother had cooked roast dinners every Sunday without fail before she was ill. But that wasn't Marilyn's fault, she had to remember that. Her mother was gone and Marilyn was back and she had made her dad happy... *would* make her dad happy.

Emma took a breath and headed into the kitchen. Marilyn was showing Dominic a car with a remote control.

'Hello,' Emma greeted, holding the wine bottle out.

'Oh, hello, Emma! Gosh, haven't you grown? What am I saying? You're not a plant, are you?' She laughed then and in one move, took the wine, put it down and caught Emma up in an embrace.

'Marilyn got me this car,' Dominic said, eyes shining.

'That's very nice of you. You shouldn't have,' Emma said as Marilyn broke the hug to attend to a saucepan on the hob.

'Nonsense! What else am I going to spend my pension on? Well, obviously there's bingo and darts but I fancied a change. Mike, take him out into the garden with it for ten minutes,' Marilyn instructed.

'Come on, Dom. I'll set up a ramp, I've got some spare wood in the shed,' Mike said, leading the way out of the room.

And then there were two. Just her and Marilyn, stood in front of her mother's cooker.

'Dominic's the spitting image of you, you know,' Marilyn remarked, looking out into the garden through the window.

'You think so?' Emma responded.

'Oh yes, definitely. So, how have you been? What's been going on? It's been so long,' Marilyn chattered on.

Yes, it had been a long time. But had it been long enough? She'd been jealous all those years ago. Jealous of this woman who made her dad happy, because they had got involved so shortly after her mother had died. She'd needed her dad. She'd needed him more than ever after Dominic came along. She couldn't have someone else there, a stranger, someone who didn't belong. And that's what she'd told her that day. *You don't belong here. I don't want you. My dad doesn't want you. You're an interfering bitch who will never take my mother's place.*

She swallowed, tears brimming at the bottom of her eyes. The words were ringing in her ears and she knew Marilyn wouldn't have forgotten them. She had to break the ice somehow. She had to let her know that it was alright now. Did she think it was alright now? Was that what she wanted to say?

'Are you alright? D'you want to sit down?' Marilyn asked, reaching out and taking Emma's arm.

'I'm so sorry, Marilyn. For all the things I said back then… for all the scowling and the tantrums and everything I did to split you and my dad up.'

The tears flooded in and before she knew it she was in Marilyn's arms again, her head resting against the perfume-infused cardigan she was wearing.

'Sshh, it's alright. Don't you think on it another minute. You was grieving. Your dad was grieving. I knew that. I told him it was too soon for us to be anything more than friends, but it just happened. Then I saw how upset it was making you and I had the chance to live somewhere exciting and I just took it. It was best for everyone. You had enough on your plate with a new baby. And what a fantastic job you've done with the lad,' Marilyn said.

The woman was talking softly in her ear and brushing her hair with her plump fingers and Emma just wanted to hold onto that feeling of security. How could she have felt threatened by this well-meaning, soft-hearted woman?

'I split up with Chris,' she blurted out.

'Oh, darlin', no wonder you brought wine. Dinner will be another half hour. Let's get us some glasses and you can tell me all about it.'

Emma wiped her eyes with her fingers. She didn't even know where to begin.

Chapter Forty-Three

He heard her come in. Despite being the tidiest person he knew she always kicked off her trainers and left them while she made coffee. She jumped when she saw him sat on the stool at the island in the kitchen.

'Guy, you make me jump. What are you doing?' she asked, her hand at her chest.

It took a few seconds to pass before she registered the suitcase.

'Are you finally taking that to be burned somewhere?' she asked, smiling.

He shook his head, getting down from the stool to stand in front of her. He could see the realisation was just starting to slowly sink in.

'What is going on?' Madeleine asked.

'I have to go,' Guy spoke. He took her hands in his.

'What do you mean you have to go?'

'It isn't working.'

He didn't know what to say. The truth was she had done nothing wrong. She just wasn't the person he wanted to be with. She had never been right, *they* had never been right. And that was his fault rather than hers.

Her bottom lip quivered. Her perfect kohl-lined eyes were

wide and moist. He had counted on anger and shouting. He hadn't considered there would be emotion like this.

'There's someone else,' Madeleine stated.

'No.' The reply was instinctive.

'Liar. There must be someone else. We have the perfect life. You have a new team, this house...'

'You can have the house. I will see to it.'

'I don't want the house. I would like an explanation.'

What could he say? She wouldn't want the real explanation. She would never understand it and she wouldn't accept it.

'I need space. Some time. All this is new. Moving here, the team, it's different...'

'So this is just temporary?' A glimmer of hope crossed her face.

'*Non.*' It was all he could manage.

A single tear traced a path down her cheek and then the defence kicked in.

'This is because of the lingerie, isn't it?'

'What?'

'You do not want me to make something for myself. You think the attention should be with you. You need to make good impression with this team. You think I will take away that focus.'

What did he say to that? Was it better to have her believe this? It was perhaps easier? Before he realised it he was nodding his head.

'You want me to give it up?' Madeleine asked him.

He hadn't expected that. Was she serious? Would she give up something so important if she believed it would save their relationship? Had he made the wrong choice choosing that scenario as a get-out? That would teach him to lie.

'No,' he responded.

'Then what? Tell me how to stop this, Guy. Why would you leave if there is no one else and it is not the lingerie?'

He struggled to take a breath, Keith's face flooding his mind. He was the curse. He was the weight he wore around his neck. He was the reason everything in his life went sour. But he could never say. Remembering was one thing, speaking it out loud was impossible. The nightmares, the palpitations he still got sometimes, the memories – they tainted everything.

'I have to go. I'm sorry.' He picked up the suitcase and walked for the door.

'No! No, you do not do this to me! You cannot do this to me! Guy! I won't be left! Guy!'

The voice became a scream and he couldn't look back. His body tensed as he opened the door, escaping, needing to feel air. He closed it behind him, hearing Madeleine's broken sobs as their relationship evaporated. It was finished.

His cell phone ringing brought him out of his thoughts. He reached into the pocket of his trousers and took the phone out.

'You haven't told the little fella yet, I take it,' Marilyn said.

Having muddled their way through a delicious roast lamb lunch, Mike and Dominic were back out in the garden while Emma and Marilyn cleared away.

'I don't know how to. He adores Chris. He'll be so upset,' Emma admitted.

'Not his decision though, is it? You've put that child first forever; you can't make love choices for him. It has to be right. Otherwise you're unhappy and he'll be unhappy and no one will be happy,' Marilyn said. She filled the washing-up bowl with water.

'There's someone else.'

Why was she sharing this information with Marilyn? Marilyn had been the enemy for so long, now it was as if she was her closest confidante. Maybe it was because she wasn't as close as Ally. Perhaps she was hoping Marilyn wouldn't judge so readily.

'I thought there might be,' Marilyn responded softly.

'Why?' Emma was taken aback.

'Because of what I just said. If it wasn't something serious you would have stayed with Chris for Dominic's sake.' Marilyn smiled.

Emma toyed with the tea-towel in her hands, thinking about what happened next. What *did* happen next?

'So, this other chap. What's he like? Where did you meet?'

Marilyn's tone was upbeat and she winked. It wasn't altogether appropriate for Emma's mood but it was entirely different to the reaction she had got from Ally. This could be a good thing. It might be the best thing that had happened in her life. Despite how they were getting there it was a happy event, wasn't it?

Before she opened her mouth to speak she knew her face was glowing, radiating everything she felt for Guy.

'We met in France, eight years ago, when Dad took my camping after... well, you know... but things didn't work out and there was Dominic and... he plays football.'

Marilyn smiled, encouraging her to carry on.

'Things happen for a reason, don't they? Sometimes things don't go right the first time and you're given a second chance,' Emma spoke.

Marilyn nodded. Emma saw the woman's eyes were filling up with tears.

'God, just like you and Dad,' Emma whispered, noticing the similarity.

'Everyone deserves a second chance, darlin'. And we all make mistakes. It's how you deal with them that counts,' Marilyn assured. She reached out and patted Emma's arm.

'Thank you for giving me a second chance,' Emma said, swallowing as she met Marilyn's gaze.

'Ah, get away! You might not be saying that after you've had pudding. It's a new recipe and I'm not sure it's turned out a hundred per cent right,' she said, laughing.

Chapter Forty-Four

September 2005

The rain was hissing. Lines, streaks, harder and faster, falling from the sky, hitting the corn and soil of the fields. Emma's eyes were closed, her ears alert to the sound, her mind in revolution as she moved naked, astride Guy on the straw-covered floor of the barn.

She loved to watch him watching her, see his expression as she ground herself against him, moving slowly at first, then deeper and harder. Starting off as a conscientious virgin, he had taught her how to appreciate herself, be unafraid of taking off her clothes, to trust him. And now they were engaged.

She put her hand against his shoulder and as she pushed into him and heard him moan, she looked at the ring on her finger. The man beneath her was going to be her husband. That knowledge flicked a switch inside her every time she thought about it. Now it made the stimulation even more intense, adding emotion to the physical pull. She could feel herself getting closer and closer to the edge of something she still didn't quite understand, something she had no control over.

'Emma... stop... *mon Dieu!*'

He reached for her, pulling her down onto his chest as his release came quick. It flooded her with warmth and she squeezed into him wanting to fall. The noise that left her lips as the orgasm rode over her sounded primal. She ached and hurt but it was so sweet and it filled every inch of her.

He shuddered beneath her, his hands in her hair, holding her head to his shoulder.

'Promise me it will always be like this.' Her words were nothing more than a whisper.

'I promise,' he responded.

This was what she really wanted. School, a career, money, they were all important but love, real love, this feeling she got when they were together, that was everything. She was an intelligent girl, she wouldn't throw her plans away for the sake of a summer romance but... this was different. Guy was different. He had made a commitment to her and he meant it. She had no doubts.

She kissed his lips, slow and drowsily and shifted from him, reaching for her dress.

'I bought a drink,' she said. Pulling her dress down over her body she reached for the carrier bag she'd abandoned on one of the hay bales.

'Merlot?' he asked, grinning.

'*Non, monsieur*, Orangina.' She held the soft drink aloft like a prize.

He shook his head, smiling at her as he pulled on his shorts.

She brought the bottle over to him as he reached for his backpack and began to take papers from it.

'What's that?' she asked.

'Some information. I get from the internet,' he responded, smoothing out the pages. 'And maps.'

They had three more days. Her dad had already started making them use up their provisions. She still didn't know how she was going to manage it. She couldn't just go without telling him. He'd called out security just because she was late back the other night. What would he do if she actually went missing? But telling him she wasn't coming home with him wasn't going to work either. There was no way he would let that happen and what father would?

'There is a bar looking for staff and a supermarket. I could work daytime and evening. We will find a place to live, whatever we can afford,' he said, showing Emma the print outs.

'I don't have any money... Dad...' she began.

'It is OK. I have some money and soon, before we go, I will have more,' Guy answered. He reached for her hand then and squeezed it in his.

'Will you get a trial at the football club? What happens? Do you telephone them or something?' She opened the bottle of fizzy drink.

'They have a time. It is next month. That will give me time to get a job and when we have more money we will find a place for Luc to go so you can study,' he continued.

There was so much hope and enthusiasm in his voice. She felt so lucky at that moment, so glad she was embarking on this new life with him.

'I can get a job too. Maybe at a nursery and Luc could

come there with me. I have an NVQ in Childcare and my first aid certificate,' she informed.

'NVQ?' he queried.

'It means I have a piece of paper that says I can do stuff.'

Guy smiled. He took her head in his hands and looked at her with those intense, green eyes as if she were the most desirable thing he'd ever seen.

'Before you come I was so lost. Now I feel like I have chance,' he whispered.

'*We* have a chance,' she told him, linking her hand with his.

He inched forward to kiss her when a cheery melody played by tubular bells rang out.

'Is there someone here?' Emma whispered, her eyes darting around the barn for evidence of company.

'*Non*,' Guy announced. He reached into the front pocket of his backpack and pulled the slim-line mobile phone from it. He pressed a button and put it to his ear.

'*Oui?*' He stood up and paced away from Emma, heading for the open door of the barn. The sound of the water hitting the roof drowned out her chance of overhearing the conversation. She didn't know he had a mobile phone. Not that she had one they could communicate with. She had had one but she'd broken it in a rage after her mum had passed. Her dad had offered to get her another but apart from Ally there was no one she'd wanted to communicate with. Whoever was on the phone now, it wasn't a good conversation. Guy was agitated. He was scuffing his bare feet on the ground, playing with the corrugated iron on the side of the barn, talking but far from sounding upbeat from what she could make out.

She was about to consider joining him, letting him know she was there, for solidarity, in case it was his mother, when he ended the call and turned back to her. For a moment she saw something like desperation in his eyes before he smiled and his face lit up again.

'Who was it?' she asked.

'David... who we meet on the boat... for work,' he added.

'I didn't know you had a phone,' Emma remarked.

He shrugged. 'It is new... for work.'

'But you're leaving.'

'I know but... no one knows yet.' He silenced her with a kiss and she put her arms around his neck and held him close.

'You have to go, don't you?' she guessed.

He nodded. 'But I do this for us. You know that.'

Yes, she knew that. And in a few days they would be far away from here and they would spend every night together. It would be hard but they would manage because they had each other. If she'd said any of this to herself before she got here she would have laughed. A life-long romance found on holiday in France – the boy who taught football at the campsite – how cliché! But she knew this was real. She felt it every time he touched her. She believed in him... in them.

He held her hand. 'I will walk you back.'

She picked up the fizzy drink and put it into the carrier bag while Guy put the papers and maps back into his backpack. He pulled his T-shirt over his head and stuffed his feet into his trainers.

Looking out of the barn she could see the rain had eased

up and the sun was making a re-appearance behind the lightening clouds.

'Ready?' he asked her. She nodded and took hold of his free hand.

They emerged from the barn, ducking their heads as the now fat, slow-falling raindrops hit them.

'When I am a famous footballer I will be able to give you and Luc everything. I will be like David Ginola. We will have the fast cars and the big house and we will eat out whenever we want,' Guy told her.

'Is that your dream? Fame and money?' Emma asked, looking to him.

He didn't answer straight away, seemed to ponder on it and consider what he was going to say. She had no desire to live her life in the spotlight.

'*Non*. I just want to have enough. I want to give Luc… and my wife, everything I can. To make them feel…look after… loved.'

Emma brought his hand to her mouth and pressed her lips against the skin there. She held it, savouring the texture and scent.

'Guy!'

As the voice called out she felt Guy tense. He pulled his hand away from her and looked to the woman down the lane.

'It is my mother. You should go,' he stated, moving away from her.

'I think I'd like to meet her,' Emma said, narrowing her lips and wondering how vile she could get away with being to this woman who had beaten her own son.

'Please, Emma. You cannot. It is better this way. Please.'

He was begging her. He looked desperate. His eyes sad and sorrowful.

He didn't wait for further reply. He took off in the direction of the woman clad in a short black dress and high-heeled shoes. She couldn't have looked less like a mother if she'd tried.

Emma watched him all the way and as he reached the woman she clipped him across the head with her hand, shouting in French. Emma flinched, as if the blow had been inflicted on her. So much for there being nothing stronger than a mother's love.

Chapter Forty-Five

Present Day

He had opened the mini-bar as soon as he got in the hotel suite. He'd wanted something smaller, something less extravagant but turning up and demanding a room for the night on the spot left him little choice. The honeymoon suite, of all rooms. It was mocking him.

The phone had rung five times and each time he had looked at it hoping for Madeleine. He would much prefer to listen to her cry or scream or beg than see Keith on the caller display and know he would never give up. All these years trying to move on, remembering everything but trying to block it out and finally it had caught up with him like he knew it would.

He turned off the TV and reached for the glass on the nightstand, filled with various miniatures from the mini-bar. He raised the glass to the ceiling and drank it down. As he replaced the glass his mobile phone rang again. A glance to the right and he saw it was Emma.

He snatched it up and answered.

'Emma.' Just saying her name had his heart rising, hope soaring.

'Hello. I… is it OK to talk?'

Over her shoulder Marilyn and Mike had Dominic involved in a game of Snakes and Ladders.

'Yes… I am not at home. I have moved out,' he responded.

'Oh. I don't know what to say. What should I say?' Emma asked.

'Say you'll meet me?'

'I can't. I have Dominic and…'

'Chris.'

'No. I… we… we broke up. He knows about you, about us,' Emma informed. There was a pause on the other end of the line. She could hear his breathing but nothing else.

'I am sorry. I am sorry for him,' he answered.

She nodded even though he couldn't see. She didn't know what else to say.

'It was what we wanted.' There was an edge to his words and she felt the same way. So much sadness and heartache. Was any of it worth it? Were they worth it?

'With Chris, you know, we weren't right together. Sooner or later this would have happened. It would probably have been later but… it would have happened,' she babbled.

'I want to see you,' he whispered. She closed her eyes and held on to the longing in his voice.

'Where are you?' she asked.

'At the Albany Hotel.'

She took a breath and took the phone away from her ear.

'Dad, would you be able to have Dom for a couple of hours?' she called.

'Of course, love. Is everything alright? Is it Ally and that pilot again?'

'Don't be so nosey! Of course we can have him, Emma. As long as he doesn't eat all the biscuits I bought,' Marilyn teased, poking her tongue out at Dominic.

'Are they Bourbons?' Dominic asked.

Emma put the phone back to her ear.

'Give me half an hour.'

She'd never felt so nervous. It was almost like when they'd first met. Him being the pin-up of the campsite, her being the nerd with the schoolbooks no one gave a second glance to. That day his football had knocked her out of her camping chair, the day he had first touched her hand had changed her whole life. Now, standing outside the honeymoon suite, it was all being brought back to her.

She raised her hand to knock but the door opened and there he was. His hair was a little dishevelled, his shirt open a few buttons and his trousers had no belt but right then he looked more beautiful than he'd ever looked.

She felt her body react to him, excitement building, adrenaline beginning to rush through her.

He opened his mouth as if to speak but closed it again, his chest expanding as he took a breath.

'I don't know what to say.' The words gushed from her mouth.

'Don't say anything,' he responded quickly.

One stride forward and his mouth was on hers, his body urging her backwards and into the suite. The door closed behind them and she was up against it, pressed to the wood as Guy's mouth explored her neck. She couldn't breathe. Everything was welling up inside, all the emotion she'd held in, not just lately, but for years, all the anger, the regret, the pain, the hurt, the desperation, all were combining now, growing and spawning, overriding all her senses. She wanted an end to it, to start a new beginning. She needed to get it all out of her system and perhaps this was the way. Right now, with his hands at the buttons of her blouse, his tongue rolling up hers, his breath hot on her cheeks, it felt like the only thing in the world she wanted to do. But it shouldn't be rushed like this. She pushed him back, gave herself some space, moved from the door.

'Emma…' he began. His expression told her he was concerned if they stopped he would lose her.

'I'm not the girl you fell in love with in France,' she said, turning back to face him.

'Yes you are.' He took a step towards her.

'No, Guy, I'm not. And you're not the same boy. We've both changed so much, we've both got older and experienced different things. Time and situations change people.'

'Why do you say this?'

'Because this has to be a fresh start, like we talked about, it has to be… for so many reasons,' she continued.

She needed to trust the man he was now. Not remember how he threw her love back in her face. They both had to be able to move on.

'I cannot pretend that I did not know you then. I cannot

tell you that my feelings now aren't because of my feelings before. But I can tell you, everything is bigger and better, stronger and clearer than ever. Love. Love... like no other.'

'Guy...'

'*Non*. I will not pretend this is not the best thing I have felt in my life. *You* are the best thing in my life. The only thing that matters in my life. I know you tell me I am not Dominic's father but I could be, if you let me. I should be. He is not here and I am... and I want to be,' he continued.

Chapter Forty-Six

He took another step closer towards her and she felt herself warming to his nearness. That buzz, the tingling of all her senses, coming alive to his proximity, it was electrifying her.

She gasped as he took a handful of her blouse and pulled her towards him. Their bodies so tight together she could feel his hardness, pressing against her thigh. She couldn't wait any longer. Didn't want to wait any longer. Any questions, any doubts had to be put to one side. Passion like this had to be given in to, it couldn't be controlled.

She opened her mouth, wetting her lips with her tongue and began to unfasten the buttons of his shirt. That tanned torso she'd so admired in her teens was about to be hers again. He closed his eyes as she loosened the shirt from his trousers and eased it back off his shoulders. The muscle definition was different, the core fitter, stronger, more man than youth but she remembered every contour of the frame, the minor blemishes, the birthmark on his thigh.

She locked his gaze as her hands explored his chest. Grazing his navel, up across his abs towards his pecs, lingering on his nipples before curling around his shoulders and pulling his body tight to hers.

*

He wanted her so badly it was already a strain to keep himself in check. He hadn't felt this way since the last time they made love. Every time with Emma he remembered how he felt like his heart would burst with joy as his body exploded inside her. It had been all-consuming then and having another chance to experience that was blowing his mind. Her touch was sweet agony, her fingertips warming his flesh with every centimetre they covered.

He wanted to touch her, taste her, make her his again. He ripped away her blouse, the buttons breaking their threads and scattering on the floor. He discarded it on the bed.

He made light work of her bra, undoing the clasp at the back with a swift tug and dragging the straps down her arms until he could pull it off from the front. It hit the wall. And there she was. Naked to the waist, with those perfect, smooth, round breasts he'd dreamed about so often.

She gasped and he brought his mouth down to her neck, his lips touching the indent at the top of her shoulder bone. His hands worked at the button of her dark jeans while his lips gave feather-light touches to her skin.

Releasing the button, he inched down the zipper and pushed the denim from her hips, all the time, his mouth making a slow, seductive journey down towards her breasts.

As he ducked his head lower she felt herself move towards him, yearning to give him what he wanted. Her breasts were swollen and obvious. Two hard peaks begging for his attention.

A sigh of pleasure escaped her mouth as his mouth,

moist, warm, probing, met one of her nipples, his tongue circling the tip, his mouth pulling it further inside. It ached and she groaned, feeling her breasts harden further still, giving away just how much she wanted this. She felt as if every fibre of her was stood to attention, alert, alive, ready.

He brought his head up, found her mouth and with his body, backed her over to the king-size bed. The edge of the mattress caught her leg and she let herself tumble backwards onto it.

He was looking down at her, his chest in time with the motion of his breath. He pulled her jeans completely from her legs and kicked them across the floor.

She wriggled slightly, enjoying the feel of the cotton-covered duvet on her back, arching herself, letting him know this was what she wanted.

He unfastened his trousers, all the time his eyes on her, as if watching her reaction, wanting to see how she felt from her expression. Tight boxers were underneath the trousers and her body tensed at the sight of him. There was no doubt his body desired her as much as she yearned for him.

Before he could move forward she shifted, sitting herself up and edging herself towards the end of the bed.

'Take them off,' she whispered, her fingers at the elastic of his shorts.

'Emma,' he said.

She knew it wasn't a protest, more a pause, but going slow wasn't an option now. She was lit up, a fusion of lust and love, bubbling and boiling with no chance of turning down the heat.

He slipped down his boxers and discarded them, standing before her. Bare.

★

This was it. This was his chance to truly put the past behind him. It was a different time, another place. He really could lose himself in her. He wasn't the naïve boy he was back then, eager to succeed, desperate for money. He'd learned so many lessons.

Her gaze made him feel suddenly self-conscious, a little vulnerable. He was proud of his physique, he worked hard to be this way for the football, but standing naked before her he wasn't worried about his flesh being on display, it was as if she could see inside him. So many secrets, so many bad, evil things were in there. He didn't want any of that to touch her.

She put her hand on his penis – so gentle – then settled her fingers at the base, guiding him towards her mouth.

It was almost more than he could stand when she folded her lips over him, moistening the skin, flicking her tongue down his length. She moved downwards agonisingly slowly. Each rhythmic stroke of her hand, followed by the pressure of her mouth, driving him mad with desire.

'Emma,' he said, his hands in her hair, caressing her scalp.

She didn't flinch or alter her position. She wanted to be as close as she could be to every part of him. The salt slick that tainted her tongue was driving her crazy with lust. She was somewhere else in her head, a different person. One who wasn't a sensible schoolteacher or a mum with several broken relationships behind her. She was the Emma she'd been before everything got messy – with the bonus of being eight years more experienced in the bedroom.

She took him further into her mouth, pulling back more urgently, increasing the pace until she felt him claw at her shoulders.

'Emma… you have to stop… I cannot…' he begged, his voice hoarse.

She withdrew, sitting back, looking at his erection. She had never seen someone so turned on, so hard. She had made him that way and that made her feel so special. She shimmied up the bed until her toes were at the bottom and her head was on the pillow.

She looked so perfect at that moment it stilled the intensity in him for a second. Her hair was fanned out on the bed clothes, her lithe body stretched out for him, only a small cotton triangle of underwear separating her from complete nakedness.

Her brown eyes held no innocence though and he knew just from looking at them what she longed for him to do. He lay down on the bed alongside her, his head next to hers, one elbow propping him up. With the flat of his hand, he began a path across her body. Brushing her nipple, moving over her ribs, the flat of her stomach and further down until he reached his target.

Thick fingers rolled her underwear downwards and he felt her arch herself to this movement, helping him remove the barrier. She shifted and he took off the underwear, pushing it off the bed. He sat up. Now he could see all of her.

★

He kissed her, exploring her mouth with his tongue while his fingers slipped inside her.

Instinctively she closed her eyes, needing to experience this with all her other senses. Touch, taste, smell…the scent of him was on her fingers, his warm breath heated up her cheeks as he kissed her, each kiss deeper, fuller, more intense. And as he caressed the inside of her mouth, his fingers were smoothing over her most intimate parts.

She let out a moan as he found the spot that made her go weak. With his thumb he started a circular motion that sent her nerves into a frenzy. With every pressure she was pulled higher, heading towards a heavenly pleasure she'd almost forgotten existed.

'Guy… I want you. I want to feel you.' She was so close to erupting already she wanted to share it with him when she did.

'Not yet.' It was almost a bark in response.

'Guy,' she begged. Her hands clutched the bed linen as she felt his fingers slip right inside her. And then they were gliding in and out of her, bumping against that sweet spot inside that had her gasping for release, begging for more but wanting it to end.

'Let go,' he willed.

'No. I want you.' She moved one hand to his head, swept her fingers into his hair.

'I want to see you let go,' he urged her.

She couldn't hold on. His words were exciting her, tipping the balance, making the difference between control and free-fall. His thumb pressed firmer, his fingers rocked her faster and she came undone with a sound that startled even her.

He pressed the flat of his hand against her, feeling the pulsating throb of her orgasm as she caught her breath, her torso stretched and taut as the ecstasy flowed over her. Seeing her like this, his need intensified. She widened the gap between her legs as he moved over her, watching every slight motion of her body, the way she was wetting her lips with her tongue, blinking her eyes, expectant.

This was what he wanted. This was all he had ever wanted. The love of this woman. This pure, wholesome, good and natural love born so long ago and still as strong.

He moved above her, studying her expression, waiting for her to come right down from the mountain of joy she'd elevated to. She shivered, then reached up, putting a hand to his cheek and holding it there.

He leaned his head into the embrace, touching her palm with his lips, closing his eyes as she caressed his hair with her fingers.

And then she let go. She spread out her fingers, travelling them wide and firm, across his torso until she reached his penis. She took it in her hand, slipping the skin back, guiding it towards her. She could see from his expression how it felt. He was keeping his eyes closed, his lips tight, a cheek muscle twitched.

When she had him in place, just on the outside edge, she took away her hand and placed both of them on his hips, shifting herself forward until they both felt the connection.

'Emma,' he said.

She felt him push against her, slow and tempting, easing his body into her.

'I want you,' she whispered. She knew what he was feeling. It had been so long and it was going to be different. But everything she'd experienced so far gave her no concerns, only sheer joy at having another chance.

He let out a groan and moved deeper into her, still controlled. He cupped her breast with his hand, his thumb flicking over her nipple until it was restored to an olive-shaped peak and she whimpered as he moved steadily inside her, back and forth, each time filling her a little more, a little harsher.

She could feel him setting light to a part of her that had lain dormant. With each thrust the delicious sensation built-up more and more until every nerve-ending was tingling with his promise.

'Guy!' she called out as he quickened his motion.

'You feel this?' he asked, dipping down low and hard.

Her breath caught in her throat and she reached out for him with a guttural sigh, turning her head to one side.

'Don't… don't stop,' she begged, rocking her hips in rhythm.

She was too far gone, she knew that. His love-making had already sensitised every part of her, inside and out. It wouldn't take much more.

'Look at me,' he urged, putting one hand in her hair and turning her face to his again.

She locked her eyes with his as he pushed further and further into her, their symmetry aligning perfectly together and in time.

'Come,' she begged, 'Come inside me.'

In his eyes she saw the boy she loved, the man she adored and his love for her. Whatever had happened in the past, they were here in the present, now, together in every way.

'*Mon Dieu... oh mon Dieu...* Emma...'

His breathing rapid, his body tensed as he pushed himself into her. As he hit her G-spot again, her toes curled and she lost it.

'Guy! Oh God, Guy!'

'I'm coming... I'm coming... Emma...'

She felt his release, so tense at first and then spasms rolling over and over, in time with hers. Her mind was doing cartwheels, every inch alive and touched with pinpricks of sensation.

Guy groaned and clenched his teeth, every ounce of energy flooding from him into her. It was like he was a surfer riding the biggest wave of his life and being carried to the shore from twenty miles out. A heart-stopping, adrenaline-fuelled thrill ride filled with utter beauty and sensitivity.

He knew he was crying but he was not ashamed. She had just given him eight years back.

'Are you OK?' she asked, reaching up and stroking her hand down his cheek.

'OK?' he asked. 'I am the happiest, luckiest man in the world.'

He lay across her, not wanting to end their connection, drawing her into his arms until they both lay on their side.

'I love you, Emma,' he told her, pressing his lips to her forehead.

'I love you too.'

'*Je t'aime.*'

'*Je t'aime.*'

Chapter Forty-Seven

She lay there, content in his arms, sated, fulfilled and relaxed for the first time in so long. She didn't know how long she'd been there. *She didn't know how long she'd been there.* She checked her watch. Horrified by what it showed she sat up, dragging back the covers.

'I have to go.' She got out of bed, looking to Guy.

'I know,' he responded. He caught her arm before she could move away.

'Dad and Marilyn have Dominic,' she said in explanation.

'I know,' he said again, his fingertips circling her elbow.

'Sorry.'

'What are you sorry for?'

'For having to leave like this. It feels wrong,' she admitted.

'You have Dominic. We will be a family. That is how this works.' He was smiling at her.

She turned back to the bed, leaned across to him, pressing her lips to his.

'We will be together next weekend and after that...' He paused.

'I need to speak to Dominic. It's too soon to think about...'

'I was not thinking. I was wishing and hoping, for the

first time knowing it will come true.' He kissed her back, lingering, his hand in her hair. She relinquished his hold.

'Where will you live? For now, I mean,' she asked, pulling on her jeans and picking up her bra.

'I will find something. Somewhere to rent maybe,' he replied.

She nodded.

'Perhaps close to you and Dominic?' he suggested.

'I would like that.' She picked up her blouse, discovering the broken buttons.

'Oh…'

'In the case. There is a T-shirt or something,' he offered, pointing.

A mobile phone began to ring. She knew it wasn't hers.

It was his. He rolled over to look at the nightstand and the phone vibrating on it. Keith.

'Who is it? Is it Madeleine? Oh God, it is, isn't it? It's too soon and I shouldn't be here,' Emma said as she got a T-shirt out of Guy's battered case.

'*Non*. No. It is not Madeleine. It is no one.'

No one he wanted in his life. Someone who should never have been in his life. He needed to do something about it, but what? Keith was not the sort of person to negotiate with.

The phone stopped vibrating and he watched her put his T-shirt over her head, then slip her trainers back on.

'This is not too soon. It has been too long.' He got out of bed, grabbing up a hotel robe and fastening it around himself.

'I know, but I feel for Chris and for Madeleine.

'We were not right for them. We are right for each other.'

He wrapped his arms around her, drawing her into him. He felt her sink into him, mould herself against his frame and he closed his eyes, savouring how it felt to hold her.

'I have to go,' she reminded, letting him go and taking another glance at her watch.

'I will call you,' he said, holding onto one hand as she moved toward the door.

She came back to him, found his lips and gave him one more kiss.

'I love you,' she whispered.

'*J'taime.*'

Smiling at him she opened the door, then closed it behind her.

As the door shut, his mobile phone vibrated anew. He would turn it off. He wouldn't allow Keith to ruin this night. The night he'd finally felt the love he thought he'd lost.

The red circle indicated a new voicemail message. His hand hovered over the power button but curiosity got the better of him.

'You have one new message. New messages,' the robotic voice began.

Keith's voice came next.

'I still have the photos.'

His heart hit the floor.

Chapter Forty-Eight

'Did he cry?'

'What?'

'Chris. Did he cry?'

'No. Why are you asking that?'

'He looked like a crier. I don't mean that in a nasty way. He just looked the type, that's all.'

Emma looked at Ally, shaking her head.

'Are you trying to make me feel worse than I already do?' she asked.

'Not at all. If it wasn't right then it wasn't right. I know I banged on about marriage and a good man but that's because I was jealous. I mean you're marriage material, aren't you? Always have been. Me, I'm wining, dining and shagging material… six months tops. No rings. No matching clothes or jointly-owned pets, not even a couple's gym membership,' Ally said, flopping down onto Emma's bed and almost upending the suitcase she was trying to pack.

'Chris and I never had any of those.'

'You had a goldfish.'

'We won it at the fair and come on, it lasted two weeks!'

'Two weeks still counts. I've called relationships that last two weeks long-term before now.'

'How are things with Jonty? You haven't said.'

'Alright. We're creeping towards five and a half months and he's got an overnight in Chicago with the beverage bimbo,' Ally informed.

'Have you actually asked him about her?'

'No! Of course not! How insecure would that make me seem? I'd look like a possessive hag – on skis.'

'But at least you wouldn't be worrying about it all the time,' Emma suggested.

'Like you, you mean. All sorted and loved up and about to go away to France for the weekend,' Ally teased.

She folded another T-shirt and added it to the small case she was packing.

'Are you sure you're OK having Dom after school? Dad's signed up to some mechanics course at the college until six on Fridays,' Emma said.

'I wouldn't have said I could have him if I couldn't. I've left Milo and Shane in charge. God knows what state the place will be in when I get back but I can't be hawk-eyed with them all the time, can I? What time does Dom get out of school again?'

'Ally! It's ten past three! You won't forget, will you? He's expecting you,' Emma exclaimed, an edge of panic to her voice.

'Of course I won't forget. So, how did *you* get out of school? Or is it a teacher training thingy-me?'

'We have to be there for those.'

'So?'

'I've called in sick.'

'Emma Barron! You lied!'

'Yes and I don't feel good about it.'

She never called in sick, even when she was sick. But that was one of the reasons why she'd done it. This weekend was important. She and Guy both needed some time to process what had happened, what was going to happen. And after the last couple of weeks she was due a break. Catching some autumn sun in France was just what was required.

'What happens if they find out? Is it lines and detention?' Ally teased.

'Worse than that. I might have to supervise the canteen for a week,' she responded, smiling.

'It's good to see you smile. You haven't smiled like that in a long time,' Ally remarked.

'Haven't I?'

'No. Mind you, if I was going to spend a weekend in France with someone hot and French I'd be wearing a grin from here to Nova Scotia. What time's your train?'

'Half ten. I'm meeting Guy at St Pancras,' she informed.

'Underneath the clock? Wearing a red rose in your lapel?'

'Will you stop?'

He'd had to give in. Despite everything his heart was telling him, he knew he had to face this. If he didn't deal with it now it would come back to bite him. Starting things anew with Emma was everything he'd ever wanted. He wouldn't let anything get in the way of that. Madeleine had phoned earlier. At first she was full of tears and pleading, but when he made it clear he would not be returning or changing his mind the attitude completely changed. She'd called him several hurtful names in French and told him she was selling her story to one of the national magazines.

He'd arrived early at the coffee shop. He didn't like the place. It was all chrome, glass and mocha, choco, skinny, triple lattes. It was overpriced and clinical. He was on his second espresso when he saw Keith enter.

Dressed in a pale grey suit, a lemon-coloured shirt beneath, he looked like the flamboyant entrepreneur he was. He stood out, but not as someone to be feared. He looked approachable, professional, someone without a care in the world.

Guy's chest tightened and he turned his gaze away. He still let him do this to him. Why? Why did this man still have power over him? He tightened his hold on the small coffee cup as, out of the corner of his eye, he saw Keith approach the table.

'Another coffee?' the man asked, seating himself opposite.

'No,' Guy refused, not raising his eyes.

'You're not going to make this difficult, are you, Guy? It doesn't have to be,' Keith said, lowering his voice.

'Just say what you have to say.' Guy raised his head, meeting his eyes.

'I've missed you,' Keith whispered. He reached across the table. Guy retracted his hands onto his lap.

'Do not say that,' he hissed in response.

'We could have had something special.'

'Stop it.'

'It's true. No denying it.'

A smile spread across Keith's mouth and he wet his lips with his tongue. 'It's fate, isn't it? Us meeting up again like this.'

'I want the photos,' Guy demanded.

'I want you. Always have.'

'No.' Guy shook his head.

'As delightful as all this defiance is and no matter how gorgeous you look when you're all brooding like that... we both know I'm going to get what I want,' Keith crowed.

Guy shook his head again, feeling his skin pimple into goose bumps.

'I hear you're off to France this weekend. Big match tomorrow.'

'I will not do what you want me to do. David set me up.' Guy could feel the bile rise from his stomach, into his throat as he forced the words out.

Keith let out a roar of laughter and banged his hand on the table as if Guy had told the funniest joke.

'You were paid handsomely. Very handsomely. I didn't hear any complaints about that.' The grin disappeared from Keith's face, his eyes narrowed and he leaned across the table, aggression radiating from him.

'If you don't do as I say I'm going to blow the whistle. No matter how you perform for France this weekend, if you don't cooperate here, the only thing the press will be talking about is what you did for a job when you were eighteen,' Keith hissed.

Guy winced, even though he knew it had been coming.

'So, all we need to arrange is a time and place. Which should be a lot easier now you've left that whiny Madeleine. Lingerie designs aren't bad but listening to her... well, I'd rather sleep with my wife!' He took a breath, reapplied his smile.

'I was thinking weekly. There have been others, Guy, I won't deny it, but...' He toyed with his tie, cleared his throat. 'Well, you never forget your first love, do you?'

He could taste the vomit in his mouth. His stomach lurching and pushing the sickness up his throat with every second that passed. He tried to focus. He couldn't let him do this to him again. He was older. He was wiser. He was stronger. What he'd got himself into back then had been born out of desperation to survive. He'd needed an escape from the poverty, a chance for him and Luc to become something they would never be in Fréjus.

'No.' The voice, despite his terror and nausea, sounded convincing and firm.

Keith nodded, tapping his fingers on the table in rhythm. Guy held himself upright, kept his eyes fixed ahead, waiting for the backlash to his refusal. He needed to pre-empt it.

'You have done well in your industry. I looked you up. You are still very rich, richer than ever now perhaps? Part of the jet set here in the UK and on many foundations. Two children's charities...' Guy began.

'I can see where this is going. Don't waste your breath,' Keith interjected.

'I think business would suffer. Clients would find someone else, friends would disappear and I cannot see foundations wanting to have anything to do with you when they find out what sort of "hobbies" you practise.'

'You were *not* a child,' Keith hissed viciously.

'I was *not* the only one,' Guy snapped back. 'How about I tell my story? Everything.'

'I know you, Guy. You haven't got the balls.'

'You don't know me. You don't know me at all. I am not eighteen anymore.' His hands were shaking as all the hatred for this man came spilling from his mouth. He knew he had raised his voice, drawn attention to their table but he didn't stop.

'If you do not leave me alone I will make sure you are ruined. I will go to the press and the police. I will tell them everything I know. I will make sure they investigate your business and everything else you have connections with. You must be a man with many contacts. Contacts with secrets. Contacts with secrets they want to keep secret… just like you,' Guy continued. He reached for his cup and put it to his mouth, only to find it was empty. He returned it to the saucer and wiped at his mouth with a napkin. Despite his firm tone, on the inside he was barely holding it together. This had to work.

'Who d'you think would come off worst?' Keith's voice was steady and controlled, the volume measured. 'You could kiss goodbye to your football career. That'd be a shame, now you've reached such dizzy heights. I can almost see the headlines now. "Footballer's Dirty Past", "Sordid Soccer Scandal". They'd not let you near the youth foundation. You'd be tainted. Don't think for a minute you'd get the world's sympathy. They might paint you as a victim at first but it wouldn't last,' Keith lowered his voice. 'And what happens then? With no career, no chance of a job in sport or anything media related, not even able to walk down the street without the name-calling and comments.'

Guy shifted in his seat, the reality of what Keith was saying sinking in. Was he prepared to go to the police? Tell the world what he'd been part of eight years ago? It had been out of dire need. People would see that wouldn't they?

'I'll give you the weekend but that's it. Come Monday I want a phone call. I'll arrange a nice room, a suite somewhere… champagne,' Keith said, wetting his lips with his tongue.

What could he say? He knew what he should say, but no words were forthcoming. He was trapped and Keith knew it. No matter what he did he was screwed.

'*À bientôt*,' Keith said, rising from his chair.

Guy didn't look up or respond. He could hear nothing but the pounding in his head. He was trapped, just like he had been in France.

Chapter Forty-Nine

Those bitches had soaked her! She'd only just dried out from the afternoon of rain and now she was sodden all over again.

It was supposed to be a team game. Filling up an empty two-litre Coke bottle, with its top cut off and stabbed with small holes, making the water rise to retrieve a plastic lemon. Instead Melody and Tasha had taken turns throwing water at her. She'd only managed to get them to stop when she'd clouted Melody in the shoulder with her bucket. She'd left her dad chortling alongside a ruddy-faced father of four from the Wirral and now she was attempting to wring out her hair before she met up with Guy.

She wished Ally was here. Ally was the type of person who carried sample-sized hair rescue and recovery packs in her bag. She squeezed the water out of each section, watching it pool on the floor. She'd need to get changed, her T-shirt was wet through and there were grubby marks on her denim shorts from the rusty bucket she'd been carrying.

That was the very last time she entered any lame games. They always seemed to end in her humiliation. Still, it was only a few more days and then everything would change.

'*Tais-toi!*'

The woman's voice was shrill and laced with venom. The ferocity and close proximity of it had Emma backing up behind the canvas of the tent. Peeking out, she saw a woman coming along the path getting closer with every tentative wobble on what looked like very high shoes. She was dressed in tight black trousers and a garish red and gold blouse. Her black hair was tousled and piled up on her head. It was almost thirty degrees and the outfit was far more disco than daywear. It was only as she drew closer and she focused on the pram the woman was pushing that she realised who it was. Guy's mother. Luc's mother. She had only seen her from a distance but now she was just a few metres away, dressed and made-up like a prostitute, directing bitter angry words at a baby. A small, innocent baby.

'*Tais-toi!*' she yelled again, bending over the pram as Luc continued to cry. '*Tais-toi! Tais-toi! Tais-toi!*'

Emma recoiled a step further, swallowing the displeasure and fear as she watched the woman lift Luc roughly from his blanket.

'*J'ai dit tais-toi!*'

And then she shook him. Emma's mouth hung open as a sickening dread crept over her. She watched in horror as Luc's fragile form vibrated under the woman's grip. His little head rocked back and forth, his cries silenced, the woman relentless in the motion.

She had to stop her. She had to confront her. She couldn't

just stand here hiding in the tent watching this brutality. She would speak up. She would protect Luc. She put one foot forward then…

'*Maman!*' It was Guy. He was wearing nothing but a pair of cut-off jeans and trainers. Shirtless and drizzled with moisture from playing football he snatched Luc from her hands. He pressed the baby to his chest, cradling his head with one olive-skinned hand.

'Where have you been? I have to get ready for work and he just scream and cry. He will not stop,' the woman shrieked, gesticulating wildly.

'He is a baby.'

The woman shook her head and made a hissing sound through her teeth.

'*Un bébé,*' Guy tried again, anger in his tone.

She turned then, sliced the side of her hand against Guy's face. He turned his body in reaction, shielding his brother from the backlash.

'*Tu penses que je suis une imbécile?*' she raved.

'*Non, Maman.*' There was desperation and exasperation inflected.

She pushed the pram towards him with force. The edge of it caught his hip as it came to a halt.

'*Tu prends lui!*' she ordered, throwing her hands up in dismissal.

Guy's face was a picture of resignation. This performance was nothing new. Just like he'd told Emma, this was his life. And now she knew just why he was so desperate to leave. If they didn't leave someone was going to get hurt… or worse.

She watched him, holding her breath, as he observed the small child. He looked into his eyes, running a finger over his cheek and placing his lips to his forehead in a soft, silent kiss.

'Guy,' she called out.

He turned then, saw her as she emerged from the tent. There were tears in his eyes and he clung to Luc as if he were a life force, the strength and purity he needed to pick himself up and refocus after his mother's tirade.

'I...' He paused, seemed to recollect. 'He is OK,' he stated. He eased Luc from his chest to let Emma see.

She didn't say anything. She didn't have the words. Instead she put her arm around him, drawing them both against her.

Chapter Fifty

'What do you think of the band, love?'

The band were terrible. They were French musicians somehow amalgamated into a Beatles/Rolling Stones/Jackson Five tribute band. One minute they were dressed as Sixties mods, the next they were donning white spangly suits with flared trousers and afro wigs.

'Hideous,' she replied.

Mike laughed and nodded, taking a glance at his mobile phone.

'Waiting for a call?' Emma asked, her head lifting out of Chaucer. She knew the answer. He'd been looking at the display all night. He was obviously waiting for Marilyn to ring.

'No. Not really. Well, I thought perhaps...'

She interrupted quickly, not wanting to hear.

'Could I have another drink?'

'Coming right up,' Mike said, picking up their empty glasses and leaving the table.

Now her dad was gone she could concentrate on watching Guy. He was clearing glasses and wiping down the tables. He did this most evenings but tonight he seemed to be spending an awful lot of time around Tasha's table.

He would take a tray of used glasses to the bar, wipe a table or two on the way and then stop back at Tasha's table. He was smiling at her, laughing, exchanging body language not usually kept for someone you didn't like. He hadn't even looked her way once. She thought what had happened earlier had brought them closer, proved how much they needed each other. This was the man she was going to marry and now he was flirting with someone else. Was he? Or was she overreacting? He couldn't be seen with her all the time. It could scupper all their plans. He was doing his job, being nice to the holidaymakers and keeping his distance so as not to arouse suspicion.

Her attention snapped away from Guy when a shattering crash reverberated around the room. All eyes turned to where a woman had staggered into a large table, knocking the contents of it on the floor. Glasses were smashed, plates were in pieces and the woman was trying with desperation to get on her feet. It was Guy's mother. Drunk again. In charge of Luc.

Before she could think about it she was moving. Heading not for Guy's mother, but for the pram.

'Get your hands off me! I said I am fine! Leave me!' Guy's mother screeched, her arms flailing about in an attempt to relieve herself of two people who were trying to assist her.

Emma could smell the alcohol on her from yards away. The woman's cheeks were ruddy, her eyes wild, her black hair falling out of what was now a loose chignon.

'What are you doing here, Mother?' Guy asked, taking hold of her arm.

'What am I doing here?! What are you doing here? You are meant to be with David,' she blasted.

At the mention of the name Guy froze. He raised his head slowly, but his eyes darted around him as if to see who might have heard. It was a mere split second before his eyes found Emma's.

His skin blanched and he seemed to plead with her with his eyes.

'I said, what are you doing here, Guy? Answer me!' she bawled.

'I am working,' he responded. His voice was weak.

'For a few Euros? Pfft! You will keep the arrangements I have made for you. I have made promises,' she carried on.

'I need to be here tonight,' Guy said. He wasn't looking at her now. He was hiding his eyes away, shifting on the spot.

Luc let out a cry of discontent and Emma put her hands on the pram handle, rolling it gently back and forth.

'You will come with me now. You have a job with me,' she ordered.

'I cannot. I have to be here,' he replied.

Without further debate, she struck out, swiping a hard hand against the side of his head.

'Stop it!' Emma yelled out at volume. The entire clubhouse seemed to quiet in an instant until the only sound to be heard was a dull murmur of hushed voices.

'You! You are the girl he has been with. The one keeping him from his job,' she sneered. The woman stepped away from Guy, took a wobbly stride towards Emma.

'And you're the so-called mother who beat him black and blue. The woman who's drunk from morning 'til night when she should be looking after a new baby! A baby she shakes when he won't stop crying!' Emma blasted.

Guy's mother raised a hand and Emma held her position,

stuck her chin out in defiance and waited for whatever was to come. This woman was a mother and she was hurting her children. She would give anything to have her own mother back. She wasn't afraid of her.

Guy intercepted the blow, catching the fist on his shoulder.

'Emma? What's going on here, love?' Mike asked, arriving at her side, drinks in his hands.

Emma opened her mouth to start to speak but caught Guy's expression. He was silently begging her to keep quiet and say no more. There were just a couple of days left here. She needed to keep things normal. They could get through this and soon it would all be a bad memory. They'd have a new life.

'She insults me!' Guy's mother screeched. She added words in French that sounded violently rude.

'I will come,' Guy spoke quickly.

'Love?' Mike said. Her dad's questioning look, coupled with the fury in Guy's mother's eyes were making it so hard to bite her tongue. If she told the truth now maybe there would be another way out. If she explained the graveness of the situation to her dad. He was a good man. If he knew they were in danger then…

'You stay away from my son!' Guy's mother shouted at Emma, taking ownership of the pram.

'*Maman*…'

'Emma, love, what's going on?' Mike tried again.

Guy put his hand on the pram, pulled it from his mother.

'Nothing, Dad. Nothing's going on,' she answered as Guy and his mother made their way to the exit.

'You're shaking, love. Do you know that woman?' Mike inquired.

'No. She was drunk, that's all,' Emma replied. She watched Guy and his mother leave the clubhouse. The woman was swaying and staggering, yelling at Guy as he pushed the pram.

'Emma?'

'I'm fine, Dad, honestly.' She smiled at her father. 'Shall we join in with bingo?'

'Well, despite our initial reservations about the band I thought they weren't too bad. The finale was good. You can't beat a Beatles medley,' Mike said. He chuckled.

Emma smiled but it didn't reach her eyes. She was thinking about Guy. She'd been thinking about him all evening. He hadn't come back. God knows what his mother was doing to him. She shuddered.

'Getting a bit nippy in the evenings now, isn't it?' Mike remarked, unzipping the tent.

Emma nodded as convincingly as she could manage.

'You alright, love?' Mike asked, turning back to face her.

'Just a bit of stomach-ache. I might pop to the shower block for the toilet,' she said, putting a hand to her midriff.

'Do you need some tablets?' Mike offered.

'No thanks, Dad. You go in. I won't be long.'

She just needed some space. She didn't want a blow-by-blow account of the Beatles/Stones/Jackson Five tribute band or the bingo in five different languages.

'Alright, love. I'll see you in a bit,' Mike said. His head disappeared into the canvas and she let out a breath of relief. She closed her eyes and let the French night wrap itself around her, revelling in the cool air as it cloaked her.

And then a pair of strong arms were around her, pulling her backwards, away from the tent. She wasn't afraid; the grip was familiar and more than welcome.

When Guy spun her around, under the shelter of the tiled entrance to the shower block, he didn't speak, just sought her lips with his.

She threaded her hands through his hair, easing his head downwards, wanting to fill herself with his taste. Finally, both out of breath, they separated their mouths and looked at each other for the longest time.

'Did she hurt you?' It was all that was important, nothing else.

He shook his head. '*Non.*'

'And Luc?'

'He is fine. Asleep. He will need milk soon. I cannot stay,' he said, looking at his watch.

'I… I'm sorry for what I said to her. I wasn't thinking. I was just so angry and…'

'Sshh. It is OK. She is not important. Just a few days and we will be somewhere else. Somewhere… *mieux.*'

She saw the release in his breath, heard the hope and promise in his tone.

She smiled. 'Tell me about St Etienne. Is it as beautiful as it looks in photographs?'

Chapter Fifty-One

Despite how they had arrived at this current situation, Emma was excited for the weekend. The last trip she'd been on involved thirty schoolchildren and a Shakespearean play. As much as she loved Richard III she'd missed most of it having to deal with Louisa and Tom who'd been trying to do a lot more than kissing in the darkness of the theatre. No, apart from day visits to the seaside and one week in a caravan in Norfolk she'd pretty much been confined to home. France sounded positively far flung.

She was nervous though. Not just for starting this new chapter with Guy, but for leaving Dominic for the weekend. She'd never left him before and that scared her a little. He was her rock. Her life had revolved around him for so long. But this weekend was just about her. Her and a lover she thought she'd lost.

★

When he saw her waiting at the entrance he was flooded with relief. After meeting with Keith, he'd almost convinced himself it was the start of everything going against him again. She was his light at the end of a long, black tunnel. She'd always been that.

He stopped walking to fully appreciate the fact she was there, waiting for him.

Black linen trousers, a T-shirt the colour of strawberries and a pair of sandals completed the look. As her hair was blown by the warm breeze his stomach contracted. She was so beautiful.

At once he felt like the most fortunate man on the planet. He started to walk again.

'Emma.'

At the sound of his voice she turned around, one hand still on her small case. He was wearing a cream-coloured checked short-sleeved shirt over blue jeans, tan trainers on his feet. Her insides rotated as he approached and she let a gasp of excitement escape her mouth.

'Am I late?' he asked, checking his watch.

'No. I was early. Like always,' she said. She let out a laugh, covering her mouth with her hand. She didn't know how to behave. All this was so new. She was almost delirious with joy.

He took her hand in his and breathed inwards, expanding his chest as he looked at her.

'Let's go back to France,' he said, his words heavy with meaning.

'I probably packed too much. I didn't know what the weather would be like. It said it would be hot but there might be thunderstorms so I have short sleeves and cardigans and my rain jacket. I know you have to go to football tomorrow but what time? Not that I mind, it's just…'

She stopped herself from talking. She was talking far too much and the train had only just left St Pancras. Guy was gazing at her, his eyes alive, a smirk on his lips.

'Sorry. I'm just… I'm so excited. I've barely left Wiltshire in eight years and…' she began.

'I know,' he responded. 'I am excited too.'

He hadn't let go of her hand since they boarded the train. They would be arriving in Paris in just under two hours now. It seemed surreal.

'When we get to Paris we will travel to the airport. I have a plane to take us to Fréjus,' he informed.

'A plane,' she said, eyes wide.

'We would have flown the whole way but I thought this… was more special.' He indicated the view outside the window as the countryside flashed past them.

'And we can carry this in our luggage as far as France.' He dipped his hand into his rucksack on the floor and lifted out a bottle of red wine.

'Merlot! Before lunch!' Emma exclaimed in mock horror.

'*Absolument*,' he replied, smiling.

'If we can't take it on the plane we'd better open it,' she suggested.

'I think we must,' he agreed, loosening the cap.

She found herself giggling again. Feeling not seventeen but about twelve.

'Tonight we will go out, have some food in Fréjus. Tomorrow I will leave in the afternoon for the game but I will be back. Midnight perhaps? A little later maybe. Sunday we have until the afternoon,' he explained, pouring her a plastic cup of wine.

He passed her the drink and she accepted it, relishing the fruity fragrance.

'To the future,' Guy said, holding his cup aloft in a toast.

'The future,' Emma agreed, raising her wine in the air.

'*Our* future,' Guy added.

'Yes,' she said.

'Together.' His eyes fixed on hers.

Could this really be happening for them at last? No sneaking around, no secrets to keep...

The wine hit her throat and the alcohol made her cough. She drank another mouthful to see if that would help and replaced the glass on the table in front of them.

'OK?' he asked her.

'Yes, sorry, I did say it was risky before lunch,' she said, recovering.

A mobile phone began to ring and Guy edged himself up on the seat to get it out of the pocket of his jeans.

It was Madeleine. He didn't know what to do. He had said all he wanted to say. He had thought he had said all he *needed* to say. The last time they had spoken she was angry but had realised it was over. What did she want now? If he answered it could be an uncomfortable conversation in front of Emma and a train full of people. If he didn't answer he would have to call her later or she would call him another time, perhaps at a worse time.

'It is Madeleine,' he spoke out loud, watching for Emma's reaction.

'Oh,' she responded.

'Would you mind? I just…' he started.

'Of course. Talk to her,' Emma urged. She stood up, allowing him to shift past her into the aisle. He pressed to answer and moved on down the train, the phone to his ear.

'Hello.'

'Where are you?' came the response.

'I am on my way to France. I have a match tomorrow. Madeleine, are you alright?'

There was something about the tone of her voice that was unsettling him. She didn't sound upset or angry; she just sounded accusing yet detached.

'You said it was because I wanted something for myself.'

'No, Madeleine, I did not say that. That is what you said.'

'You said there was no one else,' she continued.

'There is no one else.' He grimaced at the lie but he was keeping it this way for her. The break-up would have happened sooner or later regardless of Emma.

'Liar!'

His heart lurched. What did she know? How could she know?

'Madeleine…'

'There are photographs, Guy, in two of the national papers. You and some tart, some plain, ordinary-looking woman, on the balcony of the football club!'

His heart sank as reality bit him. They'd been careless and reckless. Chris had seen them that day and obviously so had an eagle-eyed guest keen on making a few pounds.

'Who is she?' Madeleine ranted.

'No one.'

He had to protect Emma from this. And Dominic. It would not be fair for the boy to have to deal with the fall out.

'Bastard!' Madeleine screamed.

He closed his eyes, thinking about what to do. He would have to call his agent, minimise the damage somehow. Right now, having Emma back, he was prepared to wear whatever the consequences of their actions were. It was worth every bit of mud the world could sling at him and more.

As that last thought rode around his mind he considered Keith's threats. Would the man really go through with telling the press about what happened in La Baume? And if he did could Guy handle it? The shame. The loss of income Keith had predicted. The football world shunning him.

It was then he realised the only real concern he had was what Emma would think of him. Her opinion was the only one that counted.

'I'm sorry, Madeleine,' he said, meaning it.

'Sorry?! You're sorry?! Do you know how much time and effort I wasted on you? You were barely anything when we met. A lesser-known footballer with bad clothes. I made you who you are! And now I have nothing!'

Could he say something right here? Could he possibly make her feel better?

'You were always the star. Now you will be a fashion designer in your own right. You can concentrate on that,' he tried.

'Pa! We have lost our manufacturer. Keith Crone called Gabriella this morning,' she shouted.

Guy gripped the luggage rack and sank against it, all energy leaving him.

She could just see Guy at the end of the carriage, still talking into his phone. She didn't feel anything about Madeleine ringing. Everything was still so raw. It had probably been as much a bolt out of the blue as with Chris. What would she do if Chris rang? Would he ring? Was he still hurting? She swallowed the nostalgia. As kind and considerate as he had been, he hadn't been her soul mate. Something that wasn't right could never last. The flaws and cracks had shown, the proposals had been turned down-it had been ending for a long time. Guy returning had been the final jolt.

She saw Guy sway with the motion of the train and sink against the metal luggage racks. Whatever Madeleine was saying it was hitting him hard. She looked away, took in the crusted, dry summer fields, through the train window. She couldn't bear to watch.

Chapter Fifty-Two

He lied and said that there had been a problem with the house. Madeleine needed the phone number of the company the football club employed to deal with matters like that. He just couldn't bring himself to tell her the truth. What good would it do to know her face was in the newspapers? That people were speculating over her identity. Right now he was pleased he had not travelled with the football team. No one knew they were arriving by train, that he was going to be staying in Fréjus. They could have some privacy. And that was all they wanted. Privacy and time to reconnect with each other again before sharing it with other people.

She didn't believe what he'd told her. Ex-girlfriends didn't phone their ex-boyfriends to get phone numbers. That was what the internet was for. Mentally, Madeleine would be in one of two places. She'd either hate his guts – she'd call anyone *but* him for help – or she was still in love with him – she'd be making up better excuses than dodgy water pipes or whatever it was in order to get him back.

Whatever the phone call was about she knew the

reason he was keeping it from her was to protect her from something. Half of her thought this was gallant and sweet, the other half was cross that he thought she couldn't deal with the truth. She'd accepted the lame excuse for now because she didn't want to spoil things. But later she would get him to tell her. They needed to start this relationship the right way and that meant putting the past behind them and dealing with whatever the future threw at them, together.

A car met them at the small airport in Fréjus and took them the few kilometres further inland to the place where she had spent that unforgettable summer.

Watching out of the window, Emma felt her whole body reconnect with both the situation and the place. A shiver ran over her as she saw so many familiar sites. The corn fields, the hue of the trees, the arable land, the cloudless sky. All of it evoking so many memories. Before she knew it, the tears were in her eyes.

'The campsite,' Guy remarked, pointing out of the window.

And there was the back entrance to the campsite. The same gate, albeit newly painted, where she had met Guy so many times before, escaping to be together. She craned her neck as the car drove on by, trying to catch a glimpse of anything she remembered, needing to see it all.

'We can go there… if you like,' Guy offered as Emma turned her head back.

'Oh, no, we don't need to, I…'

'It has changed. There are new things, two new swimming pools, archery, trampolines…'

'No more Sumo suits or darts?' she asked.

'Darts still, I think,' he responded. He laughed.

The car travelled a few more minutes and then pulled off the road onto a dirt track. As the vehicle moved along at a leisurely pace, Emma saw a house coming into view up ahead.

'Is this it?' she asked, looking through the gap in the seats and through the windscreen.

'*Oui*,' he replied.

The car swept up to an enormous two-storey farmhouse-style building. It looked made of traditional stone, had a tiled roof and bright, white, newly painted shutters adorned each window. Emma let out a gasp of pleasure. It was beautiful.

The car stopped outside the entrance and a middle-aged woman in a floral dress, an apron tied around her, came hurrying from the house, her arms outstretched.

Guy was up and out of the car and Emma watched as he gathered the woman up in his arms, swinging her off her feet. It was obvious this person meant something to him. Was it a relative? A friend? Why hadn't he told her someone would be here?

Her door opened and Guy was there, urging her to leave the car.

'Emma, this is Colette. Colette, this is Emma,' he introduced.

She had little time to adjust to the bright sunlight or her surroundings before Colette was hugging her as if they were old friends.

'Welcome back to Fréjus,' Colette said, taking Emma's hands and smiling warmly at her.

'Thank you,' she answered.

'Colette is an old friend. She looks after the house for me now I have moved to England,' Guy explained.

'I meet Guy when he sign for OGC Nice. I used to help the younger players back then. Teach them how to look after themselves. Washing machine… cooking… to shower…' Colette began.

'Hey! I always know how to shower,' Guy interrupted, acting playfully shocked.

Emma laughed, feeling a little more at ease.

The driver deposited their cases on the driveway and Guy moved to speak with him.

'You are hungry, yes? I have prepared something,' Colette said, taking Emma's arm and guiding her towards the front door of the house.

Tiled floors and oak beams greeted her inside. The interior of the house reflected modern tastes but it had obviously been sympathetically updated because nothing looked out of place. White walls and light pouring in from every window somehow managed to create a warm, bright, cosy, yet open feel.

The kitchen was state-of-the-art but the large table down the middle of it was rustic and old, a homely red and white checked tablecloth covered it. On the table was a French feast her stomach reacted to immediately. Bread, cheese, ham, grapes… the aromas were heaven sent.

'You didn't have to go to any trouble,' Emma said.

'It was no trouble. When Guy say he is returning I am pleased. I think it would be months before I see the boy again,' Colette said, smiling. She pulled a seat out for Emma who sat straight into it.

'This is such a beautiful house. I had no idea…'

'He re-build. Tear down the old one and start again.'

'Tear down?' Emma questioned.

'This is where he always live. With that wicked mother of his. He tell me all about her. So much pain and sadness in his life… losing his brother…' Colette commenced, clutching her chest as she spoke.

Emma looked away from the woman, focused on the food on the table, anything to avoid connecting with the conversation.

'Such a tragedy,' Colette carried on. 'I think that was the turning point for Guy. There was no hope for him here while *she* was still alive. It forced him to go, to make something of himself.'

'Colette, you have made food. I said we could do this!' Guy exclaimed, entering the kitchen.

'It is nothing. You sit down and enjoy. I will finish making the beds and then I will be out of your way,' she said. She pulled out a chair for Guy then bustled from the room.

Emma let out a breath she didn't even know she'd been holding as Guy sat opposite.

'Are you OK?' he asked, reaching across the table and taking her hands in his.

'Yes. I just wasn't expecting to see anyone,' she admitted.

'Colette?'

She nodded. What the woman said had brought a flood of unwelcome memories back to the surface. She should have known coming back to the place where everything had happened would do that, but she'd thought of it more as an expedition to banish the bad times, start afresh.

'She saved me back then. She picked me up when I was so down. I lived with her... after Luc... when I left,' he explained.

Emma nodded. She picked up the cheese platter and offered it to him.

'She won't be here all weekend. She lives in a cottage just a mile away. I bought it for her to thank her. Although, nothing could ever be enough to repay her for what she did.' He picked up a few grapes and put one in his mouth.

The plate slid out of her hands and she struggled to balance it.

'Are you OK with being here?' Guy asked her.

'What d'you mean? The house, it's gorgeous from what I've seen so far and...' She paused then let go of the plate, withdrawing her hands.

'I meant Fréjus. There are a lot of memories, yes?' he probed.

'I suppose.' She dropped her eyes to the table. This was what she'd been afraid of. Coming back to the place she'd left in 2005 was bound to highlight things. She could forgive Guy what had happened with Tasha, even though it gnawed at her. But she still couldn't forgive herself for her reaction to it.

'We're starting again. Something new. We can pretend we know nothing of each other if you would like,' he said.

She raised her head, saw him smile.

'I think we're a long way past a first date,' she responded.

'Sorry? What did you say your name was?' he replied, leaning across the table.

'I knew you were a ladies' man. I should never have

accepted a weekend away with a stranger,' Emma played along.

'I think we have very much in common. Over there on the bookshelf you will see I have the complete works of Shakespeare and books by a rather strange but well-respected author called Chaucer.' He indicated a bookcase just visible in what she assumed was the living room, partitioned from the kitchen-diner by a feature stone wall.

'Chaucer? I've heard of him. Writes in old English. Virtually impossible to decipher unless you're extremely clever or a thousand years old,' she bated.

'I had a good, patient and very beautiful teacher.' His eyes kept hers.

'How very fortunate. I hear that teachers these days get bullied into performing Barry Manilow musicals.'

'Chaucer would turn in his grave.'

'Græf.'

Chapter Fifty-Three

He'd given her the tour of the house but his mind was elsewhere. As she admired the simplicity of the furnishings and ran her hand over the brightly coloured woollen blanket Colette must have added to the master bed, all he could think of was getting a moment alone to call his agent. If he dealt with this matter now he could limit the damage. Not for him but for her. He knew her. She would hate to be in the spotlight. Would loathe for her life to be scrutinised like that. If she knew they'd been pictured in the press she would want to do something about it. Back out. Change her mind. End their relationship. He couldn't let that happen. Not when they'd just got back together.

He couldn't leave her to disappear and make a phone call. His hand had been on his phone in the kitchen earlier when Emma had visited the bathroom, but Colette had appeared to say goodbye and the moment had passed.

Now Emma was sat in the garden, a book open on the table, her body leaned back into the seat, embracing the warmth of the sun as it rained down on her skin. She looked so relaxed. He watched her until it seemed she sensed his presence and she turned her head towards him.

He moved, being careful to hold the tray steady in his hands.

'Should I be doing something?' she asked as he put the tray on the table and then sat down beside her.

'You want to do something?'

'No, that's not what I meant. I just… it's almost eight and I haven't lifted a finger to do anything since I got here.' She smiled at him, watched him pour them both a glass of red wine.

'You are my guest. Why should you do anything?'

'I like the idea of that,' she answered, picking up the glass and putting it to her lips.

'I have arranged a car to take us to the harbour for dinner. We have an hour,' Guy informed.

'What?! An hour? Guy, why didn't you say? I have to shower and change. I can't go anywhere like this, I…' She put the wine down and moved to stand up. He caught her arm and held her still.

'You look beautiful,' he whispered.

'We've travelled for hours, I could definitely look better,' she responded.

'Just give me a minute,' he asked.

Emma shifted in her seat, making herself comfortable again. Guy took hold of her hand and began to massage the skin with his thumb.

'Having you here, it means so much to me. When everything was happening back then, with my mother, I never thought that this place, this house, could be home for me. It was filled with bad, angry feelings, raised voices, harsh hands. But when I lost Luc, although I knew I still had to get away, I somehow always knew I'd come back. That it could be different. That making changes would set me free.'

His words banged against her soul like a door being thrown open. What if she had reacted differently? What if she had stopped and let him explain? Even if there wasn't an explanation she liked the sound of, she could have listened.

'I'm sorry I ran,' she said softly.

'I understand. I didn't understand it all back then, but I understand now,' he answered, raising her head with a finger and exploring her face with his eyes.

'I acted out of jealousy and spite and anger. I was a different person back then. I'd lost my mother and I'd put everything into loving you and you...' She stopped herself. Couldn't bring herself to say any more. 'We're doing it and we said we wouldn't. This is a conversation we shouldn't be having. I'm going to shower and change.' She got to her feet.

'Emma...'

'I won't be long,' she replied, letting go of his hands.

Along with the day of travelling, Emma tried hard to scrub off the anxiety. She should have known this would happen. It was just a question as to whether her resolve would last. And should it? Shouldn't she stop it now? Confess? Explain? Ask for forgiveness?

Towel-drying her hair she left the bathroom. As luxurious but understated as the master bedroom was, it was impersonal. There was nothing homely about it apart from the old-fashioned blanket lying across the bed that looked quite out of place. There were no photos, no pictures on the walls, just random funny-shaped ornaments in stone or wood speaking of wealth rather than taste.

As she teased strands of hair with the towel her mobile phone began to ring. Turning the towel around her, she dug her hands down into her bag until she found it. The display told her it was her dad. Straight away her chest heaved. It was going to be Dominic, something was wrong.

'Hello,' she answered, nerves in her tone.

'Hello, love. How are you? Are you there yet?' Her dad was shouting as if he had to throw his voice across the English Channel.

'Is it Dominic? Is he OK?' she breathed out quickly.

'Dom? Yes, Dom's fine, love.' She exhaled with relief and sat down on the bed.

'Is he there?' she asked. She didn't want to be one of those over-protective mothers who couldn't be parted from their offspring but... she hadn't been parted before now.

'He is, but he's teaching Marilyn some French. Brought his homework here. I'll put him on in a bit. I want to know if you're having a nice time.'

She let out a sigh. 'Marilyn told you about me and Chris, didn't she?'

'She's just worried for you, love.'

'I know. It's OK.' It *was* OK. She couldn't expect Marilyn to keep things from her dad if she was any sort of girlfriend to him. And, as unsettling as it was, it was OK.

'You haven't told Dom though?' Mike asked.

'No. I just need this weekend, Dad. Then I'll tell him,' she replied.

'So, how's the weather? Is it sunny?' Mike asked.

Emma stood up and walked over to the window. The view was outstanding. Golden fields of corn shimmered and stretched out towards the horizon, the evening sun dwindling as night closed in.

'It's beautiful,' she whispered.

'Oh, Ally told me to tell you to do everything she would do… on skis. Does that make any sense to you?' Mike asked.

'Yes,' she answered, laughing.

'Listen, love. Is everything alright? Apart from Chris. Are you alright for money? Does Dom need anything? I don't want you to think just because you're grown up you can't come to me anymore. You can come to me for anything, love.'

The sentiment in her dad's voice made her heart swell with joy and sorrow. Why hadn't she told him the truth? If not at the time, then some while later. There had been opportunities but she'd ignored them, been too fearful of the can of worms it might open and the repercussions.

'I know, Dad. Everything's fine,' she finally breathed.

'Good. Right. I'll get Dom then. You enjoy yourself,' Mike ended.

'Bye, Dad.' She touched her fingers to the rims of her eyes and tried to push the emotion away. She didn't want Dominic to know anything was wrong. Nothing *was* wrong, it was just that things were going to change a little.

'Hi, Mum. I can't talk for long. Marilyn's terrible at French. Grandad says he might take her one day so she needs practice.'

'Oh, well you'll be a fantastic teacher. She's lucky to have you. Are you having a good time?' She sat down on the bed and envisaged him. His hair would be flopping over his eyes. He'd be fiddling with something, most probably a racing car.

'Marilyn made spaghetti Bolognese and Grandad bought cake.'

'Lucky you.'

'Is Chris with you?'

She paused. What should she say? She didn't want to lie to him but it wasn't the kind of conversation to have on the telephone.

'Not this time. Listen, you be good for Grandad and Marilyn. I'll see you on Sunday,' Emma spoke.

'OK,' he replied.

'I love you.'

'Love you too. Bye.'

And then he was gone. But he was fine. He was enjoying himself and she had no concerns for him. But for her, she still held onto the one that she had been carrying around her whole life.

Chapter Fifty-Four

He looked at the ring sat in its leather box. He knew, if looked upon by others, this was too soon. But it wasn't for him. In his heart he had been engaged to Emma all this time. This ring was different. It was bought with one week's wages because he'd fought and he'd struggled and he'd succeeded professionally against all odds.

He slipped the box into his trouser pocket. He didn't know if tonight was the right time but having the ring close made him feel good. It was security. It was a real, tangible object he was going to put on the finger of the woman he loved. It was validation that everything he'd lived through had been worth it.

As she stepped into the kitchen she saw him raise his head. His eyes met hers and she saw how much he loved her in that moment. Could there finally be a happy ever after? Could she be brave enough to accept it?

'You look wonderful,' Guy said as she moved across the room, closer to him.

She brushed her hands down the yellow sundress she was

wearing. It was so similar to one she'd worn when they first knew each other. He held her hands and smiled.

'Let's go out, have fun and forget everything but us,' he suggested.

'I'd like that,' she replied.

'This restaurant is the best in Fréjus,' Guy remarked.

The car had left them at the harbour and they'd meandered along it, taking in the boats, the bustle of the night time scene, before heading for the restaurant.

'Is it very expensive?' Emma asked.

'Is that important?'

'No. I'm sorry. I don't know why I asked that.'

She did know. The life they'd talked about when they were younger had never involved money except in their dreams. To start with they were always going to be surviving day to day, scraping by, doing the best they could. Fancy restaurants had never been on the agenda. But that was why where they were now was both so similar yet so different. They'd travelled separate paths and ended up at the same place.

'They have a good Merlot,' he said, smiling at her and squeezing her hand a little tighter. The touch eased the tension.

A man in a smart black suit, teamed with a bright pink tie greeted them at the door.

'*Monsieur Duval*, welcome back to *La Mer*. Please, our best table is this way.'

The man began to lead Emma and Guy toward the rear of the restaurant. Emma pulled at Guy's arm.

'Could we sit at the front? If you think you won't be plagued by autograph hunters,' Emma said.

'Of course. We can sit anywhere you like. Excuse me, may we sit at the front?' Guy asked the waiter.

'*Absolument*. Please,' he said, turning back around. He led on to the front of the restaurant. The table he stopped at was right in the window, overlooking the street and the boats docked in the harbour.

Guy beat the waiter to pulling out Emma's chair. She smiled at him and sat down. The waiter offered the wine list but Guy waved it away.

'Your Merlot,' he ordered.

'And a glass of water,' Emma interjected.

'Perhaps a jug?' Guy suggested.

'Very good,' the waiter said. He handed them both a menu and left them alone.

'I'm too excited to think about eating. I can't believe we're here… together,' she whispered.

A smile drew across Guy's face and he clasped her hands across the table.

'You sounded just like the Emma I met all those years ago just then. So much excitement, so much youthful innocence,' he said.

'This time I want to do things properly, Guy. Before, we started so fast, rushed ahead because we had to. We don't need to do that now. We've got all the time in the world. I want to be young again. I want us to date, to hold hands, to take off our clothes and jump in the stream,' Emma said. She let out a giggle and he brought her hands to his lips, kissing the skin.

'I want to do all that too,' he agreed.

★

He returned her hands to the table and it was then he caught sight of a couple outside. Their arms were linked together and they were walking toward the restaurant. As they moved closer Guy's heart plummeted.

The waiter returned to the table with the wine and it was all Guy could do to stop himself ripping it out of his hands and filling a glass. He drummed his fingers on the table as they went through the tasting formalities.

'Are you OK?' Emma asked as Guy poured her some wine, then filled his glass to the brim.

He managed a nod but all he could concentrate on was drinking as much wine as he could in one mouthful. His flesh was creeping; a cold, damp feeling was spreading from his fingers, up his arms and deeper through his torso. They were coming in. There was nothing he could do to avoid this situation. He tried to shrink into his seat, even though he knew it would do no good. Out of the side of his eye he saw them enter. It was just a matter of time.

'Goodness! What a thrill! Tasha, look, it's Guy Duval,' Keith's voice rang out.

Emma looked up and set eyes on the girl she had spent years despising. Except now she wasn't a girl. Now, Tasha was a grown woman like her. But unlike her, Tasha was wearing something that looked designer. She was taller than Emma remembered and thinner. And surprisingly she looked completely polished, faultless, perfected. One thing she did remember about Tasha was she hadn't been polished. She'd dressed in the latest fashions, yes, but she had always been more street than princess.

'Hello, Guy. How nice to see you again,' Tasha greeted.

Emma's stomach turned over. She had to look away. This moment could stop them from having a perfect weekend. It had been ridiculous for her to think the past could stay behind them.

'Hello,' Guy responded so softly it barely reached anyone's ears.

'And you're Emma, aren't you? Do you remember Emma, Tasha? She stayed at La Baume once, years ago. Isn't it nice the four or us getting reacquainted like this?' Keith continued.

'How lovely to see you again, Emma. Are you and Guy…?' Tasha left the question open ended.

'Yes. Yes we are,' Guy answered, determination in his tone.

'Oh, how lovely. Should we celebrate do you think? Some champagne perhaps?' Keith suggested.

'There's no need. We were just going to have a quiet dinner,' Emma said. She couldn't do this. She couldn't be with this woman. Tasha had changed the course of her entire life. What she had done had made such an impact. It had altered her path irrevocably, changed her, made her make choices she never should have had to make.

'I was hoping to celebrate a little venture of my own actually.' Keith didn't wait to be invited. He pulled up two seats from another table and motioned for Tasha to sit down.

'I don't think…' Guy started.

Tasha looked to Emma and she clenched down the emotion that rose up the second the look connected. This was all wrong, this night was supposed to be special and now these people, reminders of the time when she was young and vulnerable, had burst in, shattering everything. She reached out for her wine glass and held it tight.

'I'm launching a brand new line. I'm in the lingerie business you see, Emma,' Keith told her.

Guy bit the inside of his mouth. This was the worst situation. He wanted to drag Keith away from Emma by the lapels of his jacket. Just his presence had flooded his gut with nausea he could almost taste. He knew where this was going. Keith was spreading unease, dragging Emma into the middle of a situation she had no clue about. He knew how she would be feeling. She thought Tasha was the person who had helped him break her heart. He could see just by looking at her that she was only just holding all that resentment in. He was the only one who could do something about this.

'We have to go,' Guy said, rising from his chair.

'Go? Go where? You've not eaten,' Keith yapped, indicating the untouched silverware on the table.

'I have an important match tomorrow. I did not realise the time,' he continued.

'It's barely past half nine,' Keith continued.

'Guy…' Emma started. He could see from her expression she was torn. She didn't want this woman to burst back into their lives and spoil what they'd only just begun. But she did not want to appear rude.

'Daddy, we've interrupted their dinner. We'll leave you alone,' Tasha said in a diplomatic tone.

'I'll just come right out and say it then. I'm launching a male line and I want Guy here to endorse it. I want him to be the face of… well, the body of… Mustang Lingerie.'

Tasha let out a squeal of excitement. Guy grabbed Emma's hand, hauling her up off the seat.

'We're leaving,' he stated.

'I'll give you a call. We can talk details.' Keith smirked.

'Never. Do you hear me? Never. Do what you like, tell as many reporters as you want to. It's over,' Guy hissed into Keith's face.

'Guy,' Emma began.

Rage pulsing through his veins, he pulled Euros from his wallet and dropped them to the table to cover the cost of the wine they hadn't drunk. Then he propelled Emma towards the door and out into the night.

She watched him draw breath, filling his lungs with the moist, balmy air, his eyes closed.

'Guy, tell me what's going on,' she begged, looking to him pleadingly.

It was Tasha. She knew it. The woman had destroyed things the first time around and she was set to do it again. He'd seen her... recently and not said a word.

Guy opened his eyes. The expression of pain, sorrow and pure hopelessness clawed at her heart. Whatever he was going to tell her was going to rip her world apart.

Chapter Fifty-Five

5 September 2005

Today was the day and Emma had much more than butterflies in her stomach. It was as if a whole colony of bees had invaded and were building a giant honeycomb inside her. Her dad thought they were going home together to that death-tainted house for him to move in his girlfriend and for things to carry on as before, just minus her mother. In reality, she was running away to get married to a boy she had known just a few weeks. It wouldn't be easy, but the thought of striking out on their own filled her with excitement rather than fear.

She watched her dad taking down the tent, canvas covering his head as he removed another pole.

'Do you want some help?' she offered.

'Thanks, love,' Mike replied.

She ducked under the tent and helped hold the material up. It was roasting hot under the material, the autumnal sun touching everything in its reach.

'What time do we have to leave?' Emma asked.

'I thought about two. Is that alright with you?' Mike replied.

'Yes, of course. I was just checking. I thought I might catch the wig-wam building this morning,' Emma said. In truth she was meeting Guy with a bag she'd hidden in the shower block to pass it over and finalise the details of their escape. They'd planned to leave at one. Guy had bought a cheap car from someone he knew. He'd already packed for him and Luc, taken the case and bags to the barn. They were really going to do this.

'Wig-wam building. That sounds like a caper. Once I'm packed up here I might come and have a look too,' Mike said, pulling out the last pole. The canvas fell about them and Emma's stomach lurched. She didn't want her dad leaving the camping area really.

'Are you alright, love? You look a bit peaky,' Mike remarked as they both backed out from under the tent.

'Just a bit of stomach-ache that's all. It's the end of the holiday and… we're going back home,' she said. She hated lying but she had to. Her dad would be OK. He had Marilyn.

'Things will get better, love. And, who knows, if I work hard, we might be able to afford to come back here next year,' Mike stated, smiling.

She couldn't bear it anymore. She needed to see Guy, needed reassurance that this was the right path, that their love was enough to change everything.

'I'd better go, if that's OK,' Emma said, backing away.

'Of course, love. If I don't make it I'll see you back here about half one. We can stop off for some lunch on the way to the ferry,' Mike told her.

This was it. This was the moment she was leaving her dad. He was there, rolling up the tent, oblivious to the poignancy. What should she do? Should she just back away? Leave without saying anything? She didn't want him to know but she also didn't want him to think the decision had been made without care or consideration when he looked back on things.

'I love you, Dad,' she said, tears pricking her eyes.

Mike looked up then. The intimate statement was not a usual occurrence in their family. Emotions were buried deep and not often exclaimed.

'You sure you're alright, love?' he asked. He didn't sound suspicious, just concerned. She needed to leave now. She'd said enough.

'I'm fine... *Jane Eyre*,' she said as explanation.

'Those Brontë girls again.' Mike shook his head. Emma smiled and waved her hand.

'I'll tell you all about the wig-wams.' She lowered her voice. 'One day.'

Her heart was heavier than she could have imagined. Why was it so hard? She wanted to move on with Guy, didn't want to be in a house with her dad and Marilyn, but something inside her was breaking. She looked at her watch. Guy should be here. She jumped down from the gate and looked up the path. He wasn't in sight. Where was he?

'Lost someone?'

Staring up the path one way had caused Emma not to notice the approach of Tasha's sidekick, Melody.

'No,' Emma snapped in response.

'Because if you were looking for Guy I know where he is,' Melody boasted.

She wasn't going to give her the satisfaction of acknowledging her comment. Neither Tasha or Melody had ever been anything other than obnoxious. She turned her face away from the girl, focused on the countryside scene the other side of the gate.

'About ten minutes ago he was going into Tasha's caravan. They've been getting really close, if you know what I mean,' Melody continued. Emma couldn't help but look at her. A satisfied smirk was set on her lips. Emma's heart pumped harder and faster as she let the words seep inside her. Why would Guy be with Tasha? He said he disliked her but that time in the clubhouse he'd spent so much time hanging around her table. What if... what if he'd lied to her?

'She's wearing a brand new dress today. She got it from a boutique in Fréjus,' Melody continued.

She shouldn't say anything. This was nonsense. The girls were always teasing her, trying to wind her up. She knew Guy, they were deeply in love and they'd made so many plans. He wouldn't be with Tasha. He would be changing after football and making his way to meet her. He was late that was all.

'By now, he's probably taken it off,' Melody continued.

'Shut up! You're a liar!' Emma yelled, pointing an accusing finger at the girl.

'Why would I lie? We were meant to be building a wig-wam together until she got a better offer. She wouldn't tell me what she was doing but I saw him... hot and gorgeous, no top on, going into her caravan,' Melody explained.

'I don't believe you! You're lying!' Emma screamed.

She was shaking, her hands trembling, her insides coiling up tight. This couldn't be happened. She'd given everything to this relationship, all her thoughts and feelings, all her hopes and dreams. She'd bared her soul.

'Caravan 12. It's right by the lake. Go and see for yourself if you don't believe me,' Melody challenged.

She couldn't think. There was so much information bombarding her brain. Everything Guy had told her, his declarations of love, his ideas for their future... everything was being soured by Melody's accusation. She wanted to hold on to the truth she longed to believe, but something was niggling inside her. A germ of suspicion had been planted and she needed to resolve it before it spread its deep roots.

She gave Melody a hard shove, sending her sprawling into the bushes. Then she took off up the path towards the lake. Melody picked herself up.

'It isn't my fault he doesn't want you! Maybe you should do more than read all the time!'

Her heart had been in her mouth the whole way across the campsite. Now, her stomach was clenched in so tight it felt as if her ribs were bruising her on the inside.

These caravans – *this* caravan – were unlike the others that stood at the end of the site she'd been staying on. This was luxury. This was a house with double-glazed windows and a proper front door. This was definitely it. Number 12. Her anger was reined in. Now she just felt terrified. What was going on behind the door? Was Guy really here? Was he in there with Tasha? The only thing she *did* know was she had to find out one way or another. Her whole future rested on it.

She took a step towards the set of three steps that led up to the door. Then she stopped. What was she doing? Why was she believing the word of a horrible, bitchy girl she didn't like over the assurances Guy had given her? She shook her head, prepared to retreat. Then she heard a voice. Every hair on her body reacted to the sound on instinct. It was the voice that usually sent shivers running over her body. Now, it was filling her with dread. He was in there. He was in Tasha's caravan, just like Melody said.

Her eyes filled up with tears. She didn't know what to do. From inside he spoke again, softly. Was he whispering to Tasha? Telling her he loved her?

Fired by pure white anger she mounted the steps, flinging open the door.

On the breakfast table were the remains of a picnic. A half-empty bottle of Merlot. Tears were leaking from her eyes now, but she couldn't stop. She needed to see. She needed to be sure.

She headed down the corridor to the bedrooms. Why? Why was this happening? Hadn't she given him everything? And he was throwing it away for a trampy girl from London.

There was only one door closed. She knew what she was going to see. Why did she need to see it? Because her heart was pleading with her, asking for clarification, begging her mind to give it a chance.

Her hand was on the door. As every millisecond ticked by she felt her heart drop deeper into the pit of fear her stomach was creating. If this was what she thought it was she'd wasted herself. Wasted these last weeks, sharing herself, giving him not only her body, but her dreams, her hopes, her precious memories of her mother, believing in a love that had never been.

The door flew open and there he was. Hair falling over his face, his forehead slick, his cheeks red. He was wearing only shorts. The door was ajar. She caught sight of the rumpled bed clothes, an arm and the shape of a body in the bed. He'd betrayed her. He'd slept with someone else, with Tasha.

'Emma,' he began. He reached for her. She fell back, a guttural sound coming out of her mouth. She grabbed at the walls of the corridor, righting herself, backing away as quickly as she could.

'Don't touch me!' she screamed. She couldn't balance. Her world was spinning on its axis and she was falling.

'Emma, wait, please. I can explain,' Guy called. He was putting on his T-shirt, hurriedly pulling it down as he pursued her.

'I've seen everything I need to,' she hissed. Her voice wasn't angry enough. She wanted to yell and spit. She wanted to hit him, claw at him, let him know just how much pain he had caused her. But the tears were getting in the way of everything. She was sobbing loudly, with no control, choking on emotion so thick it felt like it was coating her entire insides.

She burst out of the caravan into the hot air. Despite the heat there was a moment of relief. She was out of there. Away from the place where he'd cheated on her. She took a breath, tried to still, retain some dignity. She marched on down the steps and off up the path.

'Emma, please let me explain,' he repeated. He grabbed her arm, turned her, forcing her to look at him. The expression on his face was unreadable. What could she see there? There was sadness, regret, fear, shame, despair even. No, she couldn't fall for that. He was a liar and a cheat. He had just slept with that rough girl who showed off her underwear and had no clue who Chaucer was. How could he? The only reason there were tears in his eyes was because he'd been caught.

'Get off me! Don't you touch me! You've been touching her, haven't you?! Sleeping with Tasha like you slept with me! Have you asked her to marry you yet?' she exploded.

'It is not how you think. What I do here, it is…'

'You're half-dressed and she's in that bed! That's all I need to know! Let me go!'

His hand was still holding her arm, the velvet smoothness of his fingers pressing onto her skin. A cheater's touch. Well-practised, used many times on holidaymakers just like her. She could write into *Cosmopolitan* and tell her story when she got home. Naïve teenager falls for campsite Romeo. *Stupid. Idiot. Sucker.*

'Come with me. I will try to explain.' His fingers caressed her arm and all those lustful feelings began to stir inside her. She wrenched her arm away, her breathing heavy, her heart in overdrive. And then she lost control. She thumped him hard on the chest once, then again and again, one fist connecting after the other.

'Liar! Cheat! You're a bastard! I hate you! How could you? How could you?'

At first he accepted the blows, allowed her to hurt him but then he stopped her, blocked her attack by taking her arms.

'Emma, look at me, please,' he begged.

She was sobbing again, her eyes red and misted, her mouth agape, trying to suck in air to keep her functioning.

'I love you,' he told her.

The declaration had her yelping as it pulled at her soul. She shook her head at him.

'Emma, 'he whispered, brushing a strand of hair behind her ear.

'I never want to see you again. I'm going home,' she stated. She waited a moment for the news to sink into him and then she ran. It was over.

Chapter Fifty-Six

'Guy, stop. Where are we going?'
Emma hurried her step to prevent being dragged over. Guy was still holding her hand, marching her along the quay front. They were being stared at by everyone they passed. Every other couple walked steadily, enjoying a romantic walk, soaking in the gentle pace.

'We are going where they are not,' Guy replied. He tugged her to the right and stepped up onto the gangplank of a boat.

'What are you doing? You can't just go up on someone's boat,' Emma hissed.

'Not someone's. Mine.' He began to mount the walkway, leading her behind him.

'What?' She looked at the boat. There was something familiar about it. The white veneer, the blue hull – she'd been on this boat before. The summer they had met.

Guy was unfastening the gate at the top of the walkway. He was agitated, his hands fumbling with the lock. She had no idea what was going on. Seeing Tasha again had been a shock and if the woman had seen Guy recently and he hadn't told her, that was suspicious. What was she supposed to think? He looked like he was either going to spontaneously combust or crumple into a heap on the deck.

'You remember this boat? I brought you here. To one of David's parties,' Guy said. He was pacing down the boat, past the cabin, and she hurried to remain in step.

'Yes, I remember. It was the night you asked me to marry you. How could I forget?' she responded. He looked over his shoulder at her and gave a nod. He finally stopped walking when they'd reached the back of the boat. He put his hands on the chrome rail, looking out to sea.

'I should have told you the first moment we met again. The first chance I had. But I knew, if I did, that would be the end,' he said.

He had no idea how to get the words out. No matter what he said, however he constructed the sentences, the truth was going to shatter their happiness. But all told, that was what he deserved. He didn't warrant her love, her life. He had to keep paying for what he did. He had to be punished for hiding so many disgusting secrets.

He screwed up his eyes, blinking away the tears. His throat was so dry and Emma was gazing at him, looking so beautiful. He was about to bring her world down and crush his own.

'Is it Tasha? Have you...' Emma started.

He shook his head with vigour. 'No, never.'

'I don't understand.'

No. Of course she didn't understand. Because he'd hidden it from her from the start.

'You remember I worked for David. The man who owned this boat.' She nodded.

'My mother arranged it. She knew him from his hotel she worked at cleaning. I'm not sure she knew what was involved but... I don't know... maybe she did and she did not care.' He paused, wet his lips. 'To begin with it was just serving drinks behind the bar, chatting to the customers, making sure they were happy, having a good time. But then I saw what they did one night. I went into that room. I had no idea, you must believe that. I did not know.' He wept, more tears escaping. 'David, he promised me if I kept quiet he would pay me much more money and he would not tell my mother. It would be our secret. All I wanted was to save for the future. He was very rich and very persuasive.' He pulled in a breath, dropped his head before continuing. 'I had no choice. I would go home and we would have no money because my mother had drunk it all away and Luc would cry and... it was hundreds of Euros. I'd never seen that much money and I kept thinking if I just didn't say anything it would pay for so many things. Things for Luc, food...'

'What is it, Guy? Whatever it is you can tell me.'

'We were so poor, Emma and my mother... you know she hit me and...'

She reached for his hands, but he wrenched them off the boat rail and shoved them into his pockets. He didn't want to hurt her, but to accept her love and affection now was wrong. She needed to know the truth, then she could make a choice. Although he was more or less certain what she would do. It was what anyone would do.

He'd pulled away from her, dropped his eyes. Now she felt sick. The couple of mouthfuls of wine she'd had were swirling around in her part-empty stomach, mixing up a nausea she would have to swallow down.

'I learned what they did. I saw it one night. The men and the boys. It was a members' club. A group of rich men who got together to do things… with boys.'

Her belly went into spasm. What was he saying? She couldn't believe it. She hadn't heard it right. Boys? Men? A club?

'I… I don't understand.' The words fell from her mouth as her hands reached to console her stomach.

Guy was crying now. Audibly crying. She reached for the rail, brought herself down onto a bench. She couldn't think. His words were rolling around in her mind. What did they mean? What exactly was he telling her?

'Emma, this all started before I met you. The job at the campsite was what I loved, playing football and teaching the children but the money wasn't enough. My mother, she started me at this terrible hotel, she introduced me to David. I had to begin to make money for myself and for Luc. This was easy. I didn't acknowledge it. All I had to do was pretend it wasn't happening. I tell myself it is just a job. I zone out, I concentrate on serving drinks, that is all. And when I get the money in my hand I forget about everything else. I forget about how I got it, what they were doing. I was earning my way out of Fréjus,' he carried on.

'What are you saying? You saw them doing things to boys?' Her voice was shaking. She couldn't believe what he'd said. She needed him to spell it out because she was folding inwards.

'Yes… the men in the club… with the boys,' he responded.

'Men having sex with boys? Is that what you mean, Guy? Men having sex with underage boys?' She let out a painful sound that had her putting her knuckles to her mouth to absorb it.

She turned her face towards him then, saw the tears falling out of his eyes. She knew then it was true. She could see it written in his expression.

'You knew it was going on and you still went to work there! You let it go on,' she said, forcing the words out.

'It wasn't like that. It was a job, that is all. Just a job,' he repeated.

'A job! It's disgusting! Those men were paedophiles! How could you?! I…' She couldn't say any more. Visions of what he'd seen, what he'd turned a blind eye to were forming in her mind. She was seeing a shabby room, photographic equipment, a group of rich men, drooling over young boys forced to pose for their pleasure. Her stomach contracted and she lunged her head over the rails, vomiting into the water.

'I know it was wrong. I knew it then, but I needed the money, Emma. If I'd carried on just working at the campsite it would have taken me years to get away. I saved up thousands in just a few months. It was going to be our start together.'

He was rubbing her back as she hurled and she recoiled from his touch, forced herself away across the boat.

'So what happened then? Did you join in? Didn't they want you? Were you too old for them?'

He shook his head. 'No. I did not.'

'I can't listen to this… I just can't,' she said, steadying herself against the rails. Her mind was whirring with what this meant. The whole situation was bizarre and frightening and repellent and she didn't know what to do.

'Please, there is something else,' Guy began.

'Something else? I don't want to know… I can't know any more… I can't take any more,' she cried. She was terrified of hearing her worst fear. That these men had touched him, taken pleasure from him. Was that what he was telling her? Had they offered him more money to join their club, be one of those poor boys?

'You brought me to a party here! David was here then! Why? Why would you bring me somewhere like that?' she shrieked.

'Because I wanted him to know that I had a life. I had you. I was not like them. I could not and would not do any more than I was doing for him. It was enough that I saw and knew what they did. But he didn't like that.'

'How can I believe you?! All this time and you never said a word. Why didn't you tell me what you were doing? We could have gone to the police and put a stop to it. What they were doing was vile and illegal!' Her stomach was only just holding things together. She couldn't get the images out of her mind. Men and boys and Guy serving drinks to them like it was normal.

'I needed the money!' he yelled. 'I was desperate, Emma! I wasn't using the money for luxuries! I needed the money just to get by and to get out of there. If not for that job I might still be there, an alcoholic like my mother was, perhaps dead!' He let out a sob, palmed his hands against his face.

★

He could see from her eyes it was over. She couldn't look at him, had separated herself from him on the other side of the boat. But he couldn't stop now. He had to tell her the whole truth. She deserved to know who he was and who he wasn't.

He blew out a breath, ran his palms over his face to wipe the tears away. 'The day we were leaving. When you came to Tasha's caravan... I was not with her.'

She lifted her head from looking at the floor. There was so much fear and pain in her expression. He was sure what he was going to tell her was only going to make things worse rather than better. But it was honesty. They had never started with honesty and even if they were going to finish, at least it would be a truthful end.

'I wanted to leave with you so much. I loved you so much. Every word I said to you, every plan we made, everything we talked about, I meant everything, Emma,' he began. He saw her lips tremble. Perhaps there was a chance. If he was brave enough now to give her the whole story. Perhaps the memories he carried with him would relent if he finally let them go.

'David called me. He told me some of the group were coming to the hotel early. He asked me to collect the keys.' He paused, shook his head. 'To collect the keys from Keith.'

He closed his eyes, transferring himself back to that time, that moment when everything had been turned on its head.

'I'd been playing football with the kids. I'd taken off my shirt.' He opened his eyes, looking at her. She was waiting to hear what he was going to say and he still felt so much shame.

'There was no answer when I knocked on the door. I went in and he called to me and there he was… in the bed.'

He watched Emma put her hands to her mouth again. He knew she was caught between wanting him to stop talking and needing to hear the truth. He hated himself, had hated himself for so long, he was under no illusion that she wouldn't feel the same. He had nothing to lose now.

'Before I could do or say anything he had taken photos, of me, with no shirt. I asked him for the keys and he just laughed. He said *we both know what you're really here for*. But I wasn't. David had set me up. He knew how much I needed the money and he thought I would… but I didn't do anything, Emma, I swear it to you!'

He looked haunted. That was the only word she had for the way he looked now. The wind had risen and it was blowing his hair, his shirt rippling against his body. She was holding her breath, biting her tongue, internally begging God not to let this be what she thought it was. Was he telling her the truth?

She'd seen the bed but she hadn't seen who was in it. Guy hadn't been with Tasha, it had been Keith.

'No!' The word came out long and gut-wrenching as she sank to her knees, bowing into herself.

'I didn't do anything, Emma. I wouldn't do that. I know I took the money for keeping their secret and I know that was wrong but I wouldn't do anything else… nothing like that.'

Every ion was crying out in pain. She felt it like a thousand hammer blows on every inch of her body. She just wanted it to stop. She didn't want to know it, she wanted to un-know it.

'I walked out as soon as I realised the situation. I was leaving. Nothing happened. Then you were there and you were hurt thinking I had been with Tasha and…'

She couldn't respond. All she could do was hug herself and rock, praying she could disappear, just be evaporated into the night, never to remember his words again.

'Please, Emma, you have to believe me.'

She felt him sink to the floor beside her, heard the tears in his tone. She didn't know what to do. She didn't know what to say. She didn't know whether she could say anything. All those years she had spent thinking she couldn't be hurt any more and he had hurt her all over again, even deeper.

'Madeleine was going to work for him, for Keith. I met him at a fashion show and he started to bring it all up again. He wanted to see me…you know… and he wouldn't take no for an answer. He is trying to blackmail me over my involvement with the group and all I could think about was not the press or the football club when they found out, but you.'

She raised her head, looked at him.

'I don't know who you are. I don't think I've ever known,' she spat.

'Emma, I was trapped. I knew what they were doing was wrong. I knew what *I* was doing was wrong but I was so, so desperate.' He'd lost her. He knew it and he deserved it. All these years living in the life of luxury, on the surface having everything a man could wish for, but underneath what he'd done had scarred him for life. And now he was getting the ultimate payback. The second chance with the woman he adored was going to be taken from him because of it.

'You had a choice. Doing what was right and saying no and turning these people into the police or doing what was wrong and taking money, dirty money from them for your own benefit. You're as bad as them! You disgust me! How could you stand there serving beer and Merlot knowing what they were doing? How could you be alone in a bedroom with that man?! It's perverted! You're perverted!'

He nodded. He knew that's what she would think. It's what any normal person would think. He *had* thought of himself, but he'd also thought of his baby brother and saving him from the same fate.

'I hate myself over it… every day. I still see their faces. I still see Keith. Those few moments I've spent my whole life reliving. When I saw him again it was like a nightmare. All the things I'd done wrong coming back. And it was no more than I deserved. I know that,' he whispered.

Emma was crying now, sobbing quietly into her hands as he talked. He didn't know what to do. If he touched her she would pull away and that would mark his heart.

'What I saw in that room at the hotel, it will never leave me. The boys were corrupted and used. But I was being used too. David used me because he knew how badly I needed the money. When I met you, Emma, when we fell in love I saw myself having a real chance in life.'

She got to her feet, scrambled to pick up her bag. 'I can't listen to this anymore.' She started to walk back up the boat.

'Emma, please. Take the keys to the house. I will stay away, let you think,' he called.

'Let me think?! I've nothing to think about! I don't want you anywhere near me. This, whatever this was, is over,' she screamed.

Her words made a direct hit on his heart and he stepped back, took hold of the rail to balance.

She raced down the gangplank and out onto the quay. There they were again. The lovers, the children, the people strolling along with their lives while hers fell apart in France again. The sickness was getting worse. She needed a bathroom, a chance to puke up everything inside her and a shower to scrub herself clean. She had started out tonight feeling so happy! She had everything she wanted. The man she loved, Dominic, her dream job, her dad happy again. She should have known it was just too much. Love wasn't like that. Her life wasn't like that.

'Taxi!' she called, waving her hand at a car. The vehicle pulled over and she opened the door.

'*Camping La Baume s'il vous plaît*,' she directed as she got in. She didn't know what she was going to do when she got to the campsite but she couldn't go back to the house.

She turned herself, looking out of the back window of the car. The driver said something in French she didn't understand. She could see Guy, hurrying down the quay towards the car.

'Please, *Monsieur, vite*!' she called. Guy was just yards away, such a wounded expression on his face. She couldn't look. She turned away as the taxi pulled off and closed her eyes.

Chapter Fifty-Seven

5 September 2005

She'd run. Left the campsite, turned out of the gate, passed the barn and raced on and on towards the river. Her eyes were blinded by the tears. It wasn't fair. Why was she being punished like this? Because she'd got drunk and stupid and cautioned by the police after her mother had died? Because she'd been deliberately cruel to her dad because she blamed him for not being there when her mother passed? Hadn't she coped with enough heartache? Hadn't she tried to bury herself in her books and do the right thing? Why had life decided to hurt her again? Take away the one thing, the one person who was hers? They'd been in love. *She'd* been in love, so deeply in love it had filled her up to the brim. Guy had given her her life back. Just when she thought there was nothing but death and loss and Shakespeare, he had come along and shown her how beautiful life could be. He'd asked her to marry him and she'd believed him. She'd convinced herself it was more than a holiday romance. Fallen for the fairytale. He'd taken their love and thrown it on the bedroom floor of that caravan when he'd slept with Tasha.

She was out of breath, her lungs bursting. She jogged to a stop, bent double and put her hands on her hips as she straightened up. She should have been getting ready to leave. Leave with Guy to a new life. Instead she was here, hurt, humiliated, wanting to rage at the world for letting her down again. If there was a God, where was he? Why had he taken her mother? And why had he made this happen? He'd given her Guy and snatched him back. She wanted to scream at the heavens. She wanted to beat her fists on the ground. She wanted to get drunk again. So drunk she couldn't feel anything. It would only numb the pain for a while but even a few hours out of real life was better than nothing at all.

She hugged herself, bracing her stomach, trying to quell the torment when she heard a noise. It was a baby crying. Such a loud, distressed sound and a sound she recognised. It was Luc, she was almost sure of it. She shielded her eyes from the sun and looked around. There were fields of crops to her left but to her right was the grassland that led down to the river. She squinted against the sun, putting her hand up to her forehead to shield her eyes. There, across the grass, was Luc's pram and beside it was a figure led on a blanket on the ground.

She picked up her pace and headed towards them. It was so hot today and the pram wasn't in any shade. As she got closer she saw it was Guy's mother on the rug. She was asleep or unconscious, an empty bottle of brandy next to her. Anger gnawed at her. What sort of woman was she? She beat her eldest son, she neglected her baby and when he didn't stop crying she shook him until he did. On closer inspection Emma could see she was breathing. She was passed out and drunk. She wasn't fit to be anyone's mother. It was so unfair! Her own mother who always had time for her, always been there for school, for hugs, for chats, for everything, had been taken away, while this horrible, nasty, woman was here, wasting her life away and ruining the lives of everyone around her. She was vicious and brutal. A dangerous bully.

Emma bent over the pram and lifted Luc out.

'There now. Sshh, it's alright. Emma's here now,' she hushed, cradling his tiny body against her.

His cries lessened immediately and as she began to sing the song Guy had taught her he stilled, his breathing soft and contented. None of this was his fault. This poor little infant had been born without anyone in his life to look after him. His mother was a violent alcoholic and his brother was a liar and a cheat.

'What are we going to do, hey?' she asked the child. She put her hand to his small dark head of hair and closed her eyes.

Chapter Fifty-Eight

Present Day

Ally had told her she was on the front page of two of the tabloid newspapers. She'd also told her Mike had phoned earlier to ask if she had a spare Wii controller. She hadn't cared about either. She had let Ally talk and said 'yes' in all the right places and finally got rid of her to a Bollywood banquet night with Jonty. She'd wanted to say something, confide a little of what she was feeling to her best friend but... well, she just couldn't. It was all too ugly, too raw, too painful to recount yet, if ever.

She parted the curtains in the luxury caravan home to look out over the lake. It was the only accommodation La Baume had left. It might even be the same caravan she had found Guy in all those years ago. She'd been grateful to get anything, given how she looked. Eyes red-rimmed and swollen, hair rough and out of place. Her heart was barely functioning, her stomach felt tender and achy, her head was stuffed full of thoughts she couldn't process. How did you process something like this? Could you?

She sat down on the sofa and wrapped her legs under herself. Should she have picked up on this situation when they were together? He'd told her he worked at a hotel but she'd never asked too many questions. She'd been too caught up in the romance. She shook her head. She had been so naïve. She should have asked him for more details. She should have taken more of an interest in what he did when he wasn't with her. If she had then... then what? All this time she'd believed he'd cheated on her with Tasha and in reality... the reality was far worse.

The car had brought him home an hour ago and he hadn't moved from the kitchen floor. The cold slabs had numbed his skin and the feeling was working its way up and down his entire body. He didn't care. He didn't care about anything anymore. He had come back into her life only to break her heart again. He should have left her alone. At the opening of the fitness centre he should have just made his peace. He could have politely wished her well, been glad she was happy with another man, a good man, a man so much better than him. Instead he had opened up old wounds, pounded at her heart and relentlessly pursued her. Why? Because he was weak and selfish, like he had always been.

There was no going back now. He knew what he had to do. He reached into the pocket of his trousers for his phone. His fingers touched the small black box. He pulled out the ring and the tears began again. So many hopes for the future, broken and burned. There was nothing left to wreck. He'd singlehandedly destroyed everything.

The complimentary coffee was bitter and there weren't enough sachets of milk to make a real difference to the colour. She put the cup to her mouth and blanched her tongue. She set it back down and put her finger to the sore spot. What was she going to do? Go home the first chance she got was the obvious answer. She longed to see Dominic right now. She needed clarification of the choices she had made. Had she been right? What would have happened if Guy had confessed to her eight years ago? How would she have reacted then? What he'd done was wrong on so many levels but he had been struggling. His mother had forced him to work there, no doubt wrapped him up in guilt about him being the man of the house, the provider. She probably knew exactly what was going on, perhaps hoped he would participate for her own gain. What choice had Guy really had?

No, she mustn't make excuses for him. It was morally wrong. He knew what had been happening. He could have made an anonymous call to the police to have it stopped. Instead he went on working there, taking money from them and lying to her, hiding what he was doing behind whispered words of love and romantic rendezvous.

But what about her? What she'd done was wrong too, by most people's standards. The only difference was, nobody knew. She tried the coffee again. What if Guy hadn't been honest with her now? They would have gone on, building their second chance on a foundation of lies. She had never, ever planned to be honest with him about Dominic's parentage. Didn't that make her just as bad? Or worse?

She glanced across at her phone on the worktop. Nothing.

No messages. No missed calls. What had she expected? Him begging her forgiveness? Did he really need to? He knew what he'd done was wrong and he'd spent his whole life paying for it. And what had she done? When he'd been honest she'd let him take all the blame. She'd let him think he was the only one with a terrible secret. She should have told him. She saw how much it pained him, telling the truth and knowing how she would react. She'd acted like Little Miss Perfect. Emma Barron, the book-loving teacher, the stand-up member of the community who could never do any wrong. She shivered, hugging herself as the panic rode over her. She should have finally told him about the day she left in 2005. She should have told him about her role in Luc's death.

Chapter Fifty-Nine

They'd questioned him for four hours. They wanted details he barely remembered, names, dates, times, addresses. He should have expected nothing less, but when he'd made the call to the police he hadn't considered anything apart from confessing. After all this time, even now, after he was sure he'd lost Emma, he had to put things right. He had to do what he should have done years before. He couldn't go on with Keith's threats hanging over him. He couldn't have his whole career, his whole life under that man's control.

The police were going to investigate. They would want to talk to him again. In his mind he saw raids on the homes of David, Keith and the other names he'd given them. He couldn't care less about the ramifications for him now or in the future. He just wanted to go on with a clean slate, even if they decided to press charges against him. He would deal with it. He wouldn't shirk it. He'd done that too much and look what had happened.

He unbuttoned his shirt and shrugged it from his shoulders. It was wet with perspiration and smelt of the interview room they'd kept him in. He needed to shower.

He needed to finally unburden himself of everything he'd been holding in for so long.

The phone in his trouser pocket vibrated. He knew it would be France, the football club. He'd called them from the car on the way back. He'd told the player liaison everything. He couldn't play that night and he fully expected to be dropped from the international team for good. As far as his career with Finnerham went, well, they'd react exactly the same and who could blame them? When this hit the newspapers, which it would, he would be labelled scum.

He took the phone out and looked at the message on the screen.

She'd written the text three times, deleting parts, adding punctuation. *Adding punctuation!* Who cared about full stops when you dealing with something so vital? Her thumb hovered over the 'send' button. Could she do this? Could she really tell him the truth? She really didn't know. But what she did know was, she couldn't be a hypocrite. She couldn't berate him for keeping secrets when she was holding one so big. She pressed the button and clicked out of messages into her contacts. She pressed the key and put the phone to her ear.

'Dad, hi, it's me. Yes, I'm fine. I just... could I speak to Dominic?'

'Good morning!' Colette breezed into the house all rosy-cheeked French charm and honeysuckle perfume. He almost retched. He'd eaten nothing, drunk nothing since the mouthful of wine at the restaurant the night before. There had been water offered in the interview room but he hadn't touched it. He was sleep-deprived, dehydrated and he barely had the strength to offer her a smile. The shower had made him feel better but he was still on edge, nervous. He was meeting Emma at the campsite in half an hour. She'd contacted him. A short text asking him to meet her. His heart had soared at the message. He knew it meant nothing. He knew it probably spelt the end, but there was that little chink of hope, the tiniest chance. And if that was there he was going to grab at it with both hands.

'Guy, look at you. What has happened?' Colette appeared to be shocked by his appearance. His hair was still damp and he felt the heaviness of the bags under his eyes. He hadn't shaved and there was a hint of stubble on his face. As Colette continued to stare, he put a hand to his face, feeling the roughness.

'I… stayed out late. Too late. I didn't sleep,' he said. He couldn't tell her what had happened. She had been the rock for him when he eventually joined OGC Nice. She would know soon enough and think badly of him. He couldn't cope with her disappointment now.

'Where is Emma?' Colette asked. Her eyes moved through the kitchen, over to the lounge. 'Is she still sleeping? Tired I expect from the journey here.'

'No. She went out early. We are meeting for lunch,' he lied. He was still lying. He shook his head.

'Is everything OK? I thought you must leave this morning, for Paris, for the football game,' she queried. He knew she knew there was something wrong. He looked so terrible,

Emma wasn't at the house, he hadn't shaved, he wasn't leaving. It was obvious. But he couldn't confide in her. He was still too ashamed.

'Everything is fine, Colette. You worry too much. I have to go,' he said checking his watch.

'Shall I make something for Emma for tonight? While you are away with the football team?' she asked him.

'Perhaps a casserole?' he offered, heading for the door.

Chapter Sixty

5 September 2005

She shifted through the campsite, her head ducked low. It wasn't as if she knew lots of the holidaymakers but she didn't want to see anyone. Not the lady from three tents down, not the lifeguard with the tattoos, not Melody and definitely not Tasha or Guy. Just thinking his name brought tears of regret and shame to her eyes.

She sniffed, wiped her nose with her bare arm and shifted the two bags she was carrying up her shoulder. She had to be quick. It was almost half past one. Her dad had probably already been in touch with security.

'Oh, there you are, love. Is everything alright?' Mike appeared out of nowhere to her left and startled her.

'Hi, Dad! Yes, I'm fine, everything's fine,' she answered. She couldn't have sounded more over-the-top if she'd tried.

'Ready for the off? Said your goodbyes?' he asked.

'I didn't really have any to say. Well, apart from Sally obviously but we're going to write,' she responded, swallowing.

'That boy from the clubhouse came looking for you. You know, the one you danced with once. Did you catch up with him?' Mike queried.

That first dance. The first dance that had meant everything to her was such a long and distant memory now. So much had happened. She'd gone full circle. From grieving over her mother and having nothing but her books for solace, to finding love, getting engaged and back again. Here she was now, changed completely but still so angry with the world.

'No, I didn't but we ought to go. We don't want to miss the ferry,' Emma said, striding past her dad.

'Let me take one of those bags,' Mike said.

'No. No, it's OK.' She let out a laugh. 'I can manage.'

She smiled, her cheeks hurting with the force. What she really wanted to do was breakdown. But now wasn't the time. When she was back home she would have all the time in the world to breakdown. Her dad probably would too.

'Ready then? *Au revoir la France*,' Mike said, opening the back door for her. She put her backpack on the seat and the other bag she kept with her.

'Yes, goodbye La Baume,' she responded. She looked over her shoulder, closed her eyes for a moment and breathed in the memories. She'd never let herself be hurt like that again. Never.

Chapter Sixty-One

Walking through La Baume was like going back in time. When she'd arrived last night it had been dark, but now, in the light of the day, all of its familiarity was on show. The football court, the swimming pool, the path she'd walked every day on her way to meet with Guy. There were excited children, couples hand in hand, older guests relaxing in sun chairs enjoying the autumn sun. She just felt so isolated, not a part of any of their experiences. She wasn't here to enjoy herself now, she was here to let go of the past once and for all.

He was waiting by the gate. Sat on the wall, his head drooping, his dark hair falling forward. Apart from the better quality of his jeans and T-shirt now, he didn't look any different from the man she'd met there every day that summer. She should have trusted their love. If she hadn't been a stupid, pathetic teenager back then they would never have been parted. But then would he ever have told her about Keith, David and the club? Would he have always kept that from her? She guessed she'd never know.

He raised his head from studying the ground and saw her. She was dressed in a cream linen dress, tan sandals on her feet, her hair loose and touching her shoulders. She had never looked more beautiful. His heart should have risen at the sight of her but it had already plummeted so far south, he didn't know whether there was any going back. He didn't expect anything from her. He hoped, but he didn't expect, and he wouldn't. Ever.

He put his hands through his hair, pushing it back behind his ears and straightened up. He put his hands into his pockets and his fingers brushed the ring box. He didn't know why he'd brought it with him. Perhaps it was a comfort or a reminder of what he'd lost. He'd just instinctively known he wanted it near.

She approached him. She looked tired, nervous maybe, and when she stopped beside him she was wringing her hands together.

'Hi,' she greeted. This felt so awkward. She didn't know what to say to him. How to start or how to carry on once she had begun. She knew where it would lead and it terrified her.

'Hi,' he mouthed in response. His voice sounded hoarse.

There was silence. She looked at him, taking in his unshaven face, the frown lines enhanced on his forehead, his misted eyes.

'I am so sorry,' he broke in. He folded then, in front of her. His body convulsed as he sobbed and she didn't know what to do. It was the worst sound in the world and if it carried on she was going to break too.

She reached into his arms to find his hand. She took it, held it tightly in hers, stroking his fingers. At the moment it was all she had to give.

'I am so sorry,' he repeated in a whisper, wiping his eyes with his other hand.

She shook her head. He wasn't really the one who should be saying that now. He had given her a confession last night. Now it was her turn.

'Walk with me,' she said, turning towards the gate.

'Emma.'

'Please. Just walk with me.'

The colour of the fields, the cornflower blue of the sky looked exactly the same as they had the day she'd left. It felt surreal being here. She felt just as upset and disturbed as she had eight years ago. Time hadn't changed anything. She was still as vulnerable as she had been then. She'd hidden her heart for so long and the moment she let him in to find it, he injured it again. She began to speak.

'You have to understand that when I left you that day, I was inconsolable. Not just a bit upset, Guy. Inconsolable. It's important you know that.' She looked over at him. They had walked hand-in-hand from the campsite to where they were now, on the track, near the grass that led down to the river.

'I know that. I know what I did to you,' he responded.

She nodded, satisfied he realised the depth of her feeling. She started over to the right, stepped onto the grass, then stopped, closing her eyes. She could still see the scene. She could smell the corn, the sweet scent of fruit in the air. She could hear Luc crying.

'They were just over there.' She pointed. 'Luc was crying his little heart out and she... your mother, she was lying there on a blanket, passed out.' She didn't wait for him to make comment. She strode forward, heading towards the spot on the bank. 'She was here. Right here. Drunk. There was a bottle of brandy next to her and Luc was just screaming and screaming and she wasn't taking any notice of him. She didn't even move,' Emma continued. She turned to look at Guy as he stood alongside her, but he showed no emotion. He didn't speak or do anything. He just stood there, looking at the grass in front of them.

'I picked him up and he settled almost straightaway. He was hot and hungry so I sat on the ground and I fed him his bottle while your mother slept and I wept tears over you,' she stated.

'We found his pram down river,' Guy finally responded.

She closed her eyes tight shut and swallowed as she remembered. She'd done what she had to do. He had been better off without that woman... without Guy who lied and deceived. She'd taken away his pain. She'd got him out of that miserable existence.

'I pushed the pram into the river,' she stated, turning her tear-filled eyes to him.

He watched her fall apart in front of him. It was almost a mirror image of himself from the night before. She was crying so hard she could barely stand. Torrents of tears streamed from her eyes and she held her chest as it heaved to draw breath. He didn't speak. He didn't know quite what to say.

'I wanted to save him and punish you. You hurt me so, so much and all I could think about was that little boy, so pure and innocent, having to live with that evil woman. The woman that beat you. The woman that shook him so hard.' She paused, swallowed a knot of emotion. 'That wasn't right. And I couldn't leave him with her. Even if what I did was very wrong, I just couldn't leave him with her. You have to understand that,' she cried.

He shook his head. All these years she'd held this inside her, just like he had. A secret so deep it had scarred her entire existence.

'I took everything out of his bag apart from some milk formula, a few nappies and his toy elephant and I hid him inside it. I ran back to my dad and we left. I took Luc and I brought him up as my own, as Dominic,' she finished. Exhausted from having let it all go she sank to the grass, her head in her hands. Her brain was throbbing, her eyes aching as the stress of the situation threatened to take her over. She'd kidnapped a baby. She'd taken Guy's brother, separated a mother from her child and lied to everyone for eight years about Dominic's parentage.

'I know,' he whispered, sitting beside her.

Her eyes went wild and she shifted back, staring at him, her mouth slack. What did he just say? He knew?! How could he know? No one knew! When they'd met up again he'd told her himself that Luc was dead. She'd felt the guilt, seen the grief in his eyes.

'I knew from the moment you told me Dominic wasn't mine. If he really wasn't mine there was only one other explanation. I know you, Emma. What *I* kept from you was because I didn't want to lose you. Selfish and foolish and wicked, like you said. What *you* did wasn't out of anger like you say, it was out of love. We'd made plans together, to take care of Luc, to get him away from this place. I should have realised at the time but… I was too broken to think straight and I knew how I had hurt you. But when I saw Dominic, looking so much like me, I knew he had to be mine. I did not believe the stories of other men before me. I held you, I listened to your heart. It was always mine.'

She burst into tears and they fell, fast, hot and wet down her cheeks. Guy took her hands in his and held them strong.

'I took a child. I made you believe your brother was dead. I've kept it a secret all this time from everyone. My dad, Ally, Chris… no one knew but me. I didn't just want to protect him; I wanted him for myself because I had no one. I missed my mother so much, much more than I ever said and I thought I could cope with that if I had you. But then Dad told me about Marilyn and Chaucer was blinding me and you… did what you did and I had nothing and no one. And that baby looked into my eyes and I knew *he* needed me. I knew he was my future.'

Guy nodded. He raised a hand and brushed it down her hair. She shivered, despite the warmth of the sun on her back and wiped a hand at her eyes.

'I was too harsh with you last night and hypocritical. How could I say all those things about what you've done when I did this?' She raised her hands before dropping them back to her lap.

He shook his head. 'You did save my brother… Dominic. What you did was for the right reasons. Me, I…'

'Did exactly the same. I know how things were for you. I didn't ask questions because I was caught up in our romance like the silly little seventeen-year-old I was. I'm not excusing what you did. But I believe nothing happened with Keith. And, with your mother and Luc... you were desperate *and* vulnerable,' she said, looking up at him.

'I have told the police, last night. I go there. They questioned me and I told them everything. It is only a matter of time before the men are caught and the news is all over the press,' he stated, sighing.

'Oh, Guy. I don't know what to say,' she told him.

'Say you're not so disgusted with me that you can bear to try again. Say that you love me.'

His heart was thumping against the wall of his chest. The chink of light had grown. He saw in her eyes that she was no longer fearful of him, no longer looking at him like he was ruined for her, a shadow of the man she loved.

'I've always loved you. But *this*... you knowing *this*, about Luc... it has to change things. I have to confess too. To everyone. I broke the law. A thousand times over I expect,' she responded, her voice shaking.

He shook his head with vigour. '*Non.*'

'Dominic asks about his father every now and then. When there are shows at school or parent teacher evenings. He'll go quiet for a time and then he'll ask and every time I want the ground to open and swallow me. I never give him an answer. I say something lame like it hurts too much to speak about it and I'll tell him when he's older. Soon that isn't going to wash. I don't think it's really washing now but he hates it when I cry. He's had Chris to distract him for so long and...'

'And now he has me,' he told her. He cupped her face with his hand, pressed the pad of his thumb against her lips.

'Perhaps we're just not destined to be together, Guy. So many years have gone by, all wrapped up in so many lies,' she said.

'That is why we *are* meant to be together. Because we can get through anything. This is our chance, now everything is out in the open. My career is over, my reputation will be torn to shreds but if you say we can be together, with Dominic, as a family, then nothing else matters. Nothing.'

He held his breath. He could feel the small box pressing against the top of his thigh as he sat next to her, holding her hand. Was this the moment? Or was it too soon? There was so much forgiving to do.

Could she forgive him? Could she let him forgive her? All he had done was say nothing under pressure, been manipulated and made a misguided decision trying to get money for her, for their escape from La Baume. She had been at the forefront of his mind all the time. He hadn't cheated on her. He had meant all those things he'd whispered to her when they'd made love.

She'd spent her whole life running from that day. Covering up what she'd done. Telling lie after lie to protect herself and Dominic. Could she finally stop running? Could she consider entering the first relationship she had ever entered since she'd left Guy, with Guy, based on nothing but the truth?

'Marry me,' he said, breaking into her train of thought.

She looked at the box he offered out to her. It was open and in it was the most exquisite ring she had ever set eyes on. A thick gold band and an enormous diamond reflected the light from the sun.

'Marry me,' he repeated. 'I know after last night, with

the police and the football club, I will not have that much to share with you. I do not know what the future will hold, but whatever there is, it is yours.'

She gazed into his eyes, feeling the depth of his love wash over her and she knew then, without one single doubt, he was and always had been, the only man for her.

'I am nothing without you, Emma,' he told her.

'Yes,' she said. 'The answer is yes.'

Chapter Sixty-Two

5 September 2005

Her dad had gone for coffee just after they'd boarded the ferry and she'd stayed in the car. Luc was just starting to stir. She lifted him out of the bag and cradled him in her arms. His little fists were screwed up tight together and his tiny perfect lips were opening and closing, as he turned his head this way and that rooting for food. She was going to help him grow bigger and stronger. Protect him always.

There was one last bottle in the bag that would have to satisfy him until they got home. She un-capped the top and put the teat to his mouth.

'There we are. Who's a hungry little boy?' she asked, stroking his hair with her free hand.

She didn't see Mike come back. She didn't notice him until he'd opened the door and dropped two paper cups of coffee to the deck of the boat.

'Emma... what's going on?'

He'd gone ashen. The tan he had built up over the last three weeks had faded in an instant. She stared at her dad, not knowing what to say. She had planned to tell him when they got home, obviously, but she had been counting on a couple of hours on the boat and another few to get home before she had to face the music.

'I wanted to tell you, Dad. But… I was so frightened,' she blurted out, tears forming.

'Oh my God, love. I don't know what to say. I…' Mike started, holding onto the frame of the car door for support.

'I'm so sorry, Dad. I knew you'd be disappointed and I was ashamed. I… I had him yesterday, at the campsite and…'

'Emma… my poor sweet girl,' Mike said, shaking his head as emotion overrode him.

'I didn't want to make a fuss… I didn't want to spoil the holiday,' she continued, the tears falling. The emotion was real. She was grieving so many things. Her mother, Guy, the loss of her old future because of the hand Fate had dealt her. The future she'd chosen to take instead for this baby's sake.

'Didn't want to make a fuss?! It's a baby, love. You've had a baby,' Mike stated. He put his hand to his head. 'How did I miss this? And what do we do now?'

'I just want to go home.'

'I don't think it works like that, love. I mean he doesn't have any passport or papers or anything. What about when we get to the border in England?'

'He's been in my bag,' Emma told him as if it was the most normal sentence in the world to utter.

Mike shook his head again and she could feel his disappointment radiating off of him. She could tell he was seeing his retirement with Marilyn slipping out of sight.

'Oh, love,' Mike said, sighing.

'I know what you're thinking, Dad, but it doesn't have to mean the end of my plans for university. I can go later, in a few years,' Emma said, adjusting Luc's bottle and making him suckle louder.

'Love, why didn't you come to me? At the beginning when you first found out?'

She obviously didn't have an answer so she shrugged, hoping it would be enough.

'Who's the father? Does he know?'

She offered another shrug, focused her eyes on Luc.

'Does this little one have a name?' Mike asked.

Emma looked up then and caught the compassion mixed with shock; saw the chance to grab onto.

'Dominic. His name's Dominic.'

Chapter Sixty-Three

Present Day

'I hear they've rounded them all up,' Ally announced, pouring Emma a glass of wine.

'What?'

'The paedophiles. The ring leader's been remanded and the others have been bailed pending the trial,' she continued.

'Guy and I try not to talk about that. He has to appear at the trial to give evidence but until then we're not thinking about it. We have a wedding to plan,' Emma reminded.

'I know that! Was that a not-so-subtle hint that I ought to be arranging the hen party?' Ally asked.

'Not at all. That's the part I'm dreading because I remember the last one you made me go to that you arranged. Tequila, cowboy hats and glow-in-the-dark thongs,' Emma said, laughing.

'Great wasn't it?'

'You had more fun than the bride.'

'Ah, organiser's prerogative.'

Emma laughed.

'So, listen, miss, now I have you on your own, what I want to know is, if Guy is Dominic's father why couldn't you have just come out and told me? I mean you told me he wasn't... categorically,' Ally said.

Emma felt the loaded stare but was unmoved. She'd wanted to at least tell Dominic the truth, well a version of the truth someone his age could understand, but Guy had been adamant. He didn't want that. Not yet. When Dominic was old enough to understand, when he was safe and secure in their love, then there would come a time. Right now he was only to know one thing. That Guy and Emma were happy. That they were together and they were getting married, becoming a family.

Explaining the truth to her dad however, had been the hardest thing she'd ever done. He hadn't understood at first. She had seen the shame and hurt on his face. But Guy had held her hand the whole time, supported her through every word.

'I wasn't completely sure. We had a DNA test done,' she replied, coolly.

'Thank God for modern technology. Speaking of which, I'm still having terrible trouble with that bloody coffee machine,' Ally muttered.

The front door banged open and Dominic came sprinting into the room, two plastic bags swinging from his hands.

'They won! And you'll never guess what... Guy scored!' he announced, launching himself onto the sofa next to Emma.

'Just one? Only one?!' Ally teased, standing up and taking the bags from Dominic.

'They won, two-one,' Mike announced, as he and Marilyn entered the lounge.

'And it was flippin' freezing! I've got chilblains where they really shouldn't be,' Marilyn stated, rubbing her hands together.

'I'll serve this takeaway up, shall I? Did you remember everything, Mike? Because if I don't have my egg rolls I go green and start talking Mandarin,' Ally threatened.

'Blast!' Mike reacted.

'Don't tease the poor girl,' Marilyn chipped in, giving Mike a thump on the arm.

Guy entered the room, his kit bag over his shoulder, his hair damp from the shower.

'Hey, Guy, tell Mum about the goal. Mum, it was awesome,' Dominic enthused, grinning with pride.

'Come on, you. You've been moaning you're hungry all the way home in the car. Let's go and help Ally serve up dinner,' Marilyn suggested, taking his arm.

'Did you get chips to go with mine?' he asked, standing up and following his grandad.

Guy put down his bag and Emma stood up. He paced towards her, putting his arms around her and holding her close.

'How was it? It was the first game since... was it OK?' she asked, squeezing his body tight to hers.

'The press were outside when I arrive, lots of questions about the trial, a few accusations, unkind remarks but Finnerham, they have been so supportive to me,' he responded. He raised his head from her shoulder and held onto her hands.

'When the trial is finished it will all be over, for good,' Emma reminded him.

'We don't talk about it now. We forget it until then. We

have time to be a family, to plan the future... to organise costumes for *Copacabana*,' he said, smiling.

'Please, Guy, not tonight. Ally's still hoping I'm going to give the lead role to her,' Emma said.

He laughed and then he kissed her. A long, sensual loving kiss that told her exactly how he felt about her. She drew him in, deepening the kiss and relishing the way it felt to know she never had to let go. He pulled away, bent to unzip the top of his bag. He pulled out a string of fairy lights and shook them up and down.

'I thought... for the garden. A little food, some Merlot... do you remember?' he asked, his eyes thick with lust.

'Yes. I remember,' she said, her hand on his chest. 'I'll always remember.'

About the Author

MANDY BAGGOT is an international bestselling and award-winning romance writer. The winner of the Innovation in Romantic Fiction award at the UK's Festival of Romance, her romantic comedy novel, *One Wish in Manhattan*, was also shortlisted for the Romantic Novelists' Association Romantic Comedy Novel of the Year award in 2016. Mandy's books have so far been translated into German, Italian, Czech and Hungarian. Mandy loves the Greek island of Corfu, white wine, country music and handbags. Also a singer, she has taken part in ITV1's *Who Dares Sings* and *The X-Factor*. Mandy is a member of the Romantic Novelists' Association and the Society of Authors and lives near Salisbury, Wiltshire, UK with her husband and two daughters.

Hello from Aria

We hope you enjoyed this book! If you did let us know,
we'd love to hear from you.

We are Aria, a dynamic digital-first fiction imprint from
award-winning independent publishers Head of Zeus.
At heart, we're committed to publishing fantastic
commercial fiction – from romance and sagas to crime,
thrillers and historical fiction. Visit us online and discover
a community of like-minded fiction fans!

We're also on the look out for tomorrow's superstar
authors. So, if you're a budding writer looking for
a publisher, we'd love to hear from you.
You can submit your book online at ariafiction.com/
we-want-read-your-book

You can find us at:
Email: aria@headofzeus.com
Website: www.ariafiction.com
Submissions: www.ariafiction.com/
we-want-read-your-book

f @ariafiction
𝕏 @Aria_Fiction
◉ @ariafiction